Praise for Hunter Shea

"Hunter Shea combines ancient evil, old school horror and modern style. Highly recommended!"
—Jonathan Maberry, *New York Times* best-selling author of *The Dragon Factory*, on *Forest of Shadows*

"A frightening romp through dark terrain. The final pages will freeze your blood."
—Ronald Malfi, author of *Floating Staircase*, on *Evil Eternal*

"Hunter Shea has crafted another knockout. At turns epic and intimate, both savage and elegant, *Evil Eternal* is a harrowing, blood-soaked nightmare."
—Jonathan Janz, author of *The Darkest Lullaby*

"Bloody good read! This guy knows his monsters!"
—Eric S Brown, author of *Bigfoot War*, on *Swamp Monster Massacre*

"Hunter Shea is the real deal, folks! *Forest of Shadows* is a ghost story with attitude. Dark, intense and not afraid to get down and dirty; just the way I like them."
—Gord Rollo, author of *Valley of the Scarecrow*

"*Forest of Shadows* delves deep into the unknown. A thrill-ride of a read!"
—Alexandra Holzer, author of *Growing Up Haunted*

Look for these titles by
Hunter Shea

Now Available:

Forest of Shadows
Evil Eternal
Swamp Monster Massacre

Sinister Entity

Hunter Shea

SAMHAIN
PUBLISHING

Samhain Publishing, Ltd.
11821 Mason Montgomery Rd., 4B
Cincinnati, OH 45249
www.samhainpublishing.com

Sinister Entity
Copyright © 2013 by Hunter Shea
Print ISBN: 978-1-61921-233-6
Digital ISBN: 978-1-61921-225-1

Editing by Don D'Auria
Cover by Angela Waters

This book is a work of fiction. The names, characters, places, and incidents are products of the writer's imagination or have been used fictitiously and are not to be construed as real. Any resemblance to persons, living or dead, actual events, locale or organizations is entirely coincidental.

All Rights Are Reserved. No part of this book may be used or reproduced in any manner whatsoever without written permission, except in the case of brief quotations embodied in critical articles and reviews.

First Samhain Publishing, Ltd. electronic publication: April 2013
First Samhain Publishing, Ltd. print publication: April 2013

Dedication

For Jack Campisi, my horror co-pilot, Monster Man and brother from another mother.

"The will to disbelieve is the strongest deterrent to wider horizons."
—Hans Holzer

Ghost—the soul of a dead person, a disembodied spirit imagined, usually as a vague, shadowy or evanescent form, as wandering among or haunting living persons
—Dictionary.com

"Sleep with one eye open, gripping your pillow tight."
—Metallica, "Enter Sandman"

Chapter One

The girl walked alone.

She was oblivious to the world outside the confines of her own daydream. Pink, padded headphones blasted pop music while she texted on her phone.

Because of the false summer, she was wearing a halter top with a V-cut that just showed the swell of her firm breasts. Her shorts, denim with frayed ends, bunched up to the tops of her thighs. The olive skin of her shoulders was unblemished, perfect.

Her hips swayed as she walked, the roll of her buttocks exuding an oblivious sexuality that could only be achieved by the young and naïve. Such power, unharnessed, supercharging the air, leaving ripples of popping sparks in her wake.

It was a struggle to mirror her movements.

In the darkness, where no one else could see.

Watching, always watching.

And on days like today, imitating.

She stopped at the corner, paused to look down at her sandal and bent down to adjust the strap.

With a sudden movement, she straightened up and looked behind her, eyes narrowed.

There was no need to worry. She would only see shadows.

And in the shadows, a pair of eyes narrowed, one hand on a hip, a mirror image, a newly developed negative of the beautiful girl.

Watching...and waiting.

Chapter Two

This was the way it always started. The body reacts faster than the mind can comprehend, and a person with experience learns never to ignore what the stiff hairs on your arms are telling you. The house was quiet, had been eerily hushed for the past three hours. Silent, dark and empty.

Jessica Backman moved from her position at the end of the bed and headed to the hallway. She felt the first prickles of gooseflesh break out across her arms and the back of her neck, until every follicle on her scalp was tingling with anticipation. The sharp whine of a monitor went off in the living room below, stopping suddenly, as if smothered by someone or some*thing* that didn't want its presence to be known. Jessica's heartbeat raced as the first jolt of adrenaline coursed through her system. She had to force herself to inhale slowly from her mouth to dampen the noise of her own breathing in her head. Here, in the dark, her sense of hearing was her greatest tool.

She carefully clicked her penlight on, shining it onto her notebook so she could mark the time.

2:36am—Living Room EMF/Trifield alarm...short burst...goose bumps...not alone.

Craning her neck, she could see out the window into the empty driveway. Sometimes clients made surprise visits in the middle of the night, throwing a fat monkey wrench into the works. Unless they walked from Bedford to Bronxville, an almost thirty mile distance, the McCammon family was not the cause of the sudden change in the atmosphere. Jessica sat as still as a stone, waiting.

Pap.

Just outside the bedroom door, a slight tap, like the sound of a pebble bouncing off the carpeted hallway. The night vision camera sat on a tripod in the corner of the room, pointing at the doorway. If something had fallen onto the floor, the camera would, if she was lucky, capture it. Jessica waited for more, could feel the building tension in her chest and head. It was as if the house were gathering its strength, building and building until the air was redolent with static electricity and the pressure in her ears was ready to pop.

The sound of scratching on the walls, like a large, determined cat trapped between the rafters, echoed throughout the house. Jessica couldn't tell where it originated.

It stopped the moment she rose from the bed and took her first step back to the door. She paused, waiting a few moments for it to resume, then continued into the hallway. Leaning forward over the steel banister, she looked down into the living room and adjoining dining room.

Everything was as she had left it.

Earlier in the night, she had placed glow-in-the-dark masking tape around the perimeter of each piece of furniture, as well as the framed pictures on the walls. The glowing yellow squares, circles and rectangles gave the dark living room the appearance of an alien landscape found in the ocean depths, populated by sleeping, iridescent sea creatures. She had tacked down tape around all of the moveable objects so she could easily see what had shifted from its proper place during the course of the night. By virtue of being alone, she was assured that no one else could disturb the contents of the house.

One of the drawers in the kitchen could be heard slowly sliding open. Jessica darted down the stairs and into the kitchen, careful not to bump into anything along the way. This was her seventh night in the McCammon house and she had taken great pains to memorize every detail of its layout.

The middle drawer to the left of the sink was half-open. Jessica took a picture of the open drawer with her digital camera, shielding her eyes from the flash. A quick breeze whispered along her back in the sealed up kitchen. She had closed every window and door five hours earlier, sealing them shut with special tape as well so any manipulations by passing air could be eliminated. She shivered.

She looked once again at the drawer, the exposure of its contents mocking her, daring her to find the secret hidden within the walls of the Tudor house.

One of her Trifield meters in the upstairs bathroom squealed for several seconds before tumbling to the floor. She heard the plastic device smack the hard, unyielding tile, bouncing twice before settling to a standstill. The Trifield meter was used to measure changes in electromagnetic, electric and radio/microwave fields. She wasn't sold on its efficacy, but it was the best of the limited lot available to paranormal research. And now she was down one.

"Oh, I see," Jessica said aloud. "You want to play your games, just not with me. Can it be that you're afraid of a nineteen-year-old girl? I'm all alone and I have all night. In fact, Kristen and Tim and the girls left the house to me all weekend, so I have nothing but time."

Jessica's ears popped a split second before she saw the couch in the living room move a few inches to the right. The legs scraped across the hardwood floor and the EMF meter on the table next to it wailed like a siren.

She decided to coax the presence in the house a little further.

"Moving furniture in other rooms doesn't impress me. You did that once before and I was bored then."

Slam! The kitchen drawer shut itself with enough force to crack the wood face.

Jessica considered the intensity required to do such a thing. This was new. The EB was either getting stronger or angrier…or both. Good. At least now she knew what this presence *was not*, and that was more than she had hoped for tonight.

She pulled her digital audio recorder from the custom-designed leather holster around her waist and clicked it on. Even though there were more cameras down here, one in the kitchen and two in the living room, she wanted every piece of equipment she had at the ready to record her observations. She had also placed IR lights around the room to expand the scope of her cameras. IR lights boosted the distance her cameras could record in night-vision mode.

"Kitchen drawer just closed so hard, the wood cracked. Time is two-forty-eight a.m. I dared the EB to be more demonstrative and it's taking up the challenge. The air smells funky, like burning wires. No signs of smoke." She stopped. Something started tapping on the walls around her.

Tap, pause, *tap-tap-tap*, pause, *tap-tap*.

Jessica continued, using meditative breathing exercises to calm herself, "I hope I caught that. It's tapping out in a sequence." *Tap-tap.* "One tap, followed by three, then two. I'm not sure if it's some form of Morse code or the beat to a song or what. It just keeps tapping, and the burning smell is getting stronger," she whispered into the audio recorder. Then, much louder, "Are you trying to tell me something? If you speak into this recorder in my hand or any of the cameras, I may be able to hear you. What does the tapping mean? Or are you just trying to scare me?"

A heavy rumble shook the floor beneath her feet.

Tap-tap-tap.

Tap.

Tap-tap.

Jessica put the recorder close to her lips. "I'm going to have to check the outlets. The burning smell is getting intense. Something—*whoa!*"

The recorder was knocked from her hand and skidded across the linoleum floor. The hand that had been holding the recorder felt as if it had been dipped in a tub of ice. She gave it a few sharp shakes to halt the pins-and-needles sensation that followed.

The house was once again silent and the darkness seemed to intensify. Even though her eyes had acclimated to the night, she was finding it harder to make out the shapes of the furniture around her. It was as if a heavy, black gauze had oozed throughout the house like an obsidian blob. Sharp outlines became hazy glaucoma visions.

She took a few tentative steps toward where she assumed her digital recorder lay. The air itself was heavy and she knew she was far from alone. She fought hard to fight back the tingling dread that threatened to dance up her spine. A part of her was sure that something was very close behind her. Silently, it approached with arms wide open, edging closer with each deliberate step. If she were to turn around now, she would come face to face with all of her worst nightmares brought to life.

If only she dared to take one simple peek.

In the dark.

So close she could feel the ripples of its intrusive essence caressing the back of her neck.

Jessica stopped when she reached the threshold of the dining room and closed her eyes. She felt like a blind person in a crowded room of silent guests, no one daring to breathe lest they reveal their presence, yet eager to pounce if she gave the slightest inkling that she was aware of their claustrophobic proximity.

Her heart skipped a beat as she breathed deep. The fight-or-flight instinct was battling for control. Her body was in the throes of the primal, physical ache to flee. It would be so easy to run now. The front door was twenty feet away. Just turn a couple of locks and she could be outside.

The floorboards creaked behind her, a slight groan of wood protesting the weight of a single, heavy footstep.

Three more breaths. Her heart rate slowed to a steady rhythm.

Another creak, this time to her right, near the breakfront.

Jessica smiled and she felt the tension release its grip from her shoulders.

Breathe in, hold, breathe out.

Something hard and small smacked into the glass top of the coffee table.

Breathe in, hold, breathe out.

The sound of glass under stress, spider cracks crunching their way across the surface of the table.

Now.

Jessica spun and shouted, "Boo!"

She opened her eyes and faced the empty darkness behind her. The coffee table top exploded in a shower of crystal pebbles. Bits of glass bounced harmlessly off her leather jacket. A picture frame flew from the fireplace mantle and crashed into the opposite wall. All of the kitchen chairs slid out from under the table at once, one of them clattering to the floor. Jessica turned back toward the dining room in time to see the blinds on the front window part as if someone ran a finger from top to bottom. Upstairs, it sounded as if a brawl had broken out. The ceiling fan shook under the pounding of footsteps and falling objects.

The house was alive and it was not happy.

Jessica ducked as a couch pillow came her way. Another picture frame flipped off the wall and broke into pieces on the floor. She laughed out loud.

"That's it, get it out of your system. Get mad, madder than you've ever been. You've done enough to the McCammons. It's just you and me now. Tell me your name. I'd like to know who the gutless wonder is that hides in the shadows and terrorizes little kids. I've told you who *I* am."

An apple that had been in a bowl on the kitchen table flew at her in a lazy arc. She turned just in time to reach up and catch it.

"Nice try. Now, back to my question. *Who...the fuck...are you?*"

Chapter Three

"I have your final PK test results. I figured you'd want to hold on to these, maybe put them in a scrapbook someday."

Eddie Home dropped his suitcase on the bed and took the report from his roommate. He arched an eyebrow at his exit psychokinetic test, the last of more than he could ever count.

"Did I pass?" he asked, smiling as he dropped the report into the bottom of his suitcase.

"When do you *not* pass?" Tobi Cruz said. "It's really a shame you're leaving. Now I have to find another partner in crime."

"That should be pretty easy. I wouldn't exactly compare us to Steven Tyler and Joe Perry."

Tobi sank into his computer chair. "Yeah, you're right. Neither of us has Tyler's jack-o-lantern mouth."

They laughed as Eddie emptied the contents of his shirt drawer into his suitcase in one big heap. Tobi shook his head at the mess.

"At least we have one more night before you leave the lovely city of Durham. I've arranged a little get together at Pat's Tavern so we can send you off properly."

Eddie rolled his eyes. "Please tell me you didn't invite any of the professors. I've done my bit for science. I'd like one lab-coat-free evening before I hit the dusty."

Tobi leaned forward in his chair and said, "I don't know. You tell me."

Eddie cocked his head and sighed. "Do I really have to do this?"

"I'm afraid so," Tobi replied with a crooked smile.

"Fine." Eddie closed his eyes. He waited a moment to clear his mind.

He felt the familiar presence.

His eyelids fluttered open. A sharp intake of breath steadied his concentration.

An ethereal corpse stood behind Tobi. It rested a weightless hand on his shoulder.

Tobi shivered, but remained quiet.

The man had died when he was forty-one. His skin was pale and bloated. Dark, pink, blubbery seams had erupted here and there along his neck, legs and torso. Water was unkind to the human body.

The corpse looked down at Tobi with black, hollow eyes. He shook his head slowly.

Eddie smiled.

"Lucky for you, Bob says you didn't."

Tobi looked up. "Thank you, Bob. Man, I love that you can do that."

Bob's spirit flashed a request into the center of Eddie's mind. A brief but sharp pain made him cringe.

Eddie looked to a pile of balled up socks he'd set aside. He imagined the socks pelting Tobi in the face. A second later, without his touching them, they elevated off the bed and dashed at his friend.

"Oh, real nice," Tobi said when the fourth pair bounded off his forehead.

"Don't blame me, blame Bob."

Bob Wilson had lived in the house next door in the 1980s. On a fishing trip with his buddies, a hard-drinking band of brothers who had known each other since grade school, he tipped over the side of the boat. His head hit into one of the propeller blades. He slipped into unconsciousness, drew in cold water and died. His body was found floating near the shoreline several miles away and nine days after the accident.

He'd been their invisible roommate ever since Eddie had moved in. Bob was quiet, but loved to be around them. He was ghastly to behold, but Eddie had connected with him on levels much deeper than his appearance. It was still a mystery why he kept returning to their dorm room.

Most times, the dead kept their secrets.

Bob was also a good snitch when it came to keeping Tobi in line.

For his part, Tobi could always feel when Bob was around, but he couldn't see or communicate with him like Eddie.

Tobi said, "So, I'll see you at Pat's?"

"Of course. Who can turn down a night of free drinking thanks to his bud and roommate?"

"I don't remember anything about free drinks."

"You have a bad memory. You might want to stop at the ATM

before you go. I'm pretty thirsty."

"You're killing me, dude. Fine. I'll see you later."

"Don't forget to say goodbye to Bob."

"Yeah, yeah," Tobi said, giving a half-hearted wave.

Bob's bloated, purple lips grinned and he faded away.

Eddie looked around the room he had called home for the past year. Tobi's side of the room was neat to the point of being Spartan, while his side was a sweeping display of carnage.

"Might be easier if I just threw a match on it."

Eddie went into the bathroom to collect what he could and tossed it all into his toiletry bag. He combed his jet black hair back and smoothed the sides with his hands. At six foot two, he was lean but not skinny with a strong jaw line he inherited from his father and bright blue eyes bestowed upon him by his mother. In part because of the things he'd seen and experienced over the years, thanks to his many so-called gifts, his eyes carried the weight of a man much older, wiser and warier.

He went back into the room and removed his lacquered Duke University diploma from its place of prominence above his work desk, using his index finger to remove the layer of dust that had settled along its topmost edge. His entire four years at Duke were paid for by the nearby Rhine Research Center, the country's premier parapsychology research lab. Founded by botanist J.B. Rhine in 1935, The Rhine, as Eddie liked to call it, was dedicated to the serious study of parapsychology and human consciousness.

J.B. Rhine was an explorer in every sense of the word, devoting his life to the study of what the rest of the world considered to be the paranormal. The goal of Rhine, and now his ongoing research center, was to study and discover the truth behind things such as telepathy, ESP, psychokinesis, ghosts, poltergeists and even the existence of life after death. It was Rhine who coined the ubiquitous term ESP, as well as many of the standardized tests that are still used today to test the extra-mental capabilities of the select few chosen to take part in the institute's research.

Rhine and Eddie's family went back many, many years.

The scientist and the specimen.

But it was time to move on.

Chapter Four

For what seemed like the first time in ages, the house was gloriously quiet. No screaming kids, no husband asking where his belt was and best of all, not a single chore that had to be done.

Rita Leigh contemplated her good fortune as she sat on the chaise lounge by the window in her bedroom. Greg had taken Ricky to the office so they could spend some quality father-son time and Selena had been picked up by her friend Julie and her mother so they could spend the weekend together at her house, which was by the water and *the place to be*, as far as Selena was concerned. All of the laundry was tucked into the proper drawers and closets, dishes were clean and put away and the house was spotless.

"Now what do I do?" Rita said with a contented sigh.

She pulled back the curtain a little farther so the sun could warm her face. Even their dog Billy, an adorable brown and white Cavalier with all the energy of a nuclear reactor, was enjoying the quiet by sleeping on Selena's bed.

Rita eyed the television remote on her night table, but thought better of it. It seemed sacrilegious to shatter her domestic peace with something as predictably crass and imbecilic as daytime television. She was never one for talk or court shows and loathed soap operas. It was hard enough resigning herself to being an actual stay-at-home soccer mom. The young Rita that skipped school and listened to the Ramones and Red Hot Chili Peppers would have given her an ass whipping if she could see her now.

Rita giggled at the thought. It was amazing how priorities and preferences changed when you got older. She'd probably tell young Rita to wash off all that makeup and find a pair of jeans that didn't look as if they'd been dragged behind a truck for a week.

She picked up the latest issue of *Time* and flipped through the pages, trying to get into an article about the coming fall election and the strategies that needed to be employed to shift the balance of power in the House and Senate. She was almost asleep midway through the article.

"Okay, time to move. You've got seven hours to yourself, don't waste it sleeping."

She walked down the hall to check on Billy, who was snoring atop Selena's pillow. When her stomach gave a slight gurgle, she went down to the kitchen, started up a pot of coffee and popped some wheat bread into the toaster. Gazing out the kitchen window, she saw the mailman stop next door and decided to come out and get the mail personally.

It was nothing but a pile of bills and advertisements. No one wrote letters anymore, so much of the excitement of getting the mail was gone. The most thrilling thing she could hope for was the pack of coupons they got every month for the local businesses.

She ate her toast dry and drank her coffee black. She'd been on a health kick the past year and had managed to lose over thirty pounds, replacing much of the baby fat she had accumulated after having two children with lean muscle. She was almost in better shape than she'd been before she was married. She loved her new body and Greg certainly wasn't complaining.

Back upstairs, she stopped in front of the full-length mirror behind her door to look at her rediscovered flat stomach. She pulled up her shirt to admire the willpower and determination it took to get back in shape. Feeling giddy, she decided to take off all her clothes so she could get a complete view without worrying about one of the kids barging in.

"Not too bad, girl. Just a few more pounds to go."

She ran a hand over her hips, staying a moment on the area she targeted as her final combat zone. Her breasts had gone down a cup size, but they were firmer than before, and still larger than average. Her legs were sculpted and strong, thanks to countless hours on the treadmill, and elliptical. She'd even started hitting the tanning bed so she could be bronze all over.

She looked damn good for a middle-aged mother of two.

An idea came to her.

She walked over to her night table and rummaged around the bottom drawer, pulling aside stacks of old magazines and other accumulated junk.

"Aha, I thought that's where I put you."

It had been ages since she went to her friend Darlene's house for one of those erotica-themed parties. There had been a lot of alcohol and a so-called expert-slash-saleswoman came in to show them all the newest products and demonstrate in a funny yet almost clinical way how to use each one. Their laughter could have been heard for blocks. At the end of the party, everyone started placing orders. Not wanting to look like a prude, Rita had placed hers for some lotion that heated up when you rubbed it on your body and a vibrator. It was her first vibrator and she'd been too embarrassed to show it to Greg or even use it on herself.

Well, if today wasn't the day for it, that day would just never come.

She opened up the back to see what kind of batteries she'd need. She put on a robe and dashed downstairs to the utility closet to get a pair of C batteries. Back in her room, she closed the blinds, let the robe drop to the floor and lay back on the bed, using an extra pillow to prop up her back.

Rita gasped when she turned the vibrator on, surprised by how powerfully it shook in her hand and even more so by the noise it made. Even though it was irrational, she couldn't help thinking that her neighbors could hear its steady drone.

Thank God I never used this when the kids were home, she thought.

Twisting the little control dial down a few notches, she gently stroked the pink, plastic vibrator across her inner thighs, taking a moment to let it rest on the top of her pubic hair, as much teasing herself as hesitant to go all the way. It didn't take long for her body's response to overwhelm her mind and she moved the vibrator to exactly where it needed to be.

"Oh wow," she huskily moaned.

It felt amazing. Thanks to her and Greg's busy and conflicting schedules, it had been a while since they'd been together. Now she had something to help ease the dry spells. A torrid tingling spread to every corner of her body. Her hips gyrated as she rotated the vibrator in slow, steady circles.

Her mind was a complete blank as she lost herself in the rapidly building ecstasy.

If I'd only known, you never would have been buried in the drawer, she thought. Being raised in a strict Catholic family, masturbation had never been an option. Besides, it was something boys did because they couldn't keep their hands off themselves. Just like monkeys.

Good Lord this was good.

Blood rushed to her dampening pussy. She heard a deep groan, realizing it came from her without even feeling it escape her lips.

Pushing the vibrator to its limit, she found a perfect rhythm, and her thighs quivered with pleasure.

She was on the brink of total release when she heard the front door open and slam shut. Startled, she dropped the vibrator and jerked upright. She scrambled for her robe and almost dislocated her shoulder trying to get her arm into the sleeve. The vibrator hummed along on the comforter, rolling to the edge. Rita grabbed it, turned the dial off and threw it under the bed.

She tried to compose herself as she heard the approach of footsteps coming up the stairs.

Her cheeks had to be crimson and she was finding it hard to get her breathing under control.

Exercise! That's it. She'd say she was doing sit-ups. Wearing nothing but a robe. It was the best she could do.

"Mommy? Mom?"

Selena's voice echoed down the hall.

Rita couldn't believe it. Her one time using a vibrator and she'd almost been caught by her oldest. Maybe it was better left in the bottom of her drawer.

"I'm in here, sweetie," she said, assuming Selena must have forgotten to pack something for her little trip.

"Mommy?"

The footsteps stopped. A shiver of concern cramped her stomach. Selena only called her mommy when something was wrong. What if she was hurt?

Rita walked toward the open bedroom door.

"*Mommy.*"

"Are you okay, Selena? What can I—"

When she entered the hallway, it was empty.

But that was impossible. She distinctly heard Selena come upstairs. She must have been right outside the door the last time she called for her.

"Selena? Where did you go? Hello! Selena!"

She checked Selena's bedroom, then every room on both floors of the house, calling out her daughter's name in escalating tones. A cold lump formed in her stomach.

She was the only one in the house.

Chapter Five

The sun was out, vaporizing the morning dew, when Jessica emerged from the McCammon house. Her arms were loaded with bags of equipment and she trailed a heavy, black rolling case that housed all of her digital cameras. She piled the gear on the sidewalk by her car. A pair of chickadees was perched in the tree above her car, chirping in their familiar cadence, a musical greeting for the neighborhood early risers. She looked back at the house, amazed at the dichotomy between the interior and exterior.

Jessica lifted the flower pot under the front bay window and placed the house keys underneath.

She had spent the better part of the morning cleaning up broken glass and rearranging furniture, then packing up her own equipment. It had taken over four hours and she was bushed. All she could think of now was her own bed.

With everything packed in her hunter green Jeep, she headed back home to Rockville Centre in Long Island. Luckily for her, morning rush hour traffic was over, so the drive home from Bronxville would be less than an hour.

It wasn't until she was on the Hutchinson River Parkway that she remembered to call her aunt Eve. She hit Eve's name on her cell phone and plugged in her Bluetooth earpiece.

"I was starting to get worried about you," her aunt said.

"What, no hello?" Jessica replied. She had taken the top off the Jeep so the late spring air would keep her awake on the drive. Her shoulder-length, chestnut hair blew in every direction and she pushed the 4X4 to just under eighty miles an hour.

"Not when you go silent on me for an entire weekend, no. You know the rules," Eve coolly replied. She sounded more concerned than angry.

"You're right, I'm sorry. It was just an intense weekend and I kind of got lost in the moment."

There was a long silence before Eve asked, "How intense?"

"Let's just say I filled a garbage pail with broken glass and one of my meters is toast. On the bright side, I'm pretty sure I caught a lot of it on film."

"It really is your goal to put me in an early grave. What did the McCammon family say when they came back?"

Jessica swerved around a slow-moving car and fumbled around the center console to find her EZ Pass. "The McCammons are staying with family for the weekend, so they won't see things until they get back later tonight. I did my best to put the house back in order, but we both know that could all change between now and later."

Eve sighed heavily into the phone. "I really wish you wouldn't do these types of investigations alone. You could get hurt."

The last thing Jessica wanted to do was add more stress to Eve's life. When Jessica was just a baby, her mother passed away. One night she went to bed and simply never woke up. To make matters even stranger, her parents had won a twenty-five-million-dollar lottery on the exact same day, and her aunt Eve took it upon herself to take care of Jessica and her father as they waded through miles of grief and the ugly reality of sudden riches.

As the years went on, Jess's father became less interested in normal, everyday life, and more concerned with the paranormal, ghost hunting being one of his specialties. It was a boyhood fascination of his that, thanks to financial freedom and his newfound fears of dying, sleeping and a host of other normal activities, allowed him free reign to live in the world of the unexplained.

Jessica realized now he was just searching for her mother, any sign that she would be there waiting for him when it was his time to go. As much fun as he was to be around, there was always a deep, dark sadness lurking at the edges. He did his best to hide it from her, but kids are smarter and more intuitive than their parents think.

She thought about the last night with her father. She'd only been six years old.

The phantasm of Sharon Bolster lit up like a white-hot spotlight. Jessica and Eve slammed their eyes shut and shielded their faces with their hands. The room became exceedingly warm and the hair on their bodies stood straight up.

When she sensed the light was gone, Jessica opened her eyes.

The woman was no longer there.

A shot rang out downstairs. There was screaming, so much screaming.

They ran down the spiral staircase as fast as they could.

But it was too late.

Here she was at nineteen, driven by the same compulsions her father had. And here was Eve, trying to keep her from going over the precipice.

A solitary tear rolled down her cheek. She didn't bother to wipe it away.

"I know the risks. The book on poltergeists is that they make a lot of noise and toss a ton of stuff around, but there are no cases of anyone being seriously hurt. I asked the McCammons to leave this weekend so I could be sure it wasn't a manifestation originating from one of their daughters. I really thought Lori would have been the key. She just turned fourteen and she's loaded with your typical teenage angst. Amber and Elizabeth are too young, but you never know. Well, now I know. Hold on a sec."

Jessica slowed down to pass through the toll, holding her EZ Pass up to the window so it could be scanned. She scooted over to the left lane on the Whitestone Bridge, narrowly missing a yellow mustang. The driver gave her a New York salute. She paid him no mind as she zipped past any car in her way.

"You are one hard-headed pain in my butt," Eve said.

"Yes, but you love me."

"That I do, with all my heart. If I thought I could stop you, short of having you imprisoned, I would. Are you hungry? I can stop at the restaurant and bring something back for you. I have to meet with Anthony in a little bit to go over a few catering jobs. I'll ask Louie to whip something up."

"Thanks, but I think I'm just going to crash when I get home. Although his ravioli are even better warmed up."

"I think I can swing that. See you soon."

Jessica removed the earpiece and turned the radio on. She plugged in her iPod and cranked up the volume.

Another trait she had picked up from her father was a love of eighties and early nineties heavy metal. A day didn't go by when she didn't think of him. It was her shrink, the one she went to until she was about twelve, who had come up with the idea of connecting Jess to her father through the music he listened to most. It was odd having Megadeth blaring at her to give her comfort, but there it was.

She honked her horn at an SUV and took the entrance ramp to the Southern State Parkway. She had one more stop to make before going home.

"World without end, amen."

Jessica knelt before the small statue of Mary, where the baptismal font was kept. She was alone in St. Matthew's Church. Only a few lights were on, and the flickering candles to her right created undulating shadows against the wall.

It was quiet here. Peaceful.

Even though there was no one to disturb, she gently placed the kneeler up so as not to make a sound. Exiting the pew, she faced the altar, made the sign of the cross while kneeling on one knee. As was her ritual, she placed a ten dollar bill in the poor box, touched the long wick to one of the lit candles and transferred the flame to a new candle. She said another silent prayer for her father, and hoped he was by her mother's side.

She left the church feeling stronger, more in control. The last night had been hell. She needed a little heaven to tip the scales back toward sanity.

She had long ago reconciled her religious beliefs with her paranormal beliefs. For her, they could easily and logically coexist. Faith had the same weight as fact, and she had plenty of both. It saddened her that so many in the paranormal field either had no room for religion, or used it in excess to explain and do things that were simply not plausible.

Life was all about balance.

She gunned the Jeep out of the church parking lot, Cinderella pounding from the Bose speakers. She chuckled. *Oh yeah, I'm balanced all right.*

Chapter Six

Eddie decided to make one last stop at The Rhine.

Landscapers were weeding the garden in the front of The Rhine's relatively new home. The center had moved into the building, which looked more like a nice, large-ish house, a little over ten years ago. He nodded hello to Diego who had been tending the grounds well before Eddie started his "internship".

The reception area was empty. Eddie walked upstairs to Dr. Froemer's office. He paused to look in at the darkened testing area. He couldn't even calculate the number of hours he'd spent in there undergoing sequencing tests and predicting cards from a specially designed deck called zener cards created for psi research. Each of the five cards had a specific symbol—a star, cross, circle, wavy lines and a square. The trick was to guess which card the person holding the deck was looking at. Even a person without psychic abilities could guess correctly about twenty percent of the time. Eddie consistently *guessed* correctly well over seventy percent of the time.

His days were also filled with a multitude of psychokinetic experiments where he was asked to move objects with his mind. These particular tests were mentally and physically draining, but proved to be the most astounding of all. Eddie could pick up, shift and even levitate household items, sometimes while he was even a room away. The hours of recordings he had undergone would provide decades of study. They had even tried remote viewing, which was the ability to have a controlled out-of-body experience in order to travel to selected points on a map and describe the surroundings. Though he tested off the charts for everything, remote viewing was not his forte. He was grateful for his lack of expertise, because it was one less experimental track he had to take.

He knocked on Dr. Froemer's door.

He heard the doctor's muffled voice shout, "I said I'm not hungry. Now please, take your lunch and stop worrying about me. I'll eat only when I need to, not just because the clock says I have to eat lunch at half past noon."

Eddie eased the door open. "I hate to disappoint you, but I have no intention of getting you lunch."

Dr. Froemer pushed his glasses to the top of his head and smiled. His gaunt frame was lost amidst the plush leather chair. He had a trio of large textbooks perched on his bony lap and struggled to keep them from slipping.

"I'm so glad you stopped by, Eddie. I'm sorry about all that. You know how Danielle is always trying to force feed me. I thought she was coming back for round three."

Eddie sat opposite the doctor. "I think she got the hint. She was nowhere to be seen when I walked in."

"Hardest part about coming to work here. Everyone loves to eat." One of the books dropped onto the floor and when he went to retrieve it, the other two fell as well. Eddie went over, picked them up and put them on his desk.

Dr. Froemer gave him a quizzical look.

"I'm a little hung over today. It's best to do my light levitating manually," Eddie said with a short laugh.

"Yes, I suppose you've done your share. It's a damn shame you're taking leave of us. Is there anything I can do to convince you to stay?"

Eddie smiled. "I appreciate all you've done for me and despite how I may have reacted at times, I did enjoy this past year. I learned more about myself than I ever thought possible, which is all the more reason to leave now. Everything's been about me. It's time I went and thought about someone else for a change."

"You know, your father said the same thing to me when we had him here thirty years ago. What a talent. I wish there was a way to go back and work with your great-grandfather, D.D. Home. Like you, he absolutely vexed anyone who attempted to debunk his abilities. Did you know that Arthur Conan Doyle befriended him and was his biggest supporter?"

"I sure do," Eddie replied. It was a point of pride in the Home family that they were connected to such a legendary figure. Stories were passed down from one generation to the next. D.D. Home came out of the explosive spiritualist movement of the late 1800s. He spent decades bewitching and bewildering lay and professional people alike with a seemingly endless store of preternatural abilities. His faculties ran the gamut from ESP to levitation and talking to the dead. Every top scientist of the day had studied him. Not a single person had ever found anything that would lead them to believe his powers were anything but real. Sir Arthur Conan Doyle, a man whose interest in the paranormal was quite prodigious, found in D.D. Home the embodiment of truths greater than any known to man.

Dr. Froemer huffed. "Of course you do. Never mind an old man who tends to tell the same stories over and over again. Your great-grandfather was the gold standard in parapsychology." He raised a thin finger at him. "But you, you have all the potential to be the platinum."

"I wouldn't go that far," Eddie protested, embarrassed by the doctor's sense of his worth.

"So, what's her name?"

Eddie shook his head, confused. "What do you mean?"

Dr. Froemer laughed. "Men your age don't make big moves unless there's a woman involved. It's what keeps the species alive." A mischievous light danced behind his eyes.

Eddie reached into his back pocket and placed a printout on the desk. "And people say I'm the psychic."

"What's this?"

"The girl."

Dr. Froemer read the article. It had been posted by a now defunct paranormal team in Washington State. It described an entire Alaskan town disappearing seemingly overnight. There were rumors of multiple deaths. The catalyst may or may not have been an amateur ghost hunter and his family. It was one of the great, under-the-radar paranormal mysteries of the past twenty years. Four supposedly went to Alaska, and three made it out. One of them was a young girl. She should be just about twenty now.

"I take it you know this girl?" Dr. Froemer said.

"Never met her before. But I do have a very strong feeling that she needs my help."

The doctor arched an eyebrow. "If you never met her and there's no mention of her name that I can see in this article, how do you expect to find her?"

Eddie re-folded the paper and put it back in his pocket. He said, "Her father told me. He's the one that didn't make it out alive."

Chapter Seven

Jessica had two things to do on her checklist today. First, she had to look through the email inbox linked to her website and talk to Tom Mannerheim, her eccentric Swedish web developer who preferred to be called Swedey, about some minor changes she needed done. Then she had to sit down to do an evidence review of everything she had recorded at the McCammon house. There were hours and hours of video and audio to sift through. She always worried that the equipment would fail at the critical moment, which it sometimes did, so she wanted to get her ass in gear.

She was glad she had decided not to take any summer classes during the break this year. All set to graduate Hofstra this time next year, she wanted to devote herself full time to the business her father had created. Her ultimate plan was to take it to the next level.

School had always been easy for her, graduating South Side High School, Rockville Centre's best school, two years ahead of schedule. Being younger than her classmates made it hard to really fit in, but her eyes were always set on college and beyond. She made it into Hofstra's Honors College and was happily two semesters away from getting her B.S. in anthropology. Her goal was to pursue graduate studies in archaeology. Her obsession with the dead spanned the scope of the scientific and paranormal worlds. When she told Eve in the spring that she was going to abstain from summer classes for the first time since she'd started high school, Eve gave her full blessing.

Her break from school work was filled with all-night vigils, reviewing notes and recordings, doing background investigations on people and places and making sure her website, *fearnone.com*, stayed current and did its job of attracting more and more visitors. The website had originally been her father's, which he'd handled all on his own, and was used as a public library for all things strange and unexplained. Naturally, it died when her father passed away and she had to buy it back from its current owner when she decided to resurrect it a couple of years ago. Money was not an issue, but Jessica had a frugal streak a mile long. According to Aunt Eve, it was hereditary. At first, she tried to handle the website herself, but soon found it too much to keep up with.

This go around, she hired Swedey because she just didn't have time to devote to developing and maintaining a website amidst a full college course load and weekly paranormal investigations. And unlike her father, who was into everything from aliens to monsters, she decided to stick with what she knew—ghosts, or what she called EBs, short for Energy Beings.

She knew full well that EBs existed and made it her mission to prove it to the world. Her experience in Alaska had forever changed the six-year-old Jessica. More than just her perceptions of the world had been altered that night. Jessica's subsequent trips back to Alaska, on the spot where everything happened, brought back further proof that the dead did not, in fact, die.

"What are you up to?"

Her cousin Liam stood in her doorway holding a full bowl of chocolate ice cream. His brown hair hung over his eyes in a stringy mess. He was more like a brother than a cousin, and played the part of irritating little brother quite well when he wanted to.

"Just some work that has to be done. Today," she replied.

Liam eyed the stacks of discs and equipment on her bed.

"Cool, evidence review. You know, the whole process could go a lot easier if you let me help you."

"Your mom will kill me if I let you do that."

"So, it's not like I'm going to rush down and tell her I'm helping you. If I stayed in here and kept my bedroom door closed, she'd figure I was sleeping."

Liam had just finished his freshman year of high school and told everyone he planned to set the all-time teenage sleep record during the summer. Eve was always making noise around him to get him up and out of the house. Most times, it didn't work.

"I made a promise to your mother when I took this up that I would leave you out of it. Aside from her getting royally pissed at me, I'd be letting myself down. Ain't gonna happen. Why don't you call Steve and go to the mall or something?"

"Because I'm lazy and don't feel like showering. Come on, Jess. What's the big deal with looking at video? I see those people do it on those shows all the time and they don't run screaming from the room."

Jessica shot him a harsh look. "There are things on those tapes that you don't need to see. I'm not one of those ghost shows on TV, all right? Now go before it gets ugly."

"I forgot, you're Jessica the Super Ghost Hunter. Oooo, scary," he mocked with a mouth full of ice cream.

Jessica stood up and stared him down. "You don't want me to walk over there, do you?"

Liam thought about it for a moment, then shook his head. "I don't feel like being your kickboxing punching bag today. Have fun with your review, Jessie-poo."

She kicked the door shut when he turned to leave. Grunting to release her frustration, she turned on her laptop to send Swedey an email. She knew she was settled down when the heavy clacking of keys turned into quieter clicking.

Next, she plugged one of her twenty-six-inch monitors into her video camera and selected the file that was recorded in the living room, facing into the kitchen. The time marked on the file coincided with the moment the McCammon poltergeist, or what she thought had been a poltergeist, went into full-on crazy mode. The camera's night vision gave everything a green and gray tint. It was always uncomfortable to watch herself. She could see every emotion as they played themselves out on her face and in her body language, and she often wasn't happy with what she saw.

She, more than most, knew exactly what she was dealing with and her fear of EBs was minimal at best. Looking into the worst the unknown had to offer and walking away alive, yet deeply scarred, had a way of erasing your fears. But there it was, the first glimmer of terror as the kitchen drawer closed by itself. She could just make out the odd, rhythmic tapping on the walls. One taps, three taps, two taps. *That had to mean something.*

Jessica watched herself wrestle with her fight-or-flight response. Her father had suffered from crippling anxiety and she'd been told by more than one doctor that it could be hereditary. No matter how much bravery Jessica had in her head and heart, her body oftentimes betrayed her. It was her belief that the more she studied herself and her reactions, the more she could control them in the future.

The picture got fuzzy for a moment, and when it cleared, she saw that the couch was in a new position. Damn. The energy used to move the couch must have affected the camera. On the bright side, she *could* hear the couch legs scape against the floor.

She watched video for another four hours, cataloging events and when they happened. Intermittent bursts of static were a persistent problem and had caused her to miss key moments, like when the first picture frame flew from the shelf into the wall beside her. There might have been missing pieces, but there was enough to show the McCammons the severity of the situation and prove that they were not imagining things.

The level of activity had been increasing with each visit, the last one being a real shit storm. She had been so sure that by totally removing the family, the activity would have died down, as most poltergeist manifestations originated within the living. Not in this case. It got worse, which was a total surprise. She may not have had years of case work under her belt, but she had researched and had seen enough to know this flew in the face of conventional paranormal understanding.

There was a definite concern that the family could be hurt by flying debris, at the very least.

"You better find some answers," she muttered.

She was disappointed that she didn't get any disembodied voices or EVPs. She asked the EB for its name about a dozen times, but came up empty. *Damn.* She needed that name.

During her short tenure as a paranormal explorer, she'd discovered a welcome side effect to her curiosity. If people were at the end of their rope and just wanted a haunting to stop, Jessica could, somehow, put an end to it. How and why it worked was still a mystery to her, but she suspected it had a lot to do with what happened to her when she was little.

Before her eyes started to cross, Jessica took a break, grabbed a Gatorade from the fridge, talked to Eve for a bit about going shopping tomorrow for the dresses they'd need for a cousin's wedding in the fall, and headed back to her room. Swedey had already replied to her email and was busy at work on the changes to the site. Man, he was quick.

She wondered what he was like in person. All she knew about him she got from texts, emails, the occasional phone call and his website. He stayed off social media, preferring to keep the details of his private life to himself. In that regard, they were kindred spirits.

Now was as good a time as any to go through the website's inbox.

"Crazy, looney, horny, demented, oh, that's a maybe," she said as she scanned the subject lines and filed them into various folders to be read or deleted later.

She stopped at one that read, *I WOULD LIKE TO ARRANGE A MEETING*

"Obviously lonely, possibly demented, definitely delusional."

Before she could cast it to the deleted file, she accidentally hit the wrong key and opened it.

Hello Ms. Backman. My name is Eddie Daniel Home. I was wondering if I could possibly meet with you some day, in the public place of your choice and with as many people as you feel comfortable bringing. I'm in the process of moving to New York from Durham, North Carolina, where I've spent the majority of the past year at the Rhine Research Center.

Jessica read the rest, and went back to the beginning to read it again.

Ms. Backman. How the hell did he know her name? She'd always been careful to the point of total paranoia with the website. She only referred to herself as the *EB Explorer*. There was never mention of her real name.

Eddie Daniel Home. There was something familiar about his name. She knew full well what the Rhine Research Center was about.

Intrigue and concern did a two-step in her head.

She printed the email, posted it on the whiteboard above her desk and went back to reviewing the audio recordings. Her clients were more important at the moment than a meeting request from someone she may or may not have known.

Her voice filled the headphones.

"My name is Jessica. What's yours?"

She amped up the volume, hoping for a reply.

Chapter Eight

Eddie Home kicked the door open to his apartment while juggling a pizza box in one hand and a shopping bag in the other. His car keys, dangling from his mouth, were dropped with a flick of his head onto the kitchen counter with a heavy clang. He put the pizza box on the stovetop and plopped the bag onto the kitchen table, his bladder aching. A tiny avalanche of books slid out of the bag as it tipped to one side.

On the way to the bathroom, he stopped at his laptop that he'd left perched on the arm of the easy chair he'd found at a nearby garage sale and powered it up. By the time he was finished with his pit-stop, his email was polling for new messages.

"Come on, bring me good news."

In a way, Eddie was glad that his abilities had their limitations. He couldn't imagine how mundane life would be if he could know every event before it happened, read every thought, foretell every move. A life without anticipation, wonder, hope and even confusion just wouldn't be a life worth living.

Only one new email came through—a quick message from his mother who was an entire country away and living the renewed life of a happy divorcee. He'd read her email later, once he'd had a chance to eat, digest and mentally prepare himself. Only God knew what she was into now, or even worse, who. After discovering his father's lifetime of affairs, she had ceremoniously kicked him to the curb and was going through boyfriends like a high school cheerleader. Eddie was happy that *she* was finally happy, but he really didn't need any details about her blossoming love life.

Conversely, since the divorce, his father was, for the first time in over twenty years, *not* seeing someone and wallowing in his misery. The Home House of Dysfunction was yet another reason he took the scholarship from The Rhine to attend Duke and move three thousand miles away. The year before he'd left for Duke had been an absolute nightmare and one he would like to forget. Jesus, the fighting was epic. Both made vain attempts to recruit him to their side, even resorting to bribery. How many kids were given hotel money on prom night by their parents? Just thinking about it gave birth to an incessant pounding in his temples.

There'd been enough other things that caused his head to ache. Connecting with spirits could be unpleasant. Parental jockeying for position far exceeded psychic brain strain.

He made a mental note to call his dad after he emailed his mother. Eddie often wondered if his father's prolonged depression was brought on by the divorce or the rapid decline of his own psychic abilities. Was this a glimpse at his own fate? The thought kept him awake many nights.

He grabbed a slice of pepperoni pizza and a paper towel and sat at the table to go through the books he had purchased at a used bookstore on Fordham Road that specialized in, of all things, New Age *and* mystery paperbacks. His one-bedroom apartment in the Bronx was a short bus ride from the various shops that dotted the multicultural landscape of Fordham Road. He'd never experienced anything like it. His first week there, he'd sampled cuisine from Jamaica, India, the Dominican Republic, Cuba and Morocco until his stomach, unaccustomed to the assault of different spices and sauces, threw up the white flag. Hence the pizza, made with a chewy, thick crust that laid waste to anything he'd ever had before in North Carolina or back home in San Francisco.

Most of the books were crime novels by Robert Parker, Robert Crais, Richard Stark and Elmore Leonard, along with a handful of paperbacks dealing with various forms of meditation. Dr. Froemer had introduced him to the practice as a way to not only hone his abilities, but also to strengthen them enough so he didn't experience the same withering away of talent that almost every psychic eventually suffered. Daily meditation practice helped him in more ways than he'd ever dreamed it could.

After gobbling up three slices, he moved into the living room with one of the books, a yellow-paged, moldy-smelling text about transcendental meditation, and sat on the living room floor. The sun had set and an unexpected cool breeze drifted into his window.

His mind wandered and he recalled the very first time he had summoned the courage to speak to the dead. He'd been seeing spirits since he was a baby, but lived in terror of the daily visitations until he turned eight. On the night of his eighth birthday, his stomach filled with ice cream cake and cheese puffs, an old woman hovered over him as he lay in bed. Her long, gray hair fanned out around her deep-lined face as if she were floating in water. Her trembling, matchstick arms reached down to him, dangling inches before his face. His first reaction was to scream.

But no, he was eight now. It was time to stop being a baby.

Besides, she looked so sad, so lost. So he asked, "Are you lonely?"

The old woman's face softened, and without moving her lips, he heard her say, "My son said he will see me on Tuesday."

The question, the answer, both forged a connection that allowed him to see into her soul, to read her living past, and to know that her body was decaying in her living room chair, waiting for her son's monthly visit.

It had terrified and fascinated him at the same time. In an instant, he knew her name and where she lived and he anxiously told his father the next day. She was local, and his father said the best thing to do was read the paper each day and see if he was right. In the meantime, if she appeared again, Eddie needed to tell her she was dead, and encourage her to move on. She would have to wait some time to see her son again.

Her death was noted in a very small column in the regional section of the paper three days later. And when she came to him, again hovering over his bed, he did as his father had told him. She nodded, and faded away.

His life had never been the same since.

Eddie read the first chapter while sitting on the floor with his back against the easy chair's leg rest. Taking steady, slow breaths, he put the book down and assumed the lotus position.

He took his time, giving attention to the areas of stress in his body and releasing the tension, all the while breathing naturally, counting each breath to both focus and clear his mind of unwanted distractions. He continued until he lost count, the breaths taking over completely, bringing him into a deeper state of mind.

Feeling the nothing and everything that filled his earthbound vessel, he remained still, only his stomach moving in and out with each breath, his back and neck straight and hands atop one another in his lap. If there were noises outside, he didn't notice them. He was where he needed to be.

Eddie nudged his mind to concentrate on the energy of the being that had first reached out to him six months ago. The contact then had been all too brief and fragile as gossamer thread. With great effort, he'd worked daily on strengthening the signal, each interaction fortifying the ethereal bond between them.

The need to find the girl was overwhelming. Everything in his psi-enhanced consciousness screamed that she needed his help. So did the spirit of the man that had found him in the transom between life and death.

He thought moving to New York would supercharge the signal, a means of hardwiring himself into the direct life source of his netherworld contact. He knew this particular spirit was torn between two entry points in the plane of the living, and communication was never easy. But he had guessed correctly that being here would improve their connection.

His breathing slowed as his heartbeat calmed, until they were on a one-to-one basis—a beat, flushing blood through his semi-dormant system, followed by a short breath, with long periods of stillness between each. To the casual observer, he would look the part of the upright corpse. His skin paled and not a single muscle so much as twitched.

It was a full hour before anything happened. Eddie's conscious mind drifted in a sea of nihility, his hold on the here and now tethered by the thinnest of filaments. And then, unknown to even him, his lips began to move in whispered conversation. Disjointed words flowed from his lips, his physical body a dozen steps behind the flurry of activity occurring in his meditative mind.

His soft ramblings were the only sound in the apartment, weighed with the eerie undertones of a living haunt. It wasn't until his shoulders slumped forward that he ceased speaking, slowly lowering his head into his hands so he could rub away the arctic chill that had enveloped his head. He rested a moment, regulating his breath so he could revive his slumbering senses.

Eddie rolled onto his hands and knees with a soft groan and pushed himself off the floor. Shivering, he walked into the bedroom, wincing from the pins and needles in his feet and legs, and wrapped himself in his comforter. He looked at the clock by his bedside.

Two hours. A new record.

But it was worth it.

After warming up, he went back to the living room and woke his sleeping laptop. He carried it with him to the kitchen and turned on the oven to continue warming himself up, despite the fact it was summer and all of the windows were closed. He opened his email and typed, not all of the words his own.

Chapter Nine

A week after Jessica's last night at the McCammon house, she had completed reviewing all of the video and audio recordings and couldn't wait to show Tim and Kristen McCammon everything she had caught. This was the tricky part of the job because she was never sure how the person living in the affected home would react. The last thing she wanted to do was scare them any more than they already were, especially with three young daughters who were jumping at every noise. She was a strong believer that knowledge was power. She needed to give them that strength, and rid them of the EB that was plaguing their home.

When her best friend Angela Bastiani once asked her if she went into a home looking to debunk the claims of the paranormal like all of the people on TV went about their business—and wasn't that what made them so credible?—Jess had laughed.

"I don't even waste my time if I sense there isn't something credible there. And trust me, I know. Don't ask me how, I just know. I've been able to ever since..."

Her mind had wandered for a moment, drifting back to a cold cabin in a distant place.

"I know, honey. I know," Angela had said, reaching out to hold her hands in her own.

The physical contact had broken the pull of her past. "Yeah. Well, truth is, I don't give a shit about debunking because if there's nothing real there, I'll have that figured out at least after my first few hours in the house. The only reason I do this is to show them the truth. Maybe if more people weren't blind, life on the planet would be different. And if it's something with some bad juju, I'm there to make it disappear."

Jessica smirked at the memory as she kicked the Jeep's door closed.

The front lawn smelled of sweet, fresh-cut grass and she could hear kids splashing in a pool.

Tim and Kristen McCammon must have been waiting by the window because they opened the door a second before Jess rang the bell. Tim was wearing an extra loud Hawaiian shirt from the Tommy Bahama middle-aged-white-guy collection and khaki cargo shorts that exposed a pair of hairless legs. Kristen looked as if she had just come back from the tennis club, her tan skin in sharp contrast to her white blouse and thigh-high shorts. Neither looked as if they had been sleeping well.

"The girls are out in the back swimming with their older cousin," Kristen said as she led her into the house. "I told them not to come in so you wouldn't have to worry about showing us anything you may have recorded."

"That's good, because there's some stuff in here that's pretty intense."

"Maybe we should join the girls," Tim joked, his forced laughter unable to hide his trepidation.

Jessica put her laptop on the kitchen table and started it up while connecting a larger monitor.

"When I show you the video and you hear the audio, you have to remember that I was egging it on. I don't want you to think that this is something that will be a nightly occurrence. Like I told you, I'm kind of a lightning rod for this stuff. The good news is, we can rule out any of the girls as the catalyst."

"What's the bad news? If there's good news, there's always bad news to follow," Kristen said, pressing her hand to her heart. Tim reassuringly rubbed the tops of her shoulders.

"I wouldn't call it bad news. Let's just say I have a little more work to do. I may be young, but I'm old school when it comes to what I do. I don't just make recordings and run, which is why I've been to your house more times than the mailman the past month. There's something I still need to figure out here. I'll show you in a minute."

Her computer beeped to life and Jess entered her password to access her laptop. "Tim, if you can just sit on the other side of me, I'll go through everything I caught."

Chapter Ten

Summer had just started, but the thermometer told Greg Leigh it was in full force no matter what the calendar said. He slipped on a sleeveless T-shirt and his bathing suit, tried to comb his short, wiry, salt-and-pepper hair—though more salt than pepper lately—and admitted defeat by clamping his old Portland Sea Dogs baseball cap on his head.

Rita and Selena were sitting in the breakfast nook, talking over bowls of cereal. Selena wore pajamas that were too small and too tight on her burgeoning curves for his taste, but he'd been told numerous times by Rita to leave the dress code to her. "Where's Rick?" he asked as he reached for a box of cereal bars.

Rita answered, "He went with Sean and his mom to baseball practice. I told him I could get ready and watch him but he said he's too old to have his mom and dad there."

Selena rolled her eyes. "He almost cried when you couldn't be at practice just three weeks ago."

"He's at that age, honey," Rita said with a shrug. "One minute he wants to be a man, the next he wants to be a boy. It's not easy. Look at your father. He's still struggling with it." She smiled at Greg over her coffee mug.

"Don't be jealous of my youth," he said before shoving an entire breakfast bar in his mouth. "Anyone like seafood?" he mumbled.

"Gross, Dad. No one wants to see your chewed up food. I see what you mean, Mom."

Selena took her empty bowl to the sink and went upstairs to her room.

"Tough crowd," Greg said.

"There's nothing cool or amusing about us right now. She'll snap out of it just in time to ask you to pay for her wedding."

"I don't even want to think about that. I guess that leaves me with no helpers to change the oil and wash and wax the car, unless you want to be my buddy?" Greg tipped the bill of his cap up with a flick of his finger and sauntered over to Rita. "What say you, pardner?"

She patted his chest as she rose from her chair. "I'd love to, but I have an appointment to get my mani-pedi. After that, I have to do anything that doesn't involve changing oil or washing and waxing cars."

"You don't know what you're missing. When I'm buff and bronze from being outside all day, you'll wish you took me up on my offer."

"I'll take my chances. Have fun."

Greg watched her walk away, still disbelieving that the toned body outlined by the sun passing through her thin robe belonged to his wife of almost twenty years. He still wasn't sure how he felt about her transformation. He was equal parts impressed by her determination, turned on and, to be honest, intimidated and a bit uneasy. It was as if she were becoming a new person, and when she did, would he still have a place in her new life? He shook his head to chase the thoughts of his own insecurities away.

"Time to play with the Charger."

The air was heavy and there wasn't a cloud in the sky. He pulled the well-worn metal ramps out from under his work bench and went into the driveway to inspect the alignment. The sun warmed the back of his neck and arms. He placed a cinderblock behind each ramp so they wouldn't slip out from under his tires as he pulled up onto them. It was foolish to drive onto the ramp without a spotter, but he'd done it so many times he considered himself an expert. One wrong move and he could easily drive up and over the crest of the ramp and wedge it under his car. Shuddering at the thought, he walked back out to the driveway.

He waved to Mr. Murphy across the street. The old man was out weeding his garden, garbed in his typical yellow polo shirt, plaid shorts that had seen better days, black socks, loafers and straw hat. Rita had told him often how she would leave him if he ever developed Mr. Murphy's fashion sense in his dotage. He secretly admired the old man's lack of giving a frog's fat ass what anyone thought. That was one of the benefits of growing old. You no longer had to care about the small stuff.

Everyone considered Mr. Murphy the patriarch of the neighborhood and out of respect, couldn't bring themselves to call him by his first name, Al.

The sun felt good on Greg's skin and the air still carried a little of the dampness from the night before. If he timed things just right, he'd be done with the car around noon, which meant he could spend the rest of the day sitting back on the porch and watching the day go by with a few beers.

His black '74 Dodge Charger sat in the driveway, looking as if it had just rolled off the factory floor. He'd bought it at an auction ten years ago when it was in pretty sorry shape. Back when he was in high school and college, he and his friend Fred made it a hobby to buy old Mustangs, restore them to their former glory and resell them for a tidy profit. It beat the hell out of working in a retail store or waiting tables, and it was fun. That all changed when Fred joined the army and was sent to Fort Bliss in the searing heat of southern Texas. Rebuilding cars without Fred wasn't as much fun, so Greg put on a dress shirt and tie and got his first office job. Before he knew it, he was married and raising a family, so there wasn't any time to get dirty under a hood.

That all changed when the kids got old enough to go an hour without crying and Rita told him he needed a hobby. She didn't have to tell him twice and he knew just what he wanted to do.

The Charger was a real challenge, but damn it was worth every ounce of effort. He considered it his third child. And this one he raised all by himself.

He noticed a smudge mark by the rear quarter panel. Greg pulled out a soft cloth to buff it away.

"It sure is nice to see a real car on the block," Mr. Murphy called over. "Not like these new cars that look the same. All these rice burners have the charm of a shoe box. You do good work, Greg."

"Thanks. Someone has to keep tradition alive," he replied with a grin.

"You need any help getting it on the ramps?" Mr. Murphy fiddled with a pair of pruning shears. His straw hat, frayed at the ends and looking as if a breeze would undo the loosening weave, started to slip off. He snatched it in midair and crushed it back onto his head. Greg laughed inwardly. The old codger still had good reflexes.

"I'll be fine. Let me know if *you* need any help mowing the lawn."

Mr. Murphy waved him off. "My power mower just about does all the work by itself. All I need to do is steer the damn thing." His laughter degraded to a hacking cough. He'd been a lifetime smoker, tearing off the filters so he could get the good stuff, as he liked to call it. At age eighty, it hadn't slowed him down a bit. The man had good genes.

Mr. Murphy went back to his garden and Greg got behind the

wheel. The black leather seat was already hot enough to bake the back of his legs and the steering wheel was no better. He turned the key and the engine gave a low, steady purr. The old car vibrated like a racehorse itching to burst from the starting gate.

"Easy there, girl."

Greg dropped the gear into drive and eased off the brake. The car rolled slowly up the driveway and halfway into the garage. He stopped when he heard the scrape of the metal ramps on concrete as the front tires hit the lip. He got out to make sure the tires were lined up with the exact center of the ramps, checked the blocks behind them and slid back into the driver's seat.

This was where it got tricky. He had to give it just enough gas to get to the top of the ramp. Too much and he'd overshoot them. If he did it too fast, the pressure might cause one of the ramps to scoot forward.

He toed the gas pedal and made sure the wheel was locked in position. The Charger started its slow, steady ascent. The view out of the windshield changed as it rose higher, the ceiling now in full view.

Greg waited for the telltale *thunk* as the tires hit the depressed slots at the top of the ramp. Any second.

He looked up and gasped.

What the hell was Selena doing in front of the car?

Because he was doing it alone, he hadn't left much space between where the car would rest and the back wall. If she stayed there, she could be pinned between the car and the wall.

"Selena, get out of there!" he shouted as he slammed the brakes.

She looked at him with cold, emotionless eyes. If he hadn't just seen her fifteen minutes before, he would have sworn she was sleepwalking. She had gone through a terrifying phase of it when she was twelve. He and Rita called it *The Year Without Sleep*. Months of counseling did nothing to stop it. The day after she turned thirteen, it simply stopped. No rhyme, no reason.

Suddenly, the right side of the car dipped and the ramp shot forward like a cannon ball.

He didn't even have time to scream at his daughter to move. The ramp clanged off the wall the same time as the car slammed down on its struts. Greg was jolted to his side and lost sight of Selena.

He jammed into park and jumped out of the car, sure to find Selena in a crumpled heap on the cold floor. He cursed himself for setting the ramps up so far into the garage and for not locking the door that led to it.

His heart stopped when he looked down and saw nothing but an empty, oil-and-grease-spotted floor.

"Selena?"

Panicking, he dropped to his knees and looked under the car.

Please, please, please, don't be hurt, he silently begged.

She wasn't under the car, either.

"Selena?" he said, his voice cracking with concern.

He was answered with a muffled, "What?"

It was Selena, but she was upstairs in the room above the garage.

"Honey, are you okay? You scared the hell out of me," he called up through the ceiling.

Her footsteps walked across the floor and down the steps. She opened the door, saw the tilted car and said, "What did I do now? Why are you asking if I'm okay?"

Greg wanted to rush over and pull her in his arms. At the same time, he wanted to yell at her for walking into the garage while he was putting the car up.

He compromised, placing a hand on her shoulder and asking, "Selena, you know you're not supposed to come in here when I'm putting the car up, right?"

She looked at him as if he had just given birth to a two-headed goat. "Yeah, I know that."

"I could have killed you just now."

Selena backed out of his grip. "How? You can't blame me for dropping the car off the ramp."

Greg had to check his anger. In a measured tone, he replied, "When you popped in here, I had to jam the brakes, and then the ramp came out. I thought you were hurt, or worse."

"But I wasn't even down here. I was on the couch texting Julie."

"Honey, I know you were down here. I looked you straight in the eye. Are you sure you didn't fall asleep on the couch?"

Great. It was back to sleepwalking again. Greg shivered at the thought of going through that one more time. He also didn't want to think about the damage he had just done to the car.

"I was wide awake. Here, you can see the timeline of my texts." She held her phone out for him.

"That's not possible. You must have thought you were texting Julie."

"Look at the phone, Dad. I'm not lying."
He took her phone and scrolled up through the texts.
He swallowed hard.
She was right. She hadn't been down in the garage.

Chapter Eleven

"Take a look at this and tell me whether I should call the cops or just kick this guy's ass myself!"

Jessica dropped a folded piece of paper down on the table with a combination of revulsion and anger. Angela Bastiani slid forward in the booth and picked it up. Her fiery red hair was pulled back in a tight braid, giving her emerald eyes a chance to sparkle. Angela could have been a model, if not for the fact that she was barely five feet tall.

"You get another creep email on your website?" she asked. She knew full well that an angry Jessica could be hazardous to the health of the person pissing her off. Aside from her kickboxing and self-defense skills, her friend had a dark, angry streak that would make most people wilt.

"Read it and see for yourself."

A few nearby patrons in the diner paused to look over at the visibly irritated girl in the booth by the window. Jessica shot them a warning look that quietly advised them to go about eating and talking.

Angela's eyes grew wide as she read the printed email. "Oh wow, Jess. How is this possible?"

"I have no frigging idea. It's more than just knowing my name. Only me, you and my aunt know about the other stuff, and I'm pretty damn sure that neither of you told anyone. Hell, even Liam doesn't know that."

"You've got that right. I'd die before I told a soul."

A waitress came over to take their order. Angela asked for a Cobb salad and iced tea. Jessica ordered the double cheeseburger deluxe with a side of brown gravy and a Coke. The waitress looked her over, raising an eyebrow that said she wondered where she planned to put all the food. Sensing the tension in the air between the two girls, she darted back to the kitchen.

Once the waitress was out of earshot, Angela asked, "What are the odds that he just came out with this by chance?"

"That would be slim to none," Jessica said, fiddling with the salt-and-pepper shakers. Idle hands were never an issue for her, especially when she was upset.

Angela re-read the email, folded it back up and passed it across the table.

"Then that leaves only one thing," she said.

"Not possible," Jessica replied, keeping her eyes on the salt-and-pepper shakers.

"Actually, it's the *most* possible. My only question is, how?"

Jessica slipped the paper back into her purse. "My question is, why? I mean, why this guy? What makes him so damn special?"

Angela placed her hand over Jessica's. "You've been through and seen a lot weirder stuff. I know it hurts to think about it, but once you get past that, you have to admit that this could be important. I mean, why else would he talk to this stranger?"

The waitress brought their lunch over.

Angela poked through her salad with her fork, looking for the perfect first bite. Jessica dug into her burger like a lioness to a zebra hide. They ate in silence for a few minutes. Angela could see the wheels turning in her best friend's head.

While dipping a handful of fries in gravy, Jessica said, "I guess I should meet him, then."

"I think you should. But only on three conditions—you meet in a public place, in the daytime, with me. Does that sound fair? I know you like to kick ghost ass alone, but when it comes to real, live people, you need backup."

Jessica nodded. "Done. I'll reply to his email as soon as we're finished here. You free tomorrow?"

Angela's eyes sparkled. "Hell, even if I wasn't, I am now. I'm dying to know what the heck this is all about."

Her best friend could only mumble an unintelligible reply and brood. If what she read was true, something equal parts strange and remarkable was in store for Jessica, and Angela wasn't sure how she'd feel if she were in her friend's shoes.

Scared and confused would be a start.

Eddie Home was in the process of pouring boiling water into his noodle cup when he spied the addition to his email inbox from the corner of his eye. He sealed the top of the cup so the noodles could steep and sat down behind his laptop.

"Oh, you spammers, you must know how lonely I am."

Except for a change, the new email wasn't spam or a quick word from his mother or Tobi Cruz who was threatening to come up to New York so they could spend a weekend of debauchery in the big city.

He read it once silently, and again out loud just to make sure the words sounded as welcome, and crazy, to his ears as well as his brain.

Eddie,

Okay, you finally broke me down. I'm not too happy about the way you did it and I have some questions you better be prepared to answer. I can meet you tomorrow at Skate U in Queens at one o'clock. When you get there, rent a pair of skates and get on the rink. I'll be there. You'll know it's me because I'll be the one wearing a Slayer shirt. If you're late, well, you missed your one and only chance to talk.

Jessica

Eddie sat back and stared at the screen. He absentmindedly fumbled with his noodle cup, flipping the top off and getting hot water splashed on the back of his hand. He didn't react.

"A roller rink? I have to give her credit for originality."

Sleep did not come easy that night.

Chapter Twelve

Jessica and Angela arrived at Skate U at twelve thirty so they could get situated. Jessica carried a large duffle that looked as if it could double as a body bag. She plopped it down on a wooden bench with a loud sigh of relief.

"Please don't tell me you brought a sawed-off shotgun or something," Angela said, eyeing the bulky bag.

"Like I'd need it. No, rental skates and shoes skeeve me, so I bought us each a pair of roller skates. Ta-daa!"

She handed over a pair of white leather skates with pink pom-poms attached to the top laces.

"You didn't need to do that, Jess. I've never roller-skated in my life, and probably never will again after today. I could break my ass just as easily in rented skates."

Jessica pulled out a pair of matching skates. "It's just like roller-blading, only easier. Who knows, this might become a habit for us."

Angela looked around at the aging rink. Skate U was just the latest name for the Queens rink that had been around for close to forty years. For some reason, every time it closed, someone else was quick to buy it up, thinking *they* were the one who could make an old-time roller-skating rink a success. The wood slats of the rink were worn and scuffed by countless rubber wheels and stoppers. The entire place smelled of cheap wood polish and stale popcorn. The DJ booth that sat above the rink was manned by a young guy with an array of laptops instead of turntables. At tops, there were about twelve people in the rink.

No, Angela thought, *this is not a habit I'm about to dive into.*

"Why did you bring such a huge bag to just carry a couple of skates?"

Jess pulled aside the open flap and rooted around. Without revealing its contents, she said, "Oh, just a few little things I thought it would be smart to bring in case this dude was a psycho. Nothing to be alarmed about."

She gave Angela a mischievous grin. Angela knew better than to pry.

As they laced up, Angela asked, "So how come this place?"

Jessica gave her laces a tight tug and stood. "I figured, what better way to keep him off his feet, both mentally and physically? You said you wanted a public place, this is public. Besides, this way, I have the upper hand."

As she made to skate over to the rink entrance, her left foot slipped out from under her and she collapsed onto her butt. That got Angela laughing until her cheeks turned hot.

"Are you sure he's the one that will be off his feet?"

Angela's loud laughter brought the attention on them, resulting in some snickers from a pair of young kids who skated by Jessica. The pre-pubescent boys left a malodorous wake of greasy French fries and cheap ketchup as they passed, covering their mouths to keep from laughing like hyenas at her pratfall. Jessica looked as if she was about to lob a veiled threat in their direction but stopped herself. They were just a couple of little kids, after all.

She rolled her eyes at Angela and held out her hand. "Some back up you are. Just help me up and take your position."

Because of Jessica's threat of being late, Eddie arrived at Skate U fifteen minutes early. He sat in the parking lot for ten of them, not wanting to go inside and appear over eager. When he did go in, he walked straight to the rental counter, careful not to stare at the skaters. It would be better for her to spot him first.

The leather of the skates was so worn, they felt like wet paper. Ankle support was nil, which meant there was a high possibility of embarrassing himself. He'd never skated before in his life, leaving him to wonder if Jessica Backman knew that and used it to her advantage. Maybe he wasn't the only super psychic in town.

The music was terrible and loud. He spied the DJ, eyes closed, earphones planted on his head, positive he couldn't be listening to the mix of bad '70s disco and modern house music that he must have made in a drug-induced haze in his basement home studio. Eddie's tastes were the exact opposite, more in the Frank Sinatra era. His mother had once sung backing vocals on a Tony Bennett album, back when she was young and ready to take on the world. Growing up, his life was filled with crooners, and he never grew out of it. This stuff blasting out of worn-out speakers was intolerable.

He made it to the rink and clung to the side wall on wobbly legs.

His heart ran a steady, meth-head beat. He couldn't remember the last time he'd been so nervous.

Spotting Jessica in the thin crowd was easy. He was surprised at how naturally beautiful she was without seeming to know it herself. As promised, she was wearing a black Slayer concert shirt. Her auburn hair fanned out behind her as she breezed along on the other side of the rink. She was long and lean with small, tight curves. *Understated beauty* was what came to mind. He had to force himself not to stare.

She saw him, hanging on for dear life, and gave him a crooked smile, the way a hunter would look at her prey as it was caught in a trap.

This should be fun, Eddie thought.

The rubber stopper on her skates shrieked as she pulled up next to him.

"You must be Jessica Backman," he said. "I'd shake your hand, but I think I might fall if I tried."

"That's fine. I didn't offer to shake your hand anyway."

She looked him over from head to toe, sizing him up in more ways than he could imagine. He had to give her credit. For a single girl to meet a total stranger who had been pestering her through email, she really knew how to take complete charge. He admired both her bravery and her street smarts, two traits he was far from mastering himself.

"Is there any chance we could sit down and talk?"

She shook her head. "I prefer to do all of our talking out here."

"Somehow I knew you'd say that."

Eddie pulled himself along the wall, locking his knees to keep his feet from going out from under him. It didn't help much, and he had to use all the strength in his now shaky arms to hold himself upright. People who didn't understand the true abilities of psychics would laugh at his not foreseeing his first meeting with Jessica going down this way.

Jessica rolled beside him. "First things first," she said with barely concealed anger simmering in her voice. "Who the hell told you to write what you did? As far as I know, only two people in the world know what my father called me and where I go. I guess I was wrong. So tell me who it was so I can wring their neck."

Eddie looked over and saw her hazel eyes had turned an almost golden color. He was pretty sure she would beat the information out of him if he tried to keep his source a secret. Hell, she might beat him anyway. She may have been a thin girl, but every ounce of her was coiled muscle.

"I think I should preface my answer with a quick question. Do you know who D.D. Home was?"

His right leg shot out and he had to grip the wall to keep from falling. If she was what she promoted herself to be on her website, it was a sure bet she knew about his great-grandfather.

Without hesitation, she replied, "D.D. Home was the greatest mentalist and spiritualist of the nineteenth century. I once read where he literally floated out a second story window in front of a team of debunkers and floated back in the adjoining window. Just crazy stuff. He was the only one who was never discredited, even though countless people tried. What does a dead man have to do with this?"

Eddie stopped and faced her. "Everything."

He saw the light suddenly shine behind her eyes. "Wait, your last name is Home. Are you trying to tell me you're related?"

"A direct descendant."

"And you expect me to believe you have some psychic powers?"

"I was hoping you would."

"Well, if you're so psychic, you should have known that I don't believe in them, which then proves my point. I don't know how you did what you did. Maybe your family has special parlor tricks passed down from generation to generation. Not that I really care. It was nice meeting you."

Jessica pushed off and skated ahead of him with surprising speed.

Jesus, you're blowing it!

"Jessica, wait! Your father is the one who told me what to say!"

The DJ had just started playing Sugarhill Gang's *Rapper's Delight* and cranked up the volume. There was no way she could have heard him, and even less of a chance for him to catch up to her.

But he was wrong. She stopped on a dime and turned to him. The fire in her stare singed him from twenty feet away. Swinging her arms at her sides, she came back to his spot on the wall. Her hands were balled into fists and her mouth was pinched in a tight line.

"What did you say?"

Eddie swallowed hard and stood as straight as his legs would allow. It was make or break time.

"I've spoken to your father several times over the last few months. He was the one who told me to refer to you as *squeakpip* in my last email and also mention how much he enjoys your visits to his death site in Alaska every year."

Jessica shook her head. "This isn't possible."

"I know it sounds weird, because *it is weird*. That's kind of my specialty. I was desperate to meet you and he wanted to help."

"Out of all the people in the world, why would he talk to you?"

Eddie sighed. Great. He had her attention and she wasn't running away or hitting him. If he was lucky, things would stay that way.

"To be honest, I don't know. I was at the Rhine Research Center for the past year and I took up a specialized form of meditation. I was mostly using it to clear my mind." For now, the simplest explanation seemed best. "Then one day, he came to me out of the nothing. I could barely understand him the first couple of times we connected, but it seemed the more he reached out to me, and now me to him, the stronger our bond grew. He was the one who pointed me to your family's experience and he's the one who urged me to get in contact with you. Over the years, I'd heard about an incredible paranormal event in an Alaskan town that no longer exists, and to tell you the truth, always assumed what I heard from the grapevine had to be bullshit. From the little that is spoken about it, it sounds too crazy to be true, even for people crazy enough to believe in the impossible. Kind of like the Mothman phenomena—when something singular seems so outlandish, you tend to discard it. Your father changed my stance on that. But to tell you the truth, beyond confirming an event that happened over a decade ago and pointing me towards you, I have no clue what's supposed to happen next."

"And how did you find me?"

"He told me everything I needed to know. Then, it was just a matter of coming here and emailing the contact address on the website. Until a month ago, I was in North Carolina, so I wanted to be close in case you decided to meet. To tell you the truth, he seemed pretty insistent I meet you."

Jessica rolled back until she was flush against the wall, her fists on her hips. Eddie noticed another girl staring at them from the concession stand. She waved at Jessica with a look of concern. Jessica waved her off. The girl nodded, but didn't take her eyes off them.

Again, he was impressed. Jessica knew how to cover her bases.

Without looking at him, Jessica asked, "What was my father's favorite hockey team?"

Eddie had a feeling this would happen and was glad he had been prepared. "The Islanders."

"What town do I go to every year?"

"Shida, though your father told me it's not a functioning town anymore. People in the area won't even acknowledge that Shida ever existed."

"What would he say to me every night before putting me to bed?"

Eddie looked at her and saw the anger and distrust had been replaced by hope. This was no longer Jessica Backman, the fearless ghost hunter. This was the little girl who lost her father well before his time in an event so tragic, so beyond normal human comprehension, that it must have left scars that could never heal.

He cleared his throat, and said softly, "I love you mucho much."

"Stay right here."

Eddie's jaw tensed as he watched her skate away once again, this time to join her friend at the concession stand. They talked for several minutes and he noticed she wiped her eyes with the back of her hands a few times. When she returned, the tension in her body had eased and her eyes were red rimmed.

"Okay, Eddie Home. I'll give you one chance. I don't think my father is running a dating service from the other side, so I can only assume he sent you to help me—not that I need any help."

She gave him a business card and a pen.

"Write down your cell number, social security number, date and city of birth and current address. I'll call you later in the week. If it turns out you're just a con man, I'll fuck you up so bad, your own mother will deny ever having had you. If you're who and what you say you are, I'll put you to good use."

Eddie held the pen, too taken aback to start writing. Girls in North Carolina and San Francisco did not talk like this. "My social, really? That's kind of an odd thing to ask for."

Jessica glared at him. He realized it was an asinine question, considering what he had just dumped on her. He wrote down all of the information and handed the card back to her.

She skated away without another word or even a glance in his direction.

Chapter Thirteen

Selena Leigh lay across her bed, listening to her iPod. She had just downloaded a few tracks from Bruno Mars and Katy Perry and was content with doing nothing for the rest of the night. The school year had been extended because of extra snow days that had to be taken in February, but teachers had nothing left to teach. So, there was no homework to contend with. A small victory. She daydreamed about Hank Farley, her current crush and the best-looking baseball player in the county, and was in a very happy place when there was a knock at her door.

"Can I come in?" her mother asked.

"Yeah."

Her mother was dressed in her jogging outfit and looked as if she had just done a few miles. Her skin was shiny with sweat and the hair poking out from under her baseball cap was frizzy.

"Your father wanted me to remind you that he's picking you up after school tomorrow, so please don't forget and take the bus. You can't be late for your dentist appointment."

Selena paused her iPod and rolled onto her back. "I hate going to the dentist. Can I ask her not to scrape my teeth with those metal picks? Whenever she does that, it hurts and it makes me want to crawl out of my skin."

Her mother sat on the edge of her bed and stroked her hair. "Unfortunately, that's just something that has to be done. I feel the same way. I wonder why they haven't invented softer, plastic tools yet. Don't worry yourself too much about it. Thanks to genetics inherited from your father's side, you, my dear, have perfect teeth. It'll be over before you know it."

Changing the subject, her mother asked, "What are you listening to?"

Before Selena could answer, she had popped one bud into her ear.

"Oh, I like him," she said, swaying gently to the beat. Her mom had taken a liking to pop music right around the time she joined the gym. It was weird having a parent that listened to the same music as her and her friends, but it was also nice to have something in common.

While she listened to the rest of the song, Selena stared at the ceiling, thinking.

"Mom?"

"Yes, honey?"

"Is Dad still mad at me about the car? I swear, I was never down there."

Her mom pulled her into a hug. "No, honey, he's not mad at you at all. He's just...confused. Anyway, it just gives him more excuses to spend time with his car." She smiled but Selena could see the concern behind her eyes.

"Okay, kiddo, I have to hit the shower. Don't stay up too late texting your friends. You'll see them soon enough in school. Good night."

She gave Selena a kiss on the top of her head.

"Good night."

After her mother closed the door, Selena went over to her computer and logged on to Facebook. Five of her friends were on as well, and she started texting each. Her iPod blasted away in her ears as she also managed to read the latest issue of *Cosmopolitan*. Multitasking for her generation was a way of life and done as easily as counting to ten.

She lost herself in music, texts and articles on how to make your lips look plumper, and passed two hours without realizing it. She hummed to herself while typing to her best friend Julie about what they would do the coming Saturday, the first Saturday of summer vacation. They had to make it special. Julie's older sister had just gotten her license and agreed to drive them to the beach. She typed a reminder in her phone to pick up some sunscreen.

It wasn't a sound or a movement that broke her from her groove. It was more like a feeling, like the air in her room had suddenly changed, become thinner, the small space made even smaller.

Selena knew she wasn't alone.

That could mean only one thing.

Ricky had sneaked in and was spying on her. He was such a pain in the ass. He was in sixth grade, but he wished he were in high school and never missed a chance to see what it was that high school kids did with their time.

She spun in her chair and yelled, "Ricky, get out!"

Except he wasn't there. She removed her ear buds and walked over to her door.

It was still closed.

Knowing Ricky, he was hiding under the bed.

She dropped to her knees and whisked the comforter up, ready to scream at the obnoxious little turd.

There was nothing but a couple of shoeboxes and darkness.

"I must be losing my mind."

She was about to go back to her computer when she heard a muffled thump. It came from her closet.

Selena eyed her field hockey stick resting against her bed. If the little bed wetter wanted to play games, she was up for it. Why not make him *think* she was going to smash his face in? Hopefully it would keep him out of her room, even if only for a week or so.

She tiptoed to her closet, one hand with the raised stick, the other ready to pull the door handle open.

She paused when she heard a slight rustling, as if he was shifting amidst the clutter.

Oh, this would be fun.

Selena's left hand darted for the knob. She put on her most menacing face and pulled the field hockey stick up as high as she could.

Her overhead light flicked on and off and she felt something brush across the back of her neck, as if she had walked under a cobweb. She sensed someone right behind her, but the noises had come from the closet.

The knob twisted within her hand of its own accord and the door flung wide open.

There *was* someone in her closet.

The girl nestled amongst her clothes stared back at her, her eyes wide with shock, her mouth open in a silent scream.

She was the mirror image of Selena, only paler, with deep, dark eyes that were as unfathomable as the farthest reaches of space. The girl in the closet raised her hands in protest, her chest heaving as though she was shouting but no sounds escaped her throat.

Selena dropped the stick, trembling. She backed away on legs that had been stripped of all muscle and bone.

Her lips trembled as she sputtered, "No...no...no." Her stomach dropped and she had to pee with an urgency she had never felt before.

A jolt raced through her body when she collided with her chair. She grabbed its back to keep from falling, her gaze never leaving the phantasmagorical mirror image standing amidst her clothes and cheerleading uniforms.

The girl, Selena's twin, also moved back farther into the closet, pushing dresses aside, a look of pure terror on her face.

Selena *could* scream, and she did.

She screamed until her entire family came bursting into her room, until the girl in the closet retreated to the dark recesses, back farther than the physical limits of the closet itself, fading into the nothing from whence she came.

Selena screamed until her throat was raw and blood flecked her panicked mother's nightshirt.

Chapter Fourteen

Jessica Backman handed the manila envelope to Aunt Eve while a tornado of butterflies fluttered in her stomach. They sat on the back deck so the morning sun could warm them while they drank coffee. The birdbath in the yard was full of skittering, wet sparrows.

"I wanted you to read it first, so you can give me the thumbs-up or -down," Jessica said.

Eve used a nail to tear an opening along the top flap. She was still a very pretty woman, her smooth, lightly tanned skin and short, blonde hair making her look at least ten years younger than a woman approaching her late forties. It was only when you were close and her guard was down that you could catch brief glimpses of the sorrow that always lurked in her eyes, sometimes hiding in the tiniest corners but never, ever, entirely gone.

"And who was the one who did the background check?" Eve asked before pulling out its contents.

"Swedey, the guy who does all of my web stuff. He's one of those hacker geniuses who can find out anything about anybody. I gave him two full weeks to look up everything he could about Ed Home. I want to make sure this guy is on the level."

Eve's shoulders slumped, her face quizzical. "If you're so uneasy about him, why even bother going through all this trouble?"

Jessica looked down at her coffee. "There were some things he said that kinda stuck with me."

She offered no more in the way of an explanation. The background check was ten pages long and involved everything from Ed Home's birth certificate right up to the present.

Eve raised an eyebrow but didn't press. "This is going to take a few minutes."

Jessica eyed the sparrows, stretched her arms and took a sip of coffee. "That's okay. I have nothing but time today. It's nice being out in the morning sun for a change."

Because of her chosen profession, if she could call it that, sunlight was something she usually slept through, especially during the downtime between semesters. She felt an afternoon getting some vitamin D was in definite need.

Eve spent the next fifteen minutes reading and re-reading the report while Jessica closed her eyes and tilted her face to the sun. When Eve was finished, she placed her coffee mug atop the papers and folded her hands on the table.

"From what you said he told you, everything in there checks out. He *is* the great-grandson of D.D. Home, he *did* attend Duke University and he *was* at the Rhine Research Center over the past year. There's nothing specific about his abilities, but there's plenty mentioned about the other men in his family line. His parents are divorced and he currently lives in the Bronx. No criminal record, got all A's and B's in school, has no outstanding debt and volunteered at an animal shelter for three years, starting when he was fifteen. He sounds like the all-American boy. Being a New Yorker, that makes me suspicious. That and the fact that he found you after all of the pains we took to keep you anonymous."

With a frown that brought out worry lines on her forehead, Jessica asked, "Does he have any money?"

Eve scanned through a few pages. "Not really, no."

Guys looking to get close to her because of her money was always a concern. Eve made sure they lived normal lives and they never, ever mentioned to anyone that they had a net worth of over twenty million dollars. Jessica's father had felt money like that would only bring out the vultures, which it did when he first won the lottery. He had vowed to keep things simple, and Eve followed suit after his death.

But the lottery win was not a private thing, especially since it was coupled with the death of her mother on the same day. There were articles about it in all the local papers, articles that someone could easily come by on an Internet search or in the library. Because of that, Jessica and Eve had to be vigilant at all times when new people tried to enter their lives. Jessica often wondered if distrust was the reason Eve remained single, even though she would have made a good man exceedingly happy.

Jessica said, "Well, at least he has no debt, so he won't hit me up for a loan any time soon." She smiled. "So, what do you say?"

Eve thought things over for a bit, patting the report. "When you look at the hard facts, I'd have to say yes. I guess it can't hurt to see if he's the real deal. Maybe he *can* help you. If he was at the Rhine Research Center for a year, he must either have some strange ability or at least a good working knowledge of the stuff you investigate. In an odd way, I'd feel better if you had a partner. Safety in numbers. Plus, there are these little things I call trust and faith, which I have in abundance when it comes to you.

"Although, I am curious about what he could have said to you to make you go through all this trouble. He didn't threaten you, did he?"

Eve's eyes took on the hardened edge of a warrior. One of her hands balled into a fist. There was nothing she wouldn't do to protect Jessica and Liam. They were all survivors, and survivors knew how to look out for each other. God help the man, woman or beast who came between them with less than good intentions.

It was never spoken aloud, but Jessica suspected that Eve had been in love with her father. Losing him seemed to drain all hope of ever bonding with another man. Jessica was the last tie to her dad, and Eve was the only mother she had ever known. She sometimes wondered if there was another pair bound as close to one another as they were.

Jessica got up and kissed her on the cheek. "If he did, we'd be looking at pictures of him surrounded by a chalk outline. Thank you for loving me. I guess it can't hurt to give him a shot. I have the perfect case to test him on."

"The McCammons?"

Jessica nodded. "That place has been a thorn in my side for two months now. Maybe Mr. Eddie Home can pull it out."

Eddie nearly hit the ceiling when Jessica called him back, a week and a half later than she had said she would. He had resolved himself to defeat and was thinking of what to do next when she called. The job he had gotten working in a health food store was far from glamorous enough to keep him in New York, but the thought of going back to San Francisco filled him with dread.

"I'm going to email you the address to the house I need you to meet me at. You can Google map them or whatever," Jessica said. "Meet me there at seven sharp on Friday night. I already spoke to Tim and Kristen McCammon and got their permission to bring you on board. Rule number one, speak only when spoken to when we get there. They're going through hell and I don't want them thinking I've resorted to psychics to help them. *Capice*?"

"Can I make a quick correction?"

"As long as it's quick."

"I'm actually a psychic-medium. You kinda get the best of both worlds." When Jessica didn't respond, he gave a nervous snort.

Still silence.

"I'll be on my best behavior," he said.

"This place has a tendency to get pretty wild. Rule number two, if you run, you're done. I don't know how the presence in their house is going to react to you, so be prepared for anything."

"What should I bring?"

"Yourself, a flashlight and a change of underwear."

He thought he heard the start of a humorless chuckle as she disconnected the call.

Chapter Fifteen

They showed up at the same time in front of the McCammon house, a tidy Tudor in a neighborhood that required potential residents to have at least a couple of million in the bank. The town had once been home to the Kennedys before they became a political juggernaut and was still inhabited by the well-to-do. Jessica looked at Eddie Home's battered, olive-colored Jeep in her rearview mirror as it pulled up behind hers. At least he had good taste in cars.

She popped the trunk and got out to unload her gear. Eddie stepped out, clad all in black.

"You look like an undertaker," she said to him.

"Better I should look like a refugee from a 1988 Anthrax concert?" he shot back. A look of pained consternation washed over his face. He must have thought he was getting off on the wrong foot. She didn't bother to bail him out of his concern.

She had to admit he was a pretty good-looking guy. His thick, wavy hair and strong jawline made him look like a Disney prince or hero. He was tall with just the right amount of lean muscle, as far as she could tell. Living on Long Island, she had grown a strong aversion to muscle-bound juice-heads. No, Eddie Home was a looker.

Concentrate on the job, she scolded herself.

"Take this and follow me," she said, thrusting a black, metallic case into his hands.

Tim McCammon answered the door. The bags under his eyes were dark and heavy and his posture was one of absolute fatigue. One of his hands gripped the doorframe. It looked like the only thing keeping him upright. His breath smelled like stale beer.

"Come on in. It's been a rough night. Kristen took the kids to a hotel around midnight last night. I decided to stay, show *it* that I'm not afraid. That plan shit the bed in short order."

Jessica touched his arm and gave a warm smile. "The fact that you stayed did more than you can imagine. Trust me. Tim, this is my associate, Eddie. He's going to help me set up equipment, take notes and generally keep things from disturbing me while I work."

Eddie did as he was told and nodded in greeting.

They sat for a moment in the living room. Everything was in disarray. It looked as if Tim McCammon had thrown a party the night before with a hundred college students. Lamps were on the floor, curtains were half-hanging off their rods, every drawer was open and the floor was littered with objects that should have been on shelves.

Tim leaned forward in his chair, rubbed his hand across his face and stretched his neck until they could hear his bones crack. "Jessica, we appreciate all you've been doing for us, but to be honest, things only seem to be getting worse. I'm at a loss here. The truth is, I'm no longer sure we should be doing this. Kristen and I have been talking about selling the house. Since you told us this, *whatever it is*, isn't related to us or the children, it's best we just leave. I know you've meant well, but I don't think this is working."

The words came out softly, precisely, as if he had been rehearsing them for days.

Jessica said, "I know how you feel. I've told you before that I've had an experience similar to this. It was horrible, worse than you can ever imagine. But once my father found the key, it all ended in an instant. I know I'm close. All I ask for is one more night."

She neglected to mention that her father had lost his life finding that key thirteen years ago, but she was confident it wouldn't come to that in this case, or any other. Her childhood hell was unique and, she often prayed, singular.

Tim shook his head. "I don't know. If this house had been a stock, I would have cut and run months ago. I make a living knowing when to sell. I've gone past the acceptable holding limit here already."

Jessica was about to speak when Eddie interjected. "I promise you everything will be over when you get back in the morning. Besides, it's a buyer's market anyway. Better to hold on and wait for the market to swing in your favor."

Eddie sat back in the couch and crossed his legs. Jessica noticed how he avoided her gaze. She wanted to kill him. She should have told him rule number three, never promise the client something you're not one-hundred-percent sure you can deliver.

Tim McCammon took in a great lungful of air, closed his eyes and thought things over.

He looked at Jessica and said, "Okay, you have one more night, but that's all. I'm going to meet my family and collapse. I'll be back, alone, tomorrow at nine."

"Thank you, Tim. You look like you could use the rest. Leave the ugliness to us."

Tim nodded and headed upstairs to pack a bag. Eddie started to unlock the latches on the metal case he'd brought in. Jessica motioned for him to stop.

"Wait until he's left. I don't like setting stuff up in front of clients. It has a tendency to freak them out and he's obviously already at his limit."

Eddie stepped back from the case, palms held out. "Sorry. I'll just kick back until you tell me what you want me to do."

She took two quick strides until she was inches from his nose, glaring into his eyes. "What was the deal with your promising him this would be over tonight? Don't you realize how much of a toll something like this takes on a family? The last thing they need is false promises. No one, and I mean *no one*, can bend the paranormal to their will just because they want to. Shit, with every passing year, we dig up more questions than answers. That was very uncool."

She kept her voice low, but it was impossible to hide her anger.

Tim came down with an overnight bag.

"The keys are on the kitchen counter if you need them. I'll see you tomorrow morning. Call me if anything comes up or if you need me."

"Please say hello to Kristen and the kids for me."

"I will."

The front door closed silently behind him.

Now Jessica could raise her voice. She turned on Eddie.

"That's one strike, which is one more than I usually give anyone at any time for anything. From here on in, everything is done my way, understand?"

Eddie gave a conciliatory bow of his head. "I'm really sorry. It's just that I'm getting a serious vibe about this place and I know I can help you...a lot. You seem to forget that I have some substantiated talents on my resume."

"And you seem to forget that I don't necessarily believe in what you're selling. That's why I brought you here, to prove it. Now if you'd be so kind, please unload the Trifield meters and put them on that table there while I set up these two cameras."

Eddie picked up a Trifield meter and made a loud *tsk*.

"You have a problem?" Jessica said.

"These are superfluous. And they're not proven to be reliable. You might just as well be reacting to a natural flux of electromagnetic energy or even the neighbor's cell phone than a ghost."

"I call them EBs."

"Excuse me?"

"I don't use the word ghost. It conjures up too many hokey images." Jessica set up the two tripods with practiced ease and unscrewed the lens caps on the video cameras.

"What does EB stand for?"

"Energy Being, which is exactly what they are."

Eddie thought it over for a moment as he filled half of the table with Trifield meters.

"I like it. Hmm. EB. Makes sense," he said.

"Happy to hear it."

Jessica walked around him to get an audio recorder out of the case. She knew he would have questions as well as his own theories. He'd been at the Rhine Research Center for over a year, exposed to the entire history of paranormal research. There was a chance he knew more about the field, at least the scientific-psychological side of things, than she did. So why was she getting so damn irritated? Something about Eddie Home seemed to bring out the bitch in her.

"Anyway, if you want me to prove myself, let *me* be your Trifield meter. I guarantee that I have a much better success rate. Took a boatload of tests and passed every one."

In a way, he was right. Even though most ghost-hunting groups employed Trifield or EMF meters, there wasn't enough solid evidence to say they were the ultimate ghost detection tools. For lack of a better option, they were simply the best available. They'd steered her down a wrong path quite a number of times.

"Okay, you get to be my human EB detector. What kind of information can you tell me when you sense it?"

Eddie stopped what he was doing to face her. "Most times? Everything."

The surety of his answer, the grave look in his eyes, gave her a chill.

"If you want to know the truth," Jessica said, feeling as if it was time to ease off a bit, "I really only use the Trifield meters and cameras so I have something to show my clients. They see this stuff so much on TV that it gives them a kind of comfort. If I had it my way, I'd just come in here with an audio recorder and maybe a digital camera. I don't think you need a lot of expensive, fancy-ass equipment to capture proof of the existence of EBs. And above all, I do it to help people."

Eddie leaned against the dining room table, silent, taking everything in.

Finally, he said, "So, the stuff on your website is..."

Jessica tied her hair up in a ponytail. "It's a place where people can learn about what I do and contact me when things get bad. That's it. I try to show the world the real things I've seen and experienced, but with editing tools out there today, it's impossible for people to believe anything they see. For those who already believe, I like to think my website gives them the strength and curiosity to keep looking for themselves."

Eddie turned toward the kitchen, but Jessica thought she saw the beginnings of a smile on his face. She wondered if he'd still be smiling when the McCammon EB started flinging its shit against the fan. Well, she did want to put him to the test.

She locked the camera in place and flicked the power button. She called out to him in the next room. "You ready to experience the night of your life?"

Chapter Sixteen

"You said it yourself, something weird is going on here."

"I don't know *what's* happening. That doesn't make it total science fiction."

"Well, I'm worried about Selena. We have to do something."

There was a long, silent pause.

"I'll be damned if I know what that something would be."

Selena Leigh listened to her parents in the next room. Since the incident with her ghastly twin in her closet, she had been sleeping on a blow up mattress in her brother Ricky's room. It was late and she couldn't sleep. She was about to plug in her ear buds when she heard her parents talk about what was referred to as *Selena's Freak Out*. It aggravated her that her parents always put a name to everything. Like when her first boyfriend, Max Matthews, broke up with her and she heard them whisper, "Looks like we're in for more Heartbreak Hotel." It made her feel as if they were mocking her, that her feelings didn't matter more than earning a silly nickname.

This was different. She prayed they were taking it seriously.

Her mother pressed her father for help.

"As parents, it's our job to keep our kids safe. Our daughter no longer feels safe in her own home. I'm not feeling much better."

"It's not like you saw something in your closet."

"But I heard her call for me the day you were all out. She was miles from home, Greg."

"You must have fallen asleep and not realized."

"Trust me, I wasn't asleep. I had only been awake for a couple of hours at that point anyway, so it wasn't like I was even remotely tired."

Selena pressed her ear closer to the wall. She hadn't known that her mother had had her own experience. So that made three out of four, even though her dad refused to acknowledge that the mess with the car coming off the ramps was anything but his eyes playing tricks on him.

She looked over at Ricky, fast asleep under a sheet. He'd passed out wearing his Red Sox cap and reading a comic book. The comic was inches from sliding off the bed. He had his annoying moments, but overall he was a pretty good kid. She hoped whatever *it* was that had made an unwelcome entrance into their home decided to leave him alone. He was her brother, and only she had the right to scare him.

Her father said, "So what do you want me to do? Call the cops? Call a priest?" He sounded exasperated.

"I don't know."

The bedsprings groaned as they shifted. There was a soft click, followed by applause coming from the television.

Selena lay back, staring at the ceiling. Ricky and her mother had spent an entire afternoon sticking glow-in-the-dark stars up there last summer when he had decided he wanted to be an astronomer. It had been a short-lived dream once he realized how much math you had to know to *be* an astronomer. He hated math. A quarter of the stars had fallen off over time, and many of the rest had lost their luminescence.

She tried not to think about that night in her room, but it seeped into her consciousness like a slow-moving wave of sewage, spoiling any good feelings she had accumulated during the daylight hours and infecting the night with its foul stench of terror. Her heart raced when she recalled looking into her own face, staring back at her with sightless eyes. She shivered, wondering what would have happened if she had accidentally touched her phantom twin. She had looked real, just very, very pale with deep, dark, inhuman eyes. Was there substance to her, or would Selena's hand have passed right through her, stopping only when her fingers touched the closet's back wall? She had to clamp her jaws tight to keep her teeth from chattering.

After that night, she'd asked her parents to remove all of her belongings from the closet and she transferred them to a few storage containers. It didn't take any effort to get her mother to agree to buy the blow up mattress, though Ricky did need some convincing to share his room.

Selena knew it was putting a strain on all of them, but guilt couldn't come close to overriding her fear.

She heard muffled voices and lifted herself up to move closer to the adjoining wall.

Her father said, "Even if we found someone that may be able to help, what do we tell them?"

"We tell them exactly what's been happening."

"And what is that?"

Her mother began to sob softly, as if she had pulled a pillow close to her face.

After a while, she settled down and said, "I guess we would tell them the truth. That we're being haunted by..."

Her breath hitched and she sniffed back her tears.

"We're being haunted by our own daughter."

Selena's head jerked away from the wall as if she had been struck. She felt dizzy, as if everything in the room had just become unimaginably large and she were a mere speck, crushed by the weight of existence in a world a million times her size.

Like her mother, she started to cry. With fumbling hands, she reached for her laptop. Her fingers were cold and numb and typing was a chore. She was going to find help the best way she knew how.

So she searched, well into the night and past the dawn, until her eyes were dry and it hurt to blink, her tears long dried but for the first time in days, her spirit stronger.

Chapter Seventeen

Eddie paced around the living room in an attempt to burn off some of his nervous energy.

Jesus, he could feel it. The hairs on the back of his hands stood at attention and his scalp tingled. Something was here, all right. It was too far removed at the moment for him to draw a bead, but he knew that would change.

Jessica had placed audio recorders, ten in all, around the entire downstairs. It was hot in the house and beads of sweat dotted her hairline and the little he could see of her chest. His own shirt felt as if it had been plastered to his skin. Ducking into the foyer, he took a quick sniff of his underarms and was thankful to the scientists who invented deodorant.

He looked out the front window. The sun was still thirty minutes from setting in the western sky. Two boys zipped along the sidewalk on mountain bikes that looked to be two sizes too big for their struggling riders. It never ceased to amaze him how the regular flow of life mingled with the shadows of the unknown, most people none the wiser. There were times he wished he were part of that majority.

"So, do you want to go out and grab a bite to eat?" he said.

Jessica shook her head. "Why would we do that?"

"Well, I just assumed you would prefer to do your work in the dark. Might as well carb up before the sun goes down."

"That's ridiculous. There's no set time for EBs to show up. The only reason people do it at night is because A, things are creepier at night and they get their thrills from it and B, since cameras are often used, spirit activity just shows up better in low light. The truth is, just as much happens during the day, except we're so surrounded by activity, noise and the simple act of going through our day-to-day lives that it's almost impossible to notice any signs."

Eddie smiled. She was pretty damn perceptive.

"What are you thinking?" she said, suspicion heavy in her tone.

He recovered by throwing out a question. "But you have cameras set up, too. Don't you think you'd get better evidence if you waited until later, like say after a nice Mexican meal?"

It may have been a trick of the light, but he could have sworn she almost smiled.

"Look, at this point, I only want to help Tim and Kristen. I'm not that concerned about evidence. They already have more of that than they can handle, and it's not like I'm about to show this to anyone else. These are just here in case something odd comes up that, if it's positive, I can show them. After all, you did promise Tim that it would all be over after tonight. It might be nice to show them just how that happened."

Her sarcasm was not lost on him.

Walking over to one of the cameras, he peered into the lens and said, "So you have no intention of posting this on your website?"

"Come on, I know you've looked at everything I have up there. I post things other people send me, and only if I think it has merit. What I do is between me and my clients, unless they specifically ask me to post it in hopes of letting others know they're not alone with their own troubles. Their anonymity is the most important thing to me, just like our family's was after...well, everything. It's also why you'll never see me roll up in a car or van with some gimmicky ghost-hunting logo wearing my custom-made shirt and hat, broadcasting to every neighbor what I'm there for. People who come to me are at the end of their rope. They don't need me bumbling through their lives like a thousand-pound bear."

Score another one. Eddie had to admit, she was good. Just what he'd hoped. It made his insane gamble coming to New York worth it. And underneath it all was this reckless current that even she wasn't aware of. He hoped he was up to the task of helping her navigate through the forces surrounding her.

"So, what kind of EB do you think we've got here?" he asked.

Jessica snapped a few pictures of the room. "At first I thought it was a classic case of poltergeist energy originating from one of the kids. My last night here proved me wrong. I was a little disappointed because it would have been my first. This isn't a poltergeist at all, just a very active, pissed off EB or EBs. I couldn't be so lucky to find another Enfield poltergeist."

"You mean that case in England where the poltergeist activity tormented that woman and her two children?"

Eddie was proud of the look of shock on her face.

"See, I'm not a total novice. In fact, poltergeist phenomena is a special area of interest at The Rhine," he added.

"Did you minor in it?" she asked.

"Nah. Just a passing interest. How could I resist? *'Do not go into the light, Carol Anne!'*"

Jessica gave a rare smile. "I love *Poltergeist*. Not too crazy about the sequel."

"Not many people were," Eddie said. His stomach growled, awake and seeking attention.

"If you want to step out and grab something, go ahead. It's going to be a long night," Jessica said.

"That's okay. I'll make it."

He had to cover his stomach with his hands when it made another angry protest. Jessica reached into her backpack and tossed an energy bar his way.

"I have a bunch of them. That and Red Bull keep me going."

"Thanks. What do you want to do until—"

Eddie felt the spirit's presence storm into the room a split second before it marshaled its strength and slid a dining room chair into the wall. A sharp pain stabbed the back of his eyes just as the chair began to move. He dropped his head into his hands, squeezing his eyes so tight, bright sparks swam against the darkness.

"See, I told you," Jessica said. She took in a sharp breath when she saw him lean back against the sofa in obvious pain. "Are you okay?"

He shook his head, blinking hard. "I'm fine. Whoa, that was strong. You've got one angry bastard here." He'd never felt anything like it before. Contact with angry or upset spirits could sometimes bring a slight pressure to his head, but nothing like the whip-crack he felt in his skull.

"Or bitch."

"I can assure you, that S.O.B. is a bastard. And I'm happy to report that it's only one."

"Only one?" Jess repeated, incredulous. "Then he must be one powerful spirit. I was beginning to think I'd stumbled into an EB clubhouse."

A white-hot needle jammed itself into the center of his brain and a picture frame on the wall behind him shattered. Eddie paused to catch his breath. Jessica came to his side, concerned. The last thing he wanted was for her to perceive him as a liability.

Jessica leaned closer and touched his arm. "Do you need an aspirin or something?"

He shook her off. "Nah, it wouldn't do any good. Trust me, the pain is temporary and it's nothing medicine could cure. My mind will adjust to it the longer we're here."

They stood in silence, waiting. The pain ebbed, giving him a moment to collect his thoughts and better still, to try to piece together what he had gleaned from his brief contact with the spirit in the house.

"You said it was a bastard. Do you know who it is? Did you get a name? And please don't tell me you see a name that begins with a W. I know how that con works." Seeing that he was okay, Jessica was back in control, the hard-ass ghost hunter.

"I could feel that it was one-hundred-percent masculine, but I didn't get specific details. I do know that it's royally mad at you. It's in a kind of disbelief that you keep coming back for more. It was content to just pull the occasional prank here and there, until the McCammons brought you in. It knows what you want and what you can do and it's not about to go down easy."

Jessica scratched her head. "So, you're telling me I made things worse?"

Eddie was reluctant to answer truthfully, but he knew lying would get him in deeper water. "In a way, yes."

She kicked over one of the empty camera cases. "Damn it! I was afraid that would happen. The longer this went on, the crazier things got. When the McCammons first called me, they were concerned because they would wake up and items on shelves were on the floors, either stacked on top of one another or arranged in weird patterns. Kristen said she saw a fork jump off the kitchen table once, but all in all, it was more bizarre than anything else. Things were quiet for me the first few times here, but then stuff started to move all over the house. I thought it might have been latent energy in the girls, but even with them miles away, it got worse. Damn it! How could I have been so stupid?"

Her anger with herself was put on hold when the case skittered across the floor, back at her feet. This time, Eddie got by with only a wince.

Inexplicably, the smell of burnt toast, the kind Eddie's mother used to make by holding bread over the burners on the stove when his stomach was upset, filled the room. He dashed into the kitchen to make sure nothing was lit. He skidded to a stop when the floor vibrated beneath his feet. The flatware jangled in their drawers as if someone was running their hands through them, back and forth, back and forth.

He inched over to the kitchen drawers, the contents smashing around with increasing intensity.

"Be careful," Jessica said, just inches behind him. He nearly jumped. He had no recollection of her following him into the kitchen. "The drawers in here have a tendency to fly open. It sounds like the knives and forks are being stirred up like a shaken bottle of soda."

"That's good advice," he replied, willing his voice not to shake. They both took several steps back.

The noise stopped. The burnt toast smell disappeared. The house was still, possessing a sensation of absolute vacancy.

"Okay, that was weird," Eddie said.

Jessica clapped him on the back of his shoulder. "Not for this place. You sure you can handle it?"

Eddie shrugged. "Can of corn. Especially now that I know what you do and why it's so afraid of you."

She put a hand on her hip, raising an eyebrow. "Oh really. And what would that be?"

"I'm not sure how you make it work, but it's terrified of giving you its name, because if you know its name, you can banish it."

A look of shock washed over her face. Her mouth hung slightly open. "How...how could you know that?"

He smiled. "I told you I have a gift. And judging by the ache in my head, I'm about to put it to good use."

They both jumped when they felt a tapping right underneath their feet.

Tap. Tap-tap-tap. Tap-tap.

It did it again, the force behind the tapping stronger with each repetition.

Jessica looked down at the floor. "It did that the last time. I spent a week wondering what it could mean. I looked up Morse code on the Internet, and thought it was spelling out the initials E.S.I. I went through the records of the house and couldn't find any past residents matchingthose initials. I guess it's not Morse code."

Eddie was about to answer her when she was lifted from the floor and yanked backward, flung against the far wall like a toy tossed by an angry child. There was a loud crack and he prayed it came from the wall and not her bones. As he rushed to her aid, he was jolted by a needle of intense pain in the center of his skull.

He dropped to his knees, helpless as drawers and cabinets opened and closed in a rhythm very much like an unholy applause, the house itself cheering over the swift defeat of the two strangers, urging the presence that gripped its fibers to deliver the final blow.

Chapter Eighteen

Jessica's eyes fluttered open in time to see every kitchen drawer slam shut simultaneously. As they did, the refrigerator door opened with a loud, slow squeal of its hinges. She pushed herself up off the floor, balancing on her outstretched arm. Eddie was only a few feet from her, cradling his head in his hands, on his knees, oblivious to the world around them.

There was a popping sound, followed by a sharp *plink*. A bottle cap spun in circles, having been tossed from inside the refrigerator. A two-liter bottle of soda came crashing down, emptying its brown, sticky contents onto the linoleum. The tops of other soda bottles, condiments and juice containers rained out of the door, tapping across the floor. Their contents joined the initial slick of soda until it was a soupy mess, a concoction of pop, ketchup, tomato juice, mustard, hot sauce, barbecue sauce, milk, pickle brine and salad dressing.

The goopy blob inched steadily toward them. The stench of things better left separate was nauseating.

Jessica got to her feet on wobbly legs and leaned down to help Eddie up. Eddie pulled his hands away from his face, staring at her with unfocused eyes.

"If you don't want to ruin your clothes, you have to get up," she said to him, tugging on his arm.

He turned to where her gaze fell, registered the pungent smell and got to his feet. Jessica held his hand and led him around the mess and into the living room. They both collapsed onto the couch.

"Are you all right?" she asked. He still looked dazed, his mind wandering somewhere off the reservation.

It took him a moment, but he replied with a dry rasp, "Yeah."

Other than the mess being made in the kitchen, the rest of the house was relatively silent. It was usually like that with investigations—moments of extreme activity, followed by hours of unnatural silence. You never knew whether the EB was building its strength for another round or had decided to vacate the premises for a while. It left your nerves on fire, your senses straining to the point of exhaustion.

Jessica took an internal stock of things, realizing nothing was broken. She would have one hell of a bruise on the parts of her body that hit the wall and floor, though.

Eddie sat staring into the kitchen. He said, softly, "That was insane. Have you ever seen anything like that before?"

"Yes."

He inhaled, about to say something, paused, seemed to think better of it and exhaled.

Jessica added, "But, I've never seen the EB in here do this. That was intense."

Despite everything, she smiled. She'd been aware from a very young age that she was a lightning rod for EBs, the events in Alaska with her father having altered the DNA of her psyche or something, tuning her into frequencies unknown. It gave her a sense of satisfaction that she could cause an entity to put on such a massive display of power. It was a fighter. She liked fighters.

Eddie leaned forward and pointed. "It's down there, in the basement."

The cellar door was tucked into the back end of the kitchen, next to the door that opened into the yard.

"How do you know?"

"I just know. And it's tired...and mad. Its defenses are down. If we can get close to it, I can get its name for you."

Jessica rolled her shoulders and stretched her legs. She took a few healthy sips from a bottle of water, handing another bottle to Eddie.

"Then I guess we need to go into the basement," she said, her mood surprisingly, disturbingly, chipper.

She grabbed a tripod by the legs and held it over one shoulder like a soldier and her rifle. The camera lens pointed at the ground. Gesturing at the living room floor, she added, "Grab one of those audio recorders."

Jessica had to pull hard on the door to get it open. The old wood was swollen from the humidity and at first, she thought it was being held closed by the EB on the other side. When the edge of the door scuffed against the floor, she realized it was only the work of Mother Nature and old wood.

Eddie turned on the light from the outside wall. Eight wooden steps led down into the unfinished basement. One low-wattage bulb lit the stairs, and another one glowed feebly by the furnace. It smelled damp and musty, with a hint of mineral earthiness. *This is a place where things go to rust and wither away,* she thought.

There was a long, scarred workbench covered in boxes and dented, faded coffee cans. Ancient shovels leaned against it in one corner. Dusty milk crates jammed with old gardening tools, hardware supplies and magazines littered the floor.

"Doesn't look like Tim and Kristen come down here very much," Eddie said.

"They don't. I was only down here for a couple of hours one night but it was my first time here and I got zippo. It feels very different right now."

"This is where it goes when it's really tired. It needs a place to regroup, undisturbed."

Jessica felt a tingling at the base of her spine that danced up to the back of her neck. There was a heaviness to the atmosphere. Breathing felt like being at a higher elevation. The air itself was chilly, bordering on cold. This was the point where a lot of paranormal investigators lost their shit. It was easy to slide into a panic attack when your body was registering something before your mind had a chance to catch up.

Eddie let out a small gasp and she turned. He covered his eyes with a hand and had stopped walking.

"You getting anything?" she asked.

"Close," he said, starting to pant. "He's not making things easy."

"Where is it?"

Eddie pointed to the recessed area beyond the silent furnace, a place where the light did not penetrate. Jessica took the tripod off her shoulder and set it up so the camera could face the back of the basement. She looked through the viewfinder, set it on night vision and did a quick scan.

"Well, that's one good thing," she said, her face close to the tiny screen.

"What's that?"

"There's nothing back there for me to trip on."

She took two quick steps into the darkness. Eddie yelled, "Wait, *don't go back there!*"

There was a loud pop, and the bulb by the stairs exploded, followed by another, bathing them in total blackness. A deep, malevolent growl emanated from the deepest recesses of the basement, gaining strength as it approached them.

Chapter Nineteen

Selena met her best friend, Julie Quintana, outside the elementary school that was down the block from her house. They had become friends when Julie transferred to the school in third grade and had been inseparable ever since.

"Girl, you look like you need a twenty-hour nap," Julie said, alarmed at the dark circles under her friend's eyes. She pushed a few stray hairs from Selena's face with her fingers.

"More like twenty days. Even when I do sleep, I still wake up exhausted. I can't shut my mind down, you know."

The street darkened as an immense storm cloud passed overhead. Thunder rumbled ominously but the rain had yet to fall.

"If you want, you can sleep at my house," Julie offered. A slight wind had come with the cloud and her pin-straight brown hair flew in every direction.

"You're the best," Selena said, pulling her into a tight embrace. "How about after we meet with Crissy, we stop at my place to pick up my stuff and get some pizza to bring back to your house? I might as well have some fun before I pass out."

They walked toward Crissy's house, which was only several blocks away. The sky lit up as lightning struck in the distance. Selena and Julie counted the seconds until the clap of thunder made them jump.

"It's only about five miles away. Oh crap, my laptop bag isn't waterproof," Selena said.

"And it's a hunk of metal in a thunderstorm. Come on."

They ran the rest of the way to Crissy's and the first droplets of rain misted on them. They huddled under the aluminum awning above the porch. The rain came down in earnest the second they rang the bell, followed by a bright flash.

"One, one-thousand, two, one-thousand, three, one-thousand, four—"

Selena was breathing hard and laughed. "That was close. I really, really hate storms."

Julie said, "And I can't afford to get my hair wet. You know how hard I worked on it today? Now it's gonna get all frizzy."

The door opened and the laughter died in their throats. Crissy Davies was wearing black jeans, a ripped, black shirt from the last My Chemical Romance tour and heavy, black boots that looked as if they could kick down a brick wall. Crissy was always *Addams Family* pale. She hated the sun and all things to do with the great outdoors. Her eyelids were done up in heavy purple eye shadow and the studs from her snakebite piercings were shaped like little spiders. She was the epitome of goth and was the de facto leader of the goth circle in school.

"Hey, Selena, hey, Julie. Come on in."

The inside of her house looked like a cover from *Better Homes and Gardens*. Selena tried to think back to the last time she had been in Crissy's home. It had to have been before her father left. Crissy's mother had caught him cheating with someone from his office and threw him out of their perfect little home before he even had a chance to explain himself. It was no coincidence that Crissy became a goth not long after that. Before, she had been a regular kid, though a bit on the nerdy side, who thought listening to anything heavier than Gwen Stefani was a step away from devil worship. She loved her dad, but her mother got the better lawyer and forbid visitation. Crissy had been working overtime to annoy her mother ever since, but a steady supply of antidepressants kept her from breaking through her mother's narcotized defenses.

All that being said, Selena still considered her a friend, though their paths didn't cross very often anymore. It was just the way of high school. You spent freshman year finding your clique and stayed in their orbit until graduation. For now, she was thankful that Crissy was who she had become because she couldn't think of anyone else better to help her.

"Your mom home?" Selena asked.

Crissy rolled her eyes. "Queen Davies is out at some book club meeting or something equally asinine. You got your laptop?"

Selena patted the bag that hung by her hip.

"You have something to drink? I'm always mad thirsty before my period," Julie said.

Crissy shrugged. "Sure. Just grab whatever you want out of the fridge, except the vodka in the freezer. My mother keeps tabs on the level. Like I'd ever drink her booze."

Julie shot Selena a look that said, *what the heck have we gotten ourselves into?*, got a bottle of water and joined them in Crissy's room.

Surprisingly, it was bright and uncluttered. There were no posters of anarchy symbols or Rob Zombie and it smelled faintly of potpourri. They all sat on her bed and Crissy said, "Okay, tell me again what happened."

That was one thing about Crissy. Always eager to get to the point. She never did have time for meaningless pleasantries.

Selena took a deep breath and told her about the thing in her closet that had looked just like her, as well as what had happened to her father and mother. Crissy listened with rapt attention, asking for more details here and there. Julie pulled her knees to her chest and shivered.

When she was done recounting the weirdness in her house, Selena leaned against the headboard and massaged her temples.

"And that's why I can't eat and sleep on the floor in my little brother's room. Sounds crazy and pathetic, right?"

Crissy was lost in thought. Suddenly, she jumped from the bed and went over to her desk. "I know what it is!" she shouted, hammering at the keys on her computer. When she found what she was looking for, she tilted her monitor toward them.

"This is serious shit, Selena," she said. "What you saw in your closet is called a *doppelganger*."

"A what-a-ganger?" Julie asked.

"A doppelganger. It's German for double walker. Check this out. All throughout history, there have been reports of people coming face to face with their own double."

"You mean, like someone who looks just like them? Kinda like they say everyone has a twin somewhere?" Selena wondered.

"Not really. These doppelgangers aren't living beings. They're kind of like a phantom. Most times they appear as solid as a regular person, though there have been many cases where they're semi-transparent or their basic coloration is just off, dull. This stuff goes all the way back to Egyptian times where they believed the soul had an exact copy of itself called the *ka*. They even made special rooms for the *ka* in Egyptian tombs."

Julie moved closer to the screen. Crissy was scrolling down to read the text on a website dedicated to doppelgangers.

"OMFG," Julie said. "So these things are, like, twins to our souls?"

"It's not that simple," Crissy said, shaking her head. "There are tons of theories on the nature of doppelgangers. Some say they're simply astral projections, while others think they're independent beings, sent from the great beyond to a person's life for a very specific reason. Since no one's been able to capture one, all we have to go on is theory and conjecture. Although, some people have been known to have whole conversations with their doppelganger. This site doesn't list anything that might have been recorded about those conversations. I can't imagine what a trip that would have been."

Selena turned toward the window, watching the rain cascade down the glass in winding rivulets. She was too afraid to look at the website.

Crissy continued, "In almost all cases, people feel that the doppelganger came to warn them of an impending disaster. There are a lot of cases where famous people saw a doppelganger. Mark Twain saw and spoke to the double of a woman at a party. The real woman was miles away at the time. Percy Shelley, the poet and husband of Mary Shelley, the chick who wrote *Frankenstein*, supposedly saw his weeks before he drowned. Writers Goethe and Guy de Maupassant had their encounters as did lots of Catholic saints from Saint Ambrose to Padre Pio."

"Isn't Padre Pio that Italian priest who had the bleeding hands thing?" Julie asked.

Crissy arched an eyebrow. "It's called stigmata. How the heck did you know that?"

"My mom's into saints and stuff like that. She buys all these special candles with saints on them and reads these pamphlets the church gives her. That woman loves to pray."

Selena paced around the room clutching a tan throw pillow to her chest. "So what does this all mean? Why are we all seeing my doppelganger and what can I do to get rid of it?"

The tension in her voice was only matched by the intensity of the storm.

Crissy mumbled to herself and she worked her way down the web page. Julie came to Selena's side and rubbed her upper arms.

"Okay, in some cases, they're what they call a *bi-location* of the self, which is just a fancy way of saying an out-of-body projection. These are the kind seen by other people, like when this woman saw her brother's, even though he was in another country. His doppelganger looked and sounded exactly like her brother, except he never moved his left arm. He visited her in her living room on three successive nights, just popped in while she was sitting down to read, sat in the chair opposite her to say a few words, then walked out the door, or more like *through* the door. When her actual brother did return a month later, she fainted when she saw that his left arm was missing. He'd had an accident and lost it in a threshing machine. Communication wasn't the best back when this happened, so he wasn't able to get word to anyone until he was able to take a ship back home."

"That's crazy-eerie, Crissy. Are there other types?" Julie asked, plopping onto the bed.

Crissy drew a deep breath. "Selena, you may want to sit down for this."

Selena stopped her pacing and sat close to Julie on the end of the bed.

"The thing that is most associated with the appearance of a doppelganger, especially when it's your own, is death omens. More times than most, when people see their double, it's a warning that they're about to die soon."

Tears welled up in Selena's eyes. It was hard to breathe.

Crissy was quick to add, "But, it's not one-hundred-percent, so don't freak out just yet. If this was something that happened a lot, you would have heard it on the news by now and not on some website."

"So how do we tell this thing to get lost?" Julie said, speaking for her friend who was too shocked to form words.

"Give me a few minutes to check."

Julie pulled Selena's head to her chest and gently rocked her. "It's going to be all right, Sel. You've got me and now we have Crissy. We won't let anything hurt you."

All Selena could think was *I'm going to die*. It played over again and again, ratcheting up her fear and despair with every repetition.

After ten minutes of searching, Crissy threw her hands up. "I can't find any instances of a doppelganger being eradicated, except for this one case but it was reported by this paranormal group that I know for a fact is full of shit. It's like doppelgangers go just as mysteriously as they arrive. Selena, you said you found some places that you think could help?"

Selena wiped tears from her eyes and fumbled to get her laptop out. "I bookmarked about ten different websites."

"Good. Let's get started looking at them. We'll find the right one and email them today."

Selena could only watch with mute fascination as Julie and Crissy went through each website she had found a few nights earlier and cross-checked each on both computers. She couldn't help but be lost in her own thoughts, wondering how it could be that a sixteen-year-old girl should face her own mortality thanks to some death-omen-carrying double of herself. Everything felt too hallucinatory to be real. Yet here were her friends, accepting what she had told them, doing their best to find some answers. Maybe she did have a chance. Maybe they would find the right person to help them.

But the bigger question overrode any glimmers of hope. Why was her doppelganger here?

And what was it trying to tell her?

Chapter Twenty

The air around Eddie and Jessica filled with enough static electricity to raise the hair on their heads straight up. The sounds of growling and short chuffs surrounded them. It was like being dropped in a cage full of tigers, except they were invisible and highly agitated.

"This can't be good," Eddie muttered.

"You won't find this in any ghost hunter manual," Jessica replied from within the dark. "I told you, I seem to bring out the best in these things."

Eddie cried out with a sharp yelp before dropping to a knee. Jessica swung her arm in an arc behind her, searching for him.

"Are you okay?" she said.

Through pained breaths, Eddie choked, "Don't call...him a...*thing*. He...he really doesn't like that."

There was a loud crash behind them, but it was impossible to see what had been tossed on the floor. It sounded as if the old shovels had been picked up and launched against one of the rough cement walls.

The EB's presence was all around them, wrapping them in a cocoon of angry, crackling energy. Jessica's fingertips found the top of Eddie's head. She knelt down to whisper in his ear.

"You getting anything from him?"

Eddie paused, then replied, "Just anger. There's so much rage right now, it's like trying to spot the moon through a storm cloud."

She patted his shoulder. "Just keep your connection open or whatever it is you do. I think I detected our moment."

Before he could muster a reply, Jessica was back on her feet and shouting.

"You don't like being called a thing, huh? Well, you like to scare little kids, so that makes you a pathetic, weak, dickless *thing* in my book."

A warning rumble, like the steady gnarling of an approaching bear, echoed throughout the basement. It was meant to frighten them into leaving. It was only logical that a person would run from the house, never to return, if they were to hear such a sound in the darkest recesses of a cellar.

Jessica saw it as her chance to keep on the offensive.

"Did you like to play zoo animals when you were alive or something? How does it feel to be reduced to a *thing* that sits in a crappy basement, so impotent that you can only make lame noises and move furniture around? God, I'd hate to be a meaningless *thing* like that."

She didn't know what prompted her to duck, but she was glad she did. She felt the sharp breeze of something sail over her head. It struck the back wall with a loud clang.

Eddie, who was still on the floor, grabbed her calf.

"It's going to hurt you if you don't stop."

"Maybe."

Tiny pinpoints of white light materialized from the darkness and flitted about the dark like fireflies on a humid summer night.

"Oooh, pretty. Now we get a light show," Jessica said. She clapped her hands, loud and slow, in mock applause. "Isn't that neat, Eddie? It can make teeny little lights."

Eddie hadn't let go of her leg and she could feel his hand tense around her calf. She heard him suck in a quick breath, then groan. "My head is going to split."

"Just hang in there for a little bit more," Jessica said. Eddie released her leg and she moved deeper into the basement. Then, to the EB, she shouted, "You know what, *thing*? The McCammons are going to sell the house. Yep, you heard me, they're tired of your antics and they're moving out. But here's the part you won't like. I think I'm going to buy it from them. That way, you and I can have nice chats like this day after day after day. Just me and my *thing* in the basement."

Something grabbed her from behind and she felt herself being lifted several inches off the floor. Her shirt bunched up under her neck, making it hard to swallow. Her body felt as if it were immersed in ice water. For the first time since entering the basement, Jessica felt fear.

She gripped the collar of her shirt with both hands, swallowed back her rising terror and continued. "If you don't like me calling you the 'T' word so much, why don't you just tell me who you are?"

Her voice trembled a bit and she worried she had lost her advantage.

Eddie, in the meantime, had regained his footing and rushed up to wrap his arms around her waist. He tugged as hard as he could until her feet were back on solid ground.

"You leave her alone!" he shouted.

She heard him wheeze as he pressed his face against the back of her neck and his grip on her loosened.

When her body began to rise again, he reached out, accidentally grabbing her breasts. She didn't care. She needed him to keep her grounded, in more ways than one.

"Just don't show fear," he whispered. "He's about to crack."

Eddie let the barn doors of his mind wide open. He felt the male spirit walk right on through, bursting with unbridled fury, careless in its anger. This was the way it worked for him. When he was young, spirits came to him at their will, invading his dreams and waking hours with stories, laments, requests. It got to the point where he couldn't concentrate above the din of the dead that surrounded him.

When he turned fourteen, his dad taught him how to close them out, how to let them in when *he* was ready. His father, being raised on a farm in Iowa, had created his own mental totem, a place that stood guard at the divide between the living and the dead. He passed that totem on to Eddie, who had been using the image of the barn ever since. The big red doors were closed tight most of the time, even when he sensed the scratching of the disembodied on its wood slats.

Only now, he threw the bar that rested within the metal holders on either side of the frame free and the doors sprang open. The full image of the man's spirit raged into the barn. He was tall, rangy, with narrow eyes creased by deep crow's feet. A heavy, brown mustache drooped down past his chin. A dark, well-worn fedora was perched on his head. The spirit's lips pulled back in a sneer. Oh, it was not happy. Not at all.

Eddie stood before the door, siphoning its essence, searching for what he needed.

He got that and much, much more.

Eddie hissed in her ear, "Edwin Esposito. His name is Edwin Esposito."

Jessica's courage returned. *Gotcha!*

"Show's over, Edwin Esposito! Now I know you, and I order you to leave this place. You can go to heaven or hell, but this place is no longer your home!"

Jessica felt the temperature in the basement begin to rise and the sounds of moving objects and growling ceased. The moment the last word left her lips, the spirit of Edwin Esposito vanished into the ether.

Jessica turned the camcorder light on and scanned the basement. The place was a mess. No box had been left undisturbed and all of the old gardening utensils and tools were scattered about the floor.

"He's gone," Eddie said, his shock impossible to hide.

"That he is." She waited for him to say something else, then added, "You can let go of me now."

"Oh...yeah...right. Sorry. Just wanted to make sure you didn't float away," he said with a heavy dose of embarrassment. Jess was sure that if she shined the light in his face, it would be as red as a McIntosh.

"Come on, let's go upstairs and see what's what," she said.

With Jessica leading the way upstairs, they went through every room in the house. The kitchen floor was a disgusting mess, but nothing else had happened to it while they were in the basement. Other than the dining room, the rest of the rooms on the other floors were undisturbed. Best of all, she could tell that they were devoid of the EB's presence.

It was almost four in the morning when they finished packing things up. Jessica said she wanted to wait for Tim McCammon to get home and tell him the good news, face to face. In the meantime, she reviewed the video footage from the basement. All that had been caught was a few tools being tossed against the wall. Unfortunately, the camera hadn't been turned her way when Edwin Esposito decided to play rough and lift her off the floor.

While she watched the video, Eddie sat in an opposite chair with an icepack over his head. Even after four aspirin, the pounding in his head refused to go away.

She had just shut the camera down when Eddie asked, "How did you do it?"

"Do what?"

"You know, make Edwin's spirit take off just by saying his name and telling him to hit the bricks. I've never seen or heard of anything like it."

Jessica zipped up the camera case and rested her arms on her knees, studying him. "I don't know. I only know that it works. Better I should ask you how you got his name like that."

"I told you I could talk to the dead. No parlor tricks. But with all the things I can do, I don't have your kind of power."

"You call it power. I think they're just afraid of me. Without you down there, I wouldn't have been able to use it. He damn near choked me out. And I'll bet his name wasn't captured on any audio. It was either you getting that for me or nothing."

Eddie pulled the icepack from his head and tried to smile. It made him wince. "So, I did good?"

Jessica nodded. "Yeah, you did. We still have four hours before Tim gets back. What do you say we get some sleep so we don't look like a pair of zombies? Unless you think Edwin is still around."

"I can assure you, Mr. Esposito is someplace far, far away."

"Good."

Jessica yawned, leaned back on the couch and was asleep in seconds.

Chapter Twenty-One

Rita Leigh opened her son's door a crack, wincing when the hinges wailed in protest. Ricky was asleep in his bed, his covers already tossed on the floor. He'd always been a restless sleeper. Selena lay curled up on the blow up mattress, her back to the door. Rita watched her for several minutes to make sure Selena was asleep and not faking. The soft, gentle rise and fall of the sheet that was tugged up to her shoulders assured her that the mild sedative she had given her had done the trick.

Rita's heart broke. As a mother, she had almost gotten used to those moments that were out of her hands, like when the kids were sick and all she could do was nurse them back to health. There was nothing in the parent guidebook on how to protect your child from what she could only think was a ghost—a spirit that for some reason had decided to make itself look exactly like Selena.

It had been a couple of weeks since the incident in her closet, but Selena couldn't shake her fear and Rita's concern grew worse and worse. Selena had barely been sleeping, and it was taking its toll on her. She looked like someone who had narrowly survived a terrible accident and couldn't recover from the horror she'd seen. She spent her days in a silent fog, unable to even enjoy any time spent out of the house, too terrified to sleep.

Rita remembered the small prescription she had gotten a year ago when she herself went through a bout of insomnia, though for a very different reason. It took a lot of convincing to get Selena to take the sleeping pill, but she relented when Rita said, "Honey, if you take this, you'll sleep through the night no matter what happens. Remember when you were little and so afraid of the wind that you would make yourself fall asleep early on nights when we had a big storm coming? You'll also feel a lot better in the morning once you've had a good night's sleep in you."

My poor angel, what can I say or do to make this all go away? Rita thought as she closed the door.

She was certain there was a ghost in the house, unlike Greg, even though he had seen the thing that looked like Selena. What she couldn't understand was why now? They had lived in this house since Selena was born and nothing strange had ever happened. What triggered this thing that had insinuated itself into their lives like a cancer cell? And what would it take to convince Greg that this was real?

Rita, and her whole family for that matter, had grown up believing in ghosts. Both of her parents claimed to have seen at least one in their lives—her mother coming across the see-through phantom of a woman wearing an old frock in the basement of a hotel where she was working as a maid the summer after her senior year in high school, and her father claiming that the spirit of his grandmother had visited him in his bed on three separate occasions, all preceding major events in his life. She wished they were alive to talk to because she needed a sympathetic ear. With each passing day without a sighting, a blessing in itself, Greg became more and more convinced that it was just their imaginations, nothing more.

Greg was out playing pool with Joey Pinto tonight. They met once a month and alternated between pool and bowling. She was pissed off that he could just go out with his buddy when everyone else in the house was walking on eggshells, jumping at every odd noise.

She put a kettle of water on to make tea and sat at the kitchen table, staring into the well-lit living room. Almost every light was on in the house, and it would stay that way until it was time to go up to bed. She jumped out of her chair when, a few minutes later, the kettle started to whistle.

With shaking hands, she poured the hot water into her cup, wondering if she should take a sleeping pill herself.

Jessica walked groggily into the kitchen. Her hair was a Medusa's nest and she was still in the Anthrax shirt she had worn at the McCammons' house the night before. Liam was devouring a bowl of cereal and chugging orange juice from the carton. It was four o'clock in the afternoon, breakfast in the Backman/Powers house.

"If your mom catches you doing that, you're dead," she warned him as she poured coffee grounds into the coffee maker's filter.

"Mom's out food shopping. Have a rough night with your new boyfriend?"

A Cheerio ring popped out of his mouth when he grinned.

"You're lucky I'm too tired to wipe the floor with you."

She put two slices of bread in the toaster and laid three strips of bacon on a plate and popped it in the microwave. Tim and Kristen and the kids had all arrived at their home a little before ten o'clock. Jessica had called them ahead of time and told them it was all over. There were hugs all around and Kristen even shed a few tears. Eddie's shoulder nearly popped out of its socket when Tim couldn't stop shaking his hand, pumping his arm as if he were drawing water from a well.

"I can feel that it's gone, you know?" Kristen had said. "The house feels...empty. I don't know how to describe it."

"It's full again, now that your family is here and happy," Jess had said.

After declining money for her services, and Tim had offered a considerable amount, she and Eddie got into their Jeeps and headed to their separate homes, with a promise to be in touch in a couple of days. They both needed time to recover.

And now, the day after banishing the meanest poltergeist-like EB one could come across, she was back to sparring with Liam. It was funny. No matter how great or strange your accomplishments, life carried on. In a way, it was comforting.

She said to Liam, "By the way, what makes you think I was with a guy?"

"I'm not deaf. I do hear you and Mom talk. So, how did things work out? Is he what he says he is?"

Jessica sipped her coffee, black, no sugar, and replied, "I'm amazed to say it, but yes, he does have some ability. It really came in handy."

That ability probably saved my life, she thought.

"It figures. Some dude comes out of nowhere and gets to go with you and I'm still stuck here."

"Where you belong."

"Whatever. I'm going upstairs to take a nap."

"But you just woke up."

"I was up all night gaming. I gotta get my rest so I can start all over again tonight."

Sulking, Liam tramped back up to his room. Jess knew that he was working on his mother behind the scenes to get her to allow him to go with Jess on at least one investigation. He had a better chance getting Disney World to open its doors for free for the rest of eternity. What had happened to all of them in Alaska was a vivid memory for Eve and Jessica, one they could never forget. Liam had been a baby at the time, and they had kept the truth from him for good reason.

Because Jessica remembered the things in the cabin when she was six. How they led to her father making the ultimate sacrifice, and how she had held his heavy head in her tiny, trembling hands as he breathed his last.

If Liam knew, would he ever ask to accompany her?

Then she thought of Eddie Home, and how her father had somehow nudged him to her, and the job they had done, together, last night. It warmed her chest to think that he was still watching over her.

"I love you mucho much," she whispered. The kitchen was silent, but she knew he heard her.

Chapter Twenty-Two

Eddie Home's cell rang while he was shelving a new case of vitamins. Over the past couple of days, he appreciated the fact that his job in the health food store required very little thought and was full of enough mindless routine that he could lose himself in its repetition.

He checked the display.

Jessica Backman.

After spending so much time and energy trying to find her, his reticence at answering her call was hard for him to reconcile. The events at the McCammon house had exhausted him beyond words. The entity in their house, Edwin Esposito, had scared him, too. Finding spirits had always been as easy for him as going next door to talk to a neighbor. He had never encountered the power and rage that emanated from the faux-poltergeist.

It turned out that angry Edwin had lived in the previous house that had been on the property in the early part of the 20th century. He had died in the basement while shoveling coal on a frigid winter night. Heart attack. Nothing extraordinary. Eddie still marveled at how much he could learn through sustained contact with a spirit, or as Jessica had taught him, EB.

True to the partial theory on poltergeists, it was the combined life energies of the McCammon girls that woke his spirit from its slumber. Now awake and confused by the new house, new family and completely new time period, he began to lash out, to try to make order of things, which explained the strange stacking of household items. Odds were, he would have kept things at that unsettling, yet innocuous level. Until Jessica arrived.

When Jessica had asked him what the regular tapping had meant, Eddie laughed.

"Turns out, it wasn't Morse code at all. Old Edwin had a serious case of OCD. One of the manifestations of the disease was incessant tapping, but always in the same pattern. It must suck to die, only to have the same afflictions you had in life follow you to the hereafter," he'd said.

Jessica had replied, "That's a perfect case for instructing people, and myself, not to jump to conclusions. Wow. OCD. Never would have called that. Guess I can't assume everything I see and hear is an attempt at communication."

"That would be a big nope."

What he didn't mention to an exhausted Jessica was his burgeoning theory that if he was a communication line with the dead, she was a beacon, not just calling them forward, but imbuing them with an energy and purpose that was off the scale of human experience. Edwin Esposito's shade not only drew strength from her, he also became incensed at her attempts to communicate with him because he knew her goal was to make him go away. And go away he did, thanks to whatever it was that she could do just by repeating his name.

In a way, she was dangerous.

He answered on the fourth ring. "Hey."

"Are you home right now?" She sounded tense, but then he hadn't known her long enough to tell if that was just her regular state of being. From what he'd seen so far, tense was her middle name.

"I'm at work, elbow deep in bottles of vitamin D. What's up?"

"What time do you get out?"

Eddie checked his watch. "In about three hours."

"Do you have Skype at home?"

"No, but I can download it. Why do you ask?"

"I have something I want to go over with you that I think you'll appreciate."

"You want to show me plans for a trip to Aruba?"

Jessica was silent, then said, "Funny. Call me when you're ready and we'll talk."

The call was disconnected before he could reply. He finished putting out the vitamins, then went to the back room and crushed the box, throwing it on the pile to be dumped in the recycling bin. The rest of the day was spent cleaning out the trail mix bins and the fresh peanut butter maker. Three patrons got mad at him for denying them their ground peanut butter. He was tempted to ask them if they'd prefer dirty peanut butter, but opted to tune them out instead. His apartment didn't come free and he needed food and gas money.

When his shift was over, he hung his green apron on a peg in the employee closet, waved goodbye to Edna, the night cashier, and took the six-block walk to his apartment. The streets were buzzing with activity and loud rap music seemed to blast from every fifth passing car. He stopped to get some Chinese food and ate it slowly at his small kitchen table while listening to talk radio. He considered doing a load of laundry, but decided the pile could wait another day or two.

It wasn't until he'd been home for almost two hours before he realized that he was stalling his call to Jessica.

The top of his head was still sore, as if he'd been struck by a wooden cane and not internally by the psychic force of an angry spirit. Jessica Backman had a power that she barely knew about, much less could control. Odds were, if she kept on the path she was going, she'd end up hurt, just like her dad.

Just like her dad.

He turned on his computer, wrestling with himself to pick up the phone. He thought of Jessica the other night, suspended in the air, struggling to breathe, egging the poltergeist on so Eddie could swoop in and get that little kernel of information that she needed to use her own mysterious power. She could have died, and may have died trying, no hesitation.

He dialed her number.

"Do you have it loaded yet?" Jessica asked. She was chewing gum and filled any silences by popping it in his ear. He was beginning to gain a better understanding of her and felt she was doing it on purpose to grate on his nerves. *Just another test.* He ignored it and opened up the viewer.

"I'm in," he said.

"Okay, hold on." He could hear her typing and a few seconds later, they were face to face, in a manner of speaking. She offered him a smile and waved her fingers at the webcam.

She said, "See, isn't it nicer to see my smiling face?"

"You look better than I feel."

"What's wrong? Are you sick or something?"

She noted that his hair was a skewed mess and his eyes looked tight, pained. He couldn't argue with her observation, seeing himself in a small window on the screen and wincing at his own image.

"Or something," he replied. "Everything fine with you...you know...after the other night?"

Jessica rolled her eyes. "I was a little sore the day after, but it wasn't anything some sleep and four Advil couldn't cure. I haven't even left the house yet because I figured I'd earned a little break. I got bored, so I started going through the inbox for my website. You'll never guess what I came across."

Eddie sat back in his chair, waiting. Jessica frowned.

"That was your cue to read my mind and tell me," she said.

"It doesn't work that way."

"Oh. Well, it was worth a try." Her face disappeared from the screen as she moved out of frame. She came back holding a stack of papers. "I get tons of emails every week, most of them with photo and video attachments. Everyone who ever took a picture with an orb in it thinks they captured a ghost and wants me to put it on the website. You know, all these cheap digital cameras are going to be the death of true ghost hunting. Too many lighting issues pop up with them. Anyway, I was looking through everything, deleting most, saving a few that I would pass on to my web guy, Swedey, to load onto the site, when I came across one that literally made my jaw drop."

Eddie couldn't imagine what it was that could shock Jessica.

"I got an email from a girl in New Hampshire who is totally freaked out. She said she and her family have been seeing something that is so rare, it's beyond belief."

Eddie leaned in closer to the computer screen. Jessica's excitement was contagious.

"Well, what is it?" he asked.

"This girl—" she leafed through the pages, "—Selena Leigh, saw her *doppelganger.*"

"A doppelganger? Are you sure?"

"No shit. *She's* one-hundred-percent sure. According to her, her father saw it on a separate occasion and her mother heard it one afternoon calling to her. Needless to say, she's completely wigged out."

Eddie exhaled, long and hard. "Wow. A doppelganger that's been seen by the person it impersonates as well as other people. That's just crazy."

"I know. But I haven't even gotten to the good part yet. She sent me a video that she recorded in her friend's room. I think she was trying to convey just how serious and upset she was so I wouldn't ignore her email or throw it on the deleted pyre, you know. I'm sending it over to you now."

Eddie opened up his email and waited for her message to arrive. It took a half a minute before his incoming mail chime sounded.

Sinister Entity

"I won't say a thing until it's over," Jessica said.

"Jess, if you feel this is valid, I believe you. I don't need to see a video of a frightened girl."

"Just watch it."

Eddie double clicked the attachment and brought the video up to medium size. He could still see Jessica in the live video window. She had taken out a nail file and was working on her tips.

The video image was very clear, near HD quality, and showed a pretty girl, not much younger than Jessica, sitting before the camera. The only blemish on her good looks was the dark bags under her haunted eyes. The heads of two girls bobbed over her shoulders. One had chestnut skin and was exotic looking, must have been Latina, the other your typical teen goth, all pale makeup and facial piercings. It struck him odd that such a trio would even associate with one another. He wasn't that far removed from high school himself and remembered the rule of non-intersecting social circles.

The pretty girl spoke, "Hello, my name is Selena Leigh. I hope you had a chance to read my email. I...I never even heard of a doppelganger before until my friend Crissy just told me about it." The goth girl waved at the camera. "I saw this, uh, doppelganger that looked like me, well, kinda like me, just stranger, in my closet one night."

She went on to describe the frightened mirror image of herself in the closet and how her father had thought he'd seen her in the garage a week before that. Selena had to stop a few times to hold back her tears, and her exotic friend passed her tissues to wipe her eyes.

No doubt about it, Eddie thought, *this girl is unnerved.* He had just seen that same haunted look in Tim McCammon's eyes. It made him uncomfortable, seeing a young girl so afraid, pouring out her heart to a tiny camera in the hopes that a stranger on a website would come save her.

He noticed that Jessica had stopped filing her nails and was now watching him, watching the video. His eyes went back to Selena Leigh and her friends and her incredible story.

Just as the video was about to end, he saw something that made him squint at the screen. The video faded to black and he pulled the time bar back about ten seconds.

"Did you see it?" Jessica asked.

"Hold on."

He pressed Play, watched it a second time, then pulled back again, pausing the video.

"No freakin' way," he murmured.

Behind the girls, by the window, something had appeared between flashes of lightning.

Selena's doppelganger!

It watched them for a moment, its skin opaque, bordering on cadaverous, dressed in a knee-length, white nightgown. Then, as the flash of light from the storm outside dissipated, so did the apparition.

Neither Selena nor her friends had noticed it at the time and he assumed they didn't when they played the video back.

He closed out the video and brought Jessica up to full screen.

"It's real," he said in a soft whisper.

Jessica nodded. "Can you take a few days off work?"

Eddie had to think for a moment. "I have three days off in a row starting Monday."

"Good. Seabrook, New Hampshire is only about four hours away. I'll drive."

Chapter Twenty-Three

Greg Leigh sat in his easy chair, but he was feeling far from relaxed. Rita and Selena sat on the loveseat opposite him. They had dropped Ricky off at his friend Xavier's house earlier, then came home to drop the bomb. It had been one hell of a surprise.

"And when is this person coming?" he asked, holding off on his anger until he had all the facts.

Rita put a hand on Selena's lap and answered, "There are actually two of them and they'll be here tomorrow around noon."

Greg looked at Selena, who cast her eyes down to her mother's hand.

"I don't remember anyone asking me if this was okay," he said. He dug a nail into the armrest, trying to keep his composure.

"Selena came to me a few days ago. She and her friends did all the research and she showed it to me. I told her to contact them."

Rita looked him in the eye, defiant. She was in full on momma-bear mode. Things could get ugly, fast. Selena looked as if she was close to crying. Greg took a deep breath, hoping it would calm him. He and Rita were very much alike when it came to fighting. Both were stubborn as hell and defeat was never an option. It was why some of their more legendary arguments led to his sleeping in the guest room for as much as a week at a time.

Rita continued, "I don't know if you've been aware, but we've been living in fear the past few weeks and you didn't lift a finger to even attempt to find some answers. If bringing in the people from this website makes Selena comfortable, that's good enough for me."

She had him there. He still thought there was a rational explanation for what they had experienced, and since it hadn't happened again, it was easy to ignore. He had work, and with this being the busy season for his company, he often brought it home with him. Where would he have found time to seek help? And just where the hell did they expect him to start?

It was Rita who went to the library to see if she could find anything that would shed some light on things, but the occult section left a lot to be desired. Greg remembered coming home one day to find her sitting in bed, books on UFOs, ghosts and witchcraft on the comforter. He had joked that she looked like one of the gang from *Buffy the Vampire Slayer* and she had given him the cold shoulder in return. When that proved fruitless, she went to Father Ogden and asked him to bless the house. That was supposed to happen in another week and Greg had already made a mental note to keep busy in the yard when the padre came to the door. He thought Father Ogden was a bit of a tosspot who was well past his prime. He couldn't stand the man's sermons. They always seemed to tie back to abortion and the sanctity of life. Roe v. Wade must have really unhinged him, Greg had thought more than once.

"How much is this going to cost?"

Greg held his breath, waiting for Rita to answer. What she said next would determine whether there would be peace in the Leigh house tonight. Even in the best of times, money was tight.

"Nothing. They do this to help people, not to make money."

Greg huffed. "I'll believe that when I see it."

Selena spoke up. Her bottom lip quivered and her eyes were glassy. "Please, Daddy, don't be mad. They'll only be here for a couple of days. The woman who wrote me said she knew what we were dealing with and that she could help. I don't...I don't know how much longer I can stay here, waiting for that thing to show up again. Even when I don't see it, I can feel it. It's like I'm being watched all the time, even when I'm out of the house."

Greg almost told her to stop thinking crazy thoughts like that, but one look at her face made him swallow his retort. Jesus, she was a mess. He felt his anger, his trepidation, his wounded macho pride fade away. Whatever apprehension and doubt he felt, and it was impossible to discount, would have to be put on the back burner for now. He motioned for her to come over. Selena rose from the loveseat and melted into his outstretched arms. She buried her face in the collar of his shirt and wept.

When he looked toward Rita, she mouthed a silent thank you.

Eve looked over the questionnaire that Jessica had asked the New Hampshire girl's mother to fill out. It was standard procedure for Jessica to gather as much information as she could before she went to someone's home to take on their supernatural problem. It was essential for Eve, too, so she could get a clearer picture of what Jess was about to step into. If she didn't like what she saw, there would be no trip. She'd dismantle the Jeep herself to stop her.

The questions were pretty straightforward. They asked the experiencer to describe what they saw, when, where, the weather at the time, if there were additional witnesses, etc. From all accounts, what happened with the Leigh family was recent and brief. No prior history.

"What do you think?" Jessica asked. They were in the living room, having finished watching *Dancing with the Stars*, a guilty pleasure for them both. Jessica looked like a little girl in her long Mickey Mouse night shirt and fuzzy slippers. Eve smiled, remembering having her on one lap and Liam on the other, sitting on the same couch watching cartoons. Now here she was, being asked to give her blessing to let Jessica travel to New England to help a scared girl who wasn't much younger than her brave and stubborn adopted daughter.

"Well, from what I learned from your dad, doppelgangers are pretty rare and don't pose a threat to anyone but the person they're impersonating. I hope this is all just a misunderstanding and not a sign that something might happen to the girl. Poor kid."

"That's why I want to go. How many people have had the chance to investigate an actual doppelganger? And I want to give some peace of mind back to Selena if I can. So, can I go?"

Eve rubbed the back of her neck. "I don't know. New Hampshire isn't exactly around the corner."

"I'll only be gone for a few days."

"Yeah, but I don't like the idea of you alone in a place you've never been. There are dangers to young ladies other than ghosts, you know."

"I won't be alone. Eddie will be with me."

"And I'm supposed to be over the moon that you're going there with a boy you barely know?"

Jessica shrugged. "Wasn't it you who said you liked the idea of me having someone that would have my back? And he really did."

"What will the sleeping arrangements be?" Eve knew Jessica wouldn't be shacking up with Eddie, but it was fun to push her buttons sometimes.

"Oh jeez, we'll be in separate rooms at the Best Western. Who do you think I am, some reality show horn dog? I'd break his arms if he even suggested sharing a room."

Eve bonked Jess on the head with the rolled up questionnaire. "Sounds like you already made plans."

Jessica laughed. "It's all refundable. If I show you one more thing, will you let me go?"

"I dread to think what it could be. I know you won't be happy until you do, so let's see it."

Jessica picked her laptop off the floor and called up a video, sizing it to full screen. "Pay close attention when you get to the four-minute, thirty-three-second mark."

Eve did.

And asked her to play it again.

Even though Jessica's GPS told her to take I95 most of the way from New York to New Hampshire, Eddie had convinced her to take the more scenic route that took them along I84, then up through I495 where the road would end right at the exit to Seabrook. He had logged on to AAA the night before they left and gotten the directions from them. It meant less traffic and should save them about thirty minutes.

He wore khaki shorts and a tucked in gray golf shirt. When she picked him up, she joked that he looked as if he were going to play croquet at a country club. He commented on her choice of black jeans and faded *Ozzy Blizzard of Ozz* tour shirt as the first choice of metal heads, circa 1981.

While in Massachusetts, they passed a sign for Old Sturbridge Village. Jessica turned down the blaring radio and said, "Oh wow, I remember that place. My aunt Eve took me there for my tenth birthday. I was into American history at the time and I thought it was even cooler than Disney World."

"What is it?" Eddie asked. He kept one hand on the bar above his head and had sparingly taken his eyes off the road. Jessica laughed inside. She knew her driving took a lot of people by surprise.

"It's a replica of an old colonial times village. The people who work there dress in period pieces and they have a working blacksmith, farm, mill, you name it. I remember that I got to play tug of war on the common ground and when we won, we were given rock candy as a prize. We should go there on the way back."

She gunned the Jeep up to eighty-five to pass a car that dared to only go a tick above seventy in the middle lane. Eddie sucked air in hard through his teeth, but she gave him credit for not telling her how to drive.

"Bear in mind, I do have a job to get back to, no matter how insignificant it may be," he said.

"Well, that's if we can wrap this one up one-two-three."

Eddie shook his head. "I don't know about that. Getting a chance to investigate a recurring doppelganger is pretty rare. We don't have much history to draw from."

"That's why I have you here. I was hoping you could see or sense or hear something that I would never pick up on, maybe give us a direction to go on."

She failed to tell him about her own reticence about this particular case and how his actions with the Edwin Esposito EB made her feel safer. She knew that even if she hadn't met Eddie, she would have jumped at the chance to examine a doppelganger case. Having him around just made her more comfortable, but she'd die before letting him know that. She still didn't know much about Eddie Home. She wasn't about to spill her deepest feelings to him now.

"We'll see. I have zero experience with this type of thing," he said. "But thank you for thinking of me. Seriously. I'm happy to help."

He smiled, which was replaced by a grimace when she swerved around a tractor trailer. He did look sincere.

She said, "Okay, by my estimate, we have about two hours to go. We might as well use this time to learn a little something about each other."

"Works for me."

"Favorite movie?" she asked.

"*The 40-Year-Old Virgin.*"

Jessica laughed. "Really?"

"Really. What's yours?"

"*The Shining.*"

"I should have known."

"Speaking of which, I feel like I may be at a disadvantage here. I can ask you questions and have to take your answers at face value, whereas you can poke around my brain and see things I don't want you to see."

Eddie rolled down the window and let his hand undulate against the steady current. "That's true, I could, but I won't. I do have control over myself, and I choose to stay out of your head. I have enough nightmares as it is."

Jessica backhanded his upper arm, but not too hard.

"Okay, you ask me a question," she said.

"Well, I already know your musical tastes stopped somewhere in a metal concert in 1991. I'll tell you that my favorite modern band is the Dropkick Murphys. Other than that, I'm old-time crooners all the way. What's your major in college?"

"Anthropology. I'm not sure what I'll do with my degree when I graduate, but the subject fascinates the hell out of me. Guess I'm addicted to studying dead people."

"You ever think of taking parapsychology? There are a few schools out there that offer it as a course of study. Something like that would seem to be right up your alley."

Jessica shook her head. "I thought about it once, but I'm not interested. Parapsychologists deal with doubt and uncertainty. Their job is to assign everyday reasons for impossible events. I know what's really out there. And I bet you do, too."

Eddie moved the conversation back to lighter topics that helped make the stretch through I495 pass by quickly. They stopped for a few minutes to get gas and bottles of water, and less than an hour later, got off the first exit on I95. They only had to go another couple of miles before they pulled up to the Leigh house, a tan Cape in the middle of an entire neighborhood of similar Cape homes.

There were pretty trees in front of every house and plenty of kids playing in the streets. Seabrook looked to be a working family kind of town, and it was apparent that most people took pride in their modest homes.

The Leighs had a full second floor and an attached garage. All of the front lawns on both sides of the street were lush and well groomed. Their mailbox by the curb was shaped like a mini replica of their house.

"Quaint," Jessica said. "I wouldn't mind living here."

"Being so close to the beach doesn't hurt either."

They got out of the Jeep and were hit by a blast of heat. Since passing by the exit to Boston, they had rolled up the windows and turned on the air conditioner. Summer was in full bloom in New Hampshire.

"I thought it was supposed to be nice and cool in New England," Eddie said.

"Not in summer, do-do. Let's go, time to put on our game faces."

Jessica adjusted her hair in the car's side view mirror and walked up the drive. Eddie stayed a pace behind, she hoped trying to pick up some vibes on the place.

The door was answered by an attractive middle-aged woman and her husband, who, despite his smile, looked as if he would rather be anywhere than here at the moment.

She extended her hand. "Hi, I'm Jessica Backman from fear none dot com. This is my partner, Eddie Home. Your daughter contacted me."

"I'm Rita, this is my husband Greg. Please, come in. Selena's inside."

A tiny dog yapped at Rita's heels. It wagged its tail furiously, so she assumed it wasn't out to take a bite from her ankles.

"Billy, be quiet!" Rita said to the dog. The little ball of fur groaned and scampered into the house. "I'll let him out back in a bit so we can have peace and quiet."

Jessica smiled, letting her know that she wasn't afraid of dogs.

"My son, Ricky, is staying at a friend's house tonight. We didn't want to scare him."

"That makes perfect sense," Jessica reassured her.

As she passed by the Leighs, she heard Greg mutter to his wife, "They're kids. Are you sure about this?"

Rita waved him off.

Selena hopped out of her chair and shook their hands. Jessica could see the stress on the young girl's face as easily as if she were wearing a T-shirt that said *I'M LOSING MY MIND AND CAN'T TAKE ANY MORE*. Rita Leigh offered them some iced tea, and they all moved into the dining room to take a seat. Jessica pulled a digital recorder out of her pocket.

"You mind if I record this?" she asked.

Greg Leigh arched an eyebrow, but Rita and Selena both said, "No, it's not a problem."

"You have a real nice place here," Eddie said, admiring the comfortable, ordered living room.

"Thank you," Rita said with a flush of pride.

Jessica got down to business. Greg Leigh didn't look as if he'd be long on idle chit-chat. "Okay, Selena, I know you wrote everything that's been going on in the email you sent and even the video you recorded, but I think it would be best if each of you told us what you experienced and anything else big or small."

Selena started to talk, but the words jumbled in her throat and she looked as if she was about to cry. Her mother put her arm around her shoulders and said, "How about I start?"

I like mom, Jessica thought.

Rita Leigh proceeded to talk about the day she heard Selena calling for her when she wasn't anywhere near the house. The recorder rolled on, and Eddie followed the rule this time, keeping quiet.

Jessica hid her reaction well when Eddie grabbed her leg under the table. She followed his gaze to the stairs in the living room, catching the slight crack of a step, as if someone had just walked up and out of sight.

Chapter Twenty-Four

When they had gotten all the information they could, at least with all of the family members in the same room, consciously or subconsciously affecting one another's answers to their questions, Jessica turned off the recorder and put it back in her pocket.

"Would you mind if Eddie and I walked through the house?" she asked.

Rita Leigh rose from her chair. "Sure. I'll take you."

"If it's all right with you both, I'd like it if Selena could give us the tour."

Eddie looked over at Greg Leigh and saw the slight bulge in his neck and jaw as his muscles tensed like steel cords. Rita placed a firm hand on his shoulder to head his rejection off at the pass and said, "Only if Selena is comfortable."

Selena nodded and pushed away from the table. "Yeah, no problem. Follow me."

Eddie let Jess take the lead as they followed Selena into the living room and then into the garage. The young girl was well on her way to being a stunner. She was worn down from everything, but he sensed a very strong internal spirit within her. *This kid is not one to go down without a fight,* he thought.

"This is where your father thought he saw you?" Jessica asked. She had a small notepad in her hand and jotted down a few lines.

"He was putting his car up on those ramps so he could change the oil and he thought he saw me walk in. It made him hit the gas wrong and he tipped off the ramp. I think he's still pissed that he damaged the car...that is, after he realized I wasn't hurt or in the garage at the time."

Eddie opened up his mind, trying to pick up on any residual energies left in the wake of the incident. It wasn't something he took lightly. Letting his defense down could expose him to things better left on the other side of the barn door. But he was here to help. Time to take a chance.

Even though it had happened weeks ago, time meant very little to his abilities. What occurred a hundred years ago was just the slightest flutter of a hummingbird's wings to the various dimensions that coexisted with our current interpretation of reality. Eddie's true gift was being able to peer into those dimensions and, at times, to draw from their power and manipulate objects and people in the here and now. While the girls spoke, he let himself drift, their voices fading into the background.

Jessica pulled him by the arm so he could keep up as they moved back into the house. The upstairs hallway smelled like potpourri and Eddie thought he'd be hard pressed to find a speck of dust in any of the rooms. They went into Rita and Greg's room, where her mother had heard Selena's voice, then the bathroom and her little brother's room.

Eddie saw the blow up bed and his heart broke for Selena. She was at the age where you were supposed to think you were invincible. The universe only existed to serve you and nothing could bring you down. Sixteen was a crappy age to realize the world was a frightening place.

"It's not fun sharing my little brother's room, but I just can't sleep in my own room alone right now," Selena said. The walls were covered with Red Sox posters. Ricky's dresser was littered with handheld game systems, loose change, a smattering of polished stones and five trophies, four for baseball and one for soccer.

"Good thinking," Eddie said. He realized it was the first thing he'd said to Selena since they had entered the house. He looked over at Jessica to see if she disapproved. She didn't.

Selena hesitated when they got to the entrance to her room.

"I haven't been in there since that night. I even made my parents get my clothes and makeup and stuff out for me. Sounds kinda crazy, right?"

Jessica gave her a warm smile. "If I was in your shoes, I would have done the same thing, and I do this for a living."

Eddie gave her a mental gold star for lying to comfort the girl.

She continued, "If you're not cool with it, we can go in ourselves, check out the closet and be right back out."

Selena crossed her arms and hugged herself, nervous. "How about you go first and I'll follow you?"

Her room was like any other teenage girl's room in America. Posters of hunks in cowboy gear and R&B bands lined the walls. A hint of floral perfume permeated the walls and fabrics. Most of the normal trappings had been removed, but there was enough left behind to let even the dullest observer know who lived in it. A collection of red and gold pom-poms sat in a pile by the bed.

Selena stayed close to Eddie's back. When Jessica opened the closet door, he heard her gasp.

The closet was empty, not particularly deep or wide, and had a heavy scent of pine.

"There's nothing there," he reassured Selena. He meant it in more ways than one. When he first came into the house, he kept his totemic barn doors closed tight. When he didn't sense anything poking around the outside walls, he opened them a crack, pushing the heavy doors farther and farther back until they were wide open. Not even a whisper of a psychic breeze wafted inside.

Odd.

Other than the closet, bed and computer table, there wasn't much to see in Selena's room.

Selena looked relieved but also very happy to get out of the room. They met her parents downstairs and asked a few more questions.

Jessica pocketed her notebook and said, "Okay, I think we have what we need right now. We're going to check into our hotel and be back tonight."

"Could you come after nine? Ricky will be asleep by then," Rita asked.

"Absolutely. We'll work around your schedule, not ours. We'll see you tonight."

Greg Leigh showed them to the door, a look of relief to be rid of them for the moment on his face. When they got in the car, Jessica turned to Eddie and asked, "Well, did you sense anything?"

"Nothing. That place is like a psychic sensory deprivation chamber. I can't remember ever being somewhere that felt like such an empty void. Weird."

"I don't proclaim to be a psychic, but I have been pretty accurate when it comes to knowing something isn't right in a house," Jessica said. "In fact, it's saved me a couple of times from investing a lot of time in locations that would amount to nothing. Even knowing that there's evidence of a doppelganger, albeit unproven evidence, my internal EB meter didn't move squat."

As soon as they were out of sight of the Leighs, Jessica stamped on the accelerator.

"All right, I felt nothing, you felt nothing, but what did you *see* on the stairs? All I heard was one of the steps creak, but that's not anything to write home about when you have a humid day like this."

"I don't know. I've never been in the house before, so it just could have been a normal shadow. Maybe one of the curtains in the living room billowed out and created some light play on the wall along the stairs. Again, it was probably nothing."

"Back to the void."

Eddie exhaled and tensed as Jess zipped through a yellow light at a four-way intersection. "Yeah, back to the void, and that concerns me."

They checked in at a nearby Best Western, separate rooms, of course. Jessica had informed Eddie before the trip that hotel expenses were on her and there was no sense arguing the point.

"At least let me buy dinner," he said when they got their room keys. The hotel had put them in adjoining rooms.

Jessica agreed to it and after dropping her bag off in her room, they headed across the street where there was an Irish-pub-themed restaurant and a gas station with a little grocery. She was relieved when he came back with a menu to the restaurant. She wasn't a fan of gas station fare and refused to eat beef jerky.

They had dinner early. The restaurant was huge and empty. It was just them and several waitresses.

"Busy night," Eddie joked when he gave his order.

"It won't get much more crowded than this on a Monday," the waitress replied. "You should come back when it's *Monday Night Football*. We have awesome wing and drink specials."

Eddie thanked her, gave a wink and she winked back.

"Please don't tell me you're planning on making any moves on her. I *am* in the next room, you know, and I didn't bring any headphones."

Eddie waved her off. "I just spent five years in North Carolina. Down there, they call that southern hospitality."

"In New Hampshire, they call that flirting with the waitress."

Jessica took a big gulp of her soda. She said, "So, what do you think of the Leighs?"

"I'm sure the same you do. Rita seems nice enough, and worried. Selena is completely freaked out, which lends credence to her story. And Greg would like to see us head back to New York in short order."

"He doesn't seem to be the warm and fuzzy type."

"I can't say that I blame him. He obviously doesn't believe what *he* saw, much less a couple of people from a paranormal website. I'm sure he's worried that we're feeding into his wife and daughter's irrational fears and will only make things worse."

Jessica's cell phone rang and she saw that Eve was calling. She excused herself from the table and took the call outside, letting her know that they made it in one piece and all was well. Eve sounded relieved and made her promise to check in once each morning and once each night.

"Guess who came into the restaurant for lunch?" Eve said.

"I don't know, was it Brad Pitt?" Jessica smiled.

"I wish. One of the Baldwin brothers came in, had our veal parmigiana and left Cassie an amazing tip."

"That's so cool! Which one was it?"

"I have no idea. They all look alike to me," Eve said with a laugh. "Look, be careful up there. If you need me, you just call and I'll be there before you know it. And email me everything you find out along the way. I may not be physically there, but I'm going to be with you every step of the way."

Jessica sighed. "I know, and I love you for it. I gotta go. My dinner should be ready any minute now, and I don't have any Baldwins to gawk at. Talk to you tomorrow."

After the call, she walked into the gas station and bought a pack of cigarettes. She smoked, on average, half a pack a month, and felt the need for a pre-dinner cig.

By the time she got back to the restaurant, the waitress was putting their plates on the table.

Eddie crinkled his nose. "I didn't know you smoked."

"While it's still not a crime," she said.

After a few bites of her fried clam strips, she asked, "I've been wondering. What have you heard about my family and Alaska?"

He took a huge swig from his root beer. "Just bits here and there. You go on enough message boards and you get little snippets. The word is that a man, your father, moved his family into a haunted house in some little town that's no longer on the map. There were paranormal events off the scale of believability. People were hurt. A lot of people died. It's hard to tell the fact from fiction. Most people don't equate others getting killed with hauntings, so they don't want to believe it happened. Nothing in the story is verified. It's just word of mouth, like a legend from a long time ago."

If Dad only knew he was going to create a legend, she thought.

"Hm. Just curious," she said, tucking back into her dinner.

She could see that he was waiting for her to fill in the blanks, to tell him if he was right or wrong, to give him the true story. It wasn't a subject she was about to discuss in detail.

From then on, they ate mostly in silence, then walked back to the hotel where they changed, took a nap and met by the car. Eddie noticed that she wasn't carrying one of her black cases.

"Traveling light tonight?" he asked.

"I just want to get used to the house, get a feel for the place and the family. I'm hoping you can provide even better insight. Maybe later it won't register as such a zero with you."

"I hope, because everyone and every place has something attached to it. If I'm still coming up with nothing, it can only mean that something is actively blocking me. You didn't tell Selena in your correspondence about me or what I can do, did you?"

"Are you crazy? No way."

"Well, if she doesn't know, someone must."

Jessica shivered despite the heat, adding, "Or some*thing*. We are, after all, dealing with a doppelganger."

They climbed into her car and hit the road.

Jessica said, "That's the one aspect that concerns me. I mean, what do we really know about doppelgangers? I come to places to help people. I keep thinking, if we come face to face with this, what the hell can I do to help them? There's no manual on this."

He let her concern hang in the air. When she pulled into the driveway, her Jeep's lights briefly illuminated the top windows. They saw Selena at the window, quickly pulling back the curtains and fading from view.

Eddie jumped out of the car before it came to a stop.

"What are you doing?" Jessica called after him.

He ignored her and rang the bell. She had just caught up to him when Selena answered the door. She saw their faces and looked startled.

"Selena, where were you just now?" Eddie asked.

"I was in the kitchen making a cake. Sometimes when I'm nervous, I bake. Why?"

Now Jessica knew why Eddie had run out of the car.

It was in the house.

Chapter Twenty-Five

Eddie sprinted up the stairs. Jessica was close behind. Greg Leigh jumped out of his easy chair and shouted at them.

"What the hell do you think you're doing? My son is asleep!"

Eddie stopped and turned to talk to Greg. Jessica saw her chance and slipped ahead of him, proceeding up the stairs. She heard Greg Leigh say, "You have no right to come barging in here like a couple of lunatics. You're scaring the shit out of my daughter."

While Eddie tried to talk him down, Jessica slipped into the room where she believed she had seen Selena. It was the master bedroom. A small bedside lamp was on, but the room was empty. She looked behind the curtains, then checked under the bed and the closet. Nothing.

As she walked over toward Selena's room, Greg pointed to her from the stairs. "Hey, I'm talking to the both of you."

She pretended she didn't hear him and stepped into Selena's room. The only illumination came from the half-moon shining through the window.

Better not scare it if it's in here, she thought, abstaining from flipping on a light. She walked around the room, careful not to make too much noise.

The closet door beckoned. Maybe Selena's closet was where it felt safest. It made sense. When it came to EBs, almost all had a remote corner that was less traveled than others to call home. Just like Edwin Esposito in Bronxville. She'd yet to fully grasp why that was, but had come to expect it.

She walked softly toward the door. She could hear Greg and Eddie going back and forth in the hallway now, but Eddie knew to keep the rabble from Selena's room, at least for a few more moments.

The wind picked up outside and something pinged against the window pane. Jessica gave a slight start, but returned her attention to the closet door. She reached out, grasped the knob. It felt cool against her damp palm. She took a breath, steadied herself and turned.

The door pulled back to reveal nothing but a few shirts and skirts on hangers and scattered shoeboxes. Jessica put her hand between the clothes, reaching until she could touch the back wall. It was completely empty.

Then she thought about the inside corners by the doorframe and poked her head inside, expecting to see a pair of glowing eyes greeting her from within the darkness.

That's when Eddie and Greg came in. Greg hit the ceiling light, chasing the gloom away.

"Find anything you like?" he said, his voice dripping with sarcasm.

"Nothing that I had hoped to find, no," Jessica replied.

Eddie said, "I told him what we saw when we pulled up, which is why we felt there was no time to waste."

"Which I find hard to believe," Greg shot back. "I mean, no one has seen anything for weeks and suddenly you're here and you see something right away? Please don't yank our chains. Go find another place to sensationalize for your little website."

Jessica held up her hands. "Mr. Leigh, I apologize for the way we burst in here just now, but believe me, we only did that because we thought we could get to the bottom of this right here, right now. This isn't the way I usually work. I promise we will both be discreet. No more running around."

Greg scowled. "Save it. I want you both out of here, now."

Eddie stepped between them. "Greg, please, just give us another chance. I take full responsibility. If anything, I'll go and Jessica will stay."

Greg seemed to think about it for a brief moment, but his face clouded over and he said, "Both of you, out, before I lose my temper."

Jessica knew they weren't going to get anywhere by begging or apologizing. She pulled Eddie by the arm and left the room without another word. She was mad at herself, angrier than Greg was with her. She prided herself on always conducting herself in a professional manner. When they reached the living room, she could see the fear on Selena's and Rita's faces and realized she had done the exact opposite of what she had set out to do. In just a few minutes, she had managed to create a complete clusterfuck.

Greg was hot on their heels, his rage a physical force compelling them toward the front door.

Jessica looked at Selena and said, "I'm so sorry."

Rita turned to Greg, said, "Honey, what happened? Why are they leaving?" She looked on the verge of tears.

He didn't offer her an explanation. He opened the door for them, and closed it with a soft click the moment they stepped outside. Jessica thought she heard muffled crying behind the door.

It was the first time she'd ever been thrown out of a house.

Eddie avoided her gaze, walking like a dog with its tail between its legs and into the passenger seat.

Jessica cranked the ignition, punched the roof of the car as hard as she could and sped off.

Eddie knew enough to not say anything during the tense ride back to the hotel. When they pulled into the lot, he expected Jessica to tell him to grab his things from his room because they were heading home.

She surprised him by saying, "We might as well get some sleep, head out in the morning."

"Jessica, I'm sorry about the way things went down."

She stopped him with a look. "We both screwed up. I don't want to talk about it right now, okay? I'll see you at breakfast."

Jessica didn't look back at him as she walked to her room and locked the door. He leaned back against the Jeep, taking in the night air, amazed by the number of stars in the sky. This was what he called a country sky. The air had cooled and smelled faintly of salt from the nearby Atlantic.

Well, this is the last time she has you along for the ride, he thought. And he couldn't blame her. When he thought about how scared Selena looked when they left, he wanted to kick himself, hard. Talk about amateur hour.

But then again, he *was* an amateur, at least as far as field investigating went. His expertise was being a lab rat.

Why the hell couldn't he detect anything? Even tonight, the house and everyone in it came up as a complete blank. For once, he saw something with his own eyes before sensing it within his mind, and to wonderful results. Had the altercation with Edwin Esposito's spirit taken so much out of him that his extra senses were dulled to the point of being nearly nonexistent? Meditation was in order tonight, if anything to help restore some balance.

Before that, though, he wanted to get a better view of the stars. He walked behind the hotel to the closed pool area, and farther back into the tree line where the hotel lights couldn't reach. It was breathtaking. He couldn't remember ever seeing so many stars. They were so numerous and bright and clustered together, it seemed as if the sky were on fire. Crickets chirped around him, their harmony just short of hypnotizing.

At least there was one perk to their short-lived disaster in New Hampshire.

As tempting as it was to stay out all night, he willed himself to go back and meditate. He walked across the street and bought a bottle of water and a pack of cocktail peanuts from the twenty-four-hour market at the gas station. At the counter, he saw a souvenir magnet in the shape of New Hampshire and added it to his bill. *Might as well commemorate the night you fucked it all up with something you can stick on your fridge.*

He looked at Jessica's door and thought of knocking, but he was too afraid to face the consequences. She needed to decompress. She didn't need his traveling pity party right now.

Back in his room, he ate the peanuts and drank half the bottle of water, then changed into a T-shirt and boxers and sat on the bed in the lotus position. After ten minutes, he began to realize that his mind was in too agitated a state to get anywhere close to where he needed to be. He wished he had the meditative abilities of a Buddhist monk, then realized how wishing to be something was a cause of suffering and only adding to his lost cause.

He considered jerking off to help ease the tension that was humming through both his mind and body, but after a few futile attempts he shot that idea down. It was impossible to bring up any of his stable of fantasies without drifting back to the debacle at the Leighs' house and Jessica's look of disgust when she left the car.

Frustrated, he gathered all the pillows behind his head and turned on the television.

"No peace for you tonight, dumbass," he said.

He flipped through the channels, unable to find anything that could hold his attention, finally stopping at an old Spencer Tracy movie. It was the one where he was a one-armed guy coming to a town that held a huge secret. He'd missed the first twenty minutes but he didn't care. Consider it a very small penance.

His heart jumped when there was a knock at his door.

He looked at the clock and rubbed his eyes in disbelief. It was three o'clock. He glanced at the TV. The Spencer Tracy movie was long gone. Claudette Colbert was on a train with Clark Gable now, the two of them bickering.

"I'll be there in a sec," he said, coughing to clear his throat. He grabbed his jeans from the floor and yanked them on. He was about to pull the safety chain and unlock the door when he realized he had no idea who was on the other side. It was, after all, the middle of the night.

"Is that you, Jess?"

There was no answer, just another couple of raps on the door.

Eddie opened his mind and felt Jessica sleeping in the next room. Her dreams, or at least the emotional vibe from them, were troubled, agitated, but she was most certainly under the covers and not outside his door.

"Wonderful," he huffed.

He looked around the room for a weapon, settling on his belt. Indiana Jones had his whip, Eddie Home had his belt. It wasn't as if he'd been expecting a confrontation in a New Hampshire Best Western.

Knock. Knock. Knock.

Eddie's heart pulsed in his throat. Steeling himself, he moved his face to the door, stooping to look through the peephole. The glass had been smeared by years of dirt and neglect. He could just make out the shape of a person standing inches from the door. He attempted to connect with the person's mind, to gain an insight into their identity and intentions. Nothing.

Just like at the Leighs'.

"Holy crap," he said.

He darted back to the door that connected his and Jessica's room and whispered through the crack, "Jessica, wake up, it's Eddie!"

It was followed by the sounds of the bed creaking and covers shifting. He knocked softly and whispered again, louder.

When the lock clicked he nearly jumped. He undid the lock on his side and opened the door. Jessica looked tired, angry, disheveled and confused. She had been sleeping in her clothes.

"This better be fucking good," she said drowsily.

"One way or another, I'm pretty sure it will be."

The steady, sure knocking resumed at his door.

"You call for room service?" Jessica said while trying to smooth her hair.

"Yeah, at three in the morning," he said.

"Well, who is it?"

"I can't see and I can't sense a thing, just like I couldn't get a read on anything at the Leigh house."

Realization dawned on Jessica's face. She ran back to her room and returned with her phone. "Just in case we need to call for help."

Together, they crept to the door. The knocking happened again, three raps on the door, then silence.

Eddie turned to Jessica. "You open the door and stay behind it. I'll face whoever it is."

He didn't feel half as brave as he sounded. He motioned for Jessica to open the door.

She tugged with all her strength in an attempt to startle the person on the other side.

It didn't work.

Chapter Twenty-Six

Jessica saw the look of surprise on Eddie's face when she pulled the door open and her heart stopped. He stood silent for a few seconds that seemed to last an eternity. She was about to peek around the door, having already dialed 9-1 in her phone when he said, "Selena! What are you doing here?"

She joined Eddie's side and faced the girl. Selena didn't speak, barely moved, her skin pale as milk in the moonlight. She looked as if she was in shock. Her dark eyes were wide and unblinking.

Jessica asked, "Selena, honey, are you all right? Come inside and sit down."

Selena Leigh didn't answer or move.

When Jessica reached out to touch her arm, Selena took a step back, keeping the same distance between them.

Eddie leaned into her ear and whispered, "How did she know we're staying here? Better yet, how did she know this is my room?"

Everything had happened so fast, her brain hadn't had time to think beyond the immediacy of the situation. Now that Eddie mentioned it, nothing was making sense. She felt a chill drop down her back.

"Selena, can you tell me why you're here?"

The girl stared back at them with black, emotionless eyes.

Jessica handed Eddie her phone. She whispered, "Just click the button in the middle to take pictures. I'm going to make a rush for her."

"What?"

"Just do it," she hissed.

She put up her hands to show she was defenseless and meant no harm. "I want to help you, honey, but I have to know what's bothering you. I'd really like it if you could come inside and talk to us. Isn't that why you're here, to talk to us?"

Without warning, she dashed out of the room. Selena took several quick steps backward, avoiding her touch, before turning her back and running into the gloomy parking lot. Jessica heard the click of her phone as Eddie snapped away. She sprinted after her, but Selena, or the thing that looked like her, was too fast. She took off like a world-class sprinter. Jessica jumped when the girl ran into a car's side view mirror, shearing it off with a loud crash. It didn't even slow her down and in seconds she had passed under the last streetlight and out of sight, into the night.

Jessica gave chase for several blocks, her bare feet hardly registering the pain from pounding on the hard concrete, until she gave up, realizing there was no way she would catch up with her. Eddie pulled up a moment later, panting. He bent over and clasped his knees, trying to catch his breath.

"Man, she's freaky fast."

"That's because she wasn't real."

He looked up at her. "She seemed pretty real when she took out that mirror. I admit, she was a little strange with the wide-eyed and silent routine, but I don't think doppelgangers can tear metal and glass off of cars."

"Let me see the phone."

She hit the Back button to flip through the photos Eddie had snapped. Most were too dark and grainy to make out any detail.

He continued, "I mean, I'm no doppelganger expert, but I doubt they could pull off something as real as that. She's going to wake up with one hell of a bruise in the morning."

Jessica clicked through to the very first photo he had taken, just as she had approached Selena outside the door. She stared at it for a while, tuning Eddie out as he expounded on his theory that only a real, flesh-and-blood person could have done what Selena did to the car.

She walked back to the hotel, Eddie by her side, still out of breath.

When they were back in the parking lot, she knelt by the remains of the mirror. The glass was cracked and the metal bent where it had connected with the door. It belonged to an old Mustang, an eighties vintage. Not their best decade. The mirror weighed more than most new car bumpers. She carried it with her to the porch outside their rooms.

"You want to see how I know you're wrong?" she asked.

Eddie leaned against the open doorway. "Does the mirror have ectoplasm or something on it?"

"You're a totally different guy at night, you know that?"

"I get cranky when I get woken up by troubled, Olympic track star teens."

She smiled. "Well, be cranky no more."

She held the phone's display to his face, deriving great satisfaction when she saw his jaw go slack.

"You've gotta be kidding me," he muttered.

Chapter Twenty-Seven

The next morning, Jessica and Eddie met in the breakfast area at nine. The room was packed with people loading plates with bagels, muffins, boxes of cereal and fruit. Everyone seemed to be of the same mind that a free continental breakfast meant you had to gather up enough food to hold you over until dinner. Most of the kids were already in their bathing suits and quite a few moms were wearing straw sunhats.

Eddie peeled an orange and asked to see her phone again. He studied the picture for several minutes while she chomped on a bland toasted bagel with cream cheese and grape jelly. "I was thinking that this would all seem very different in the light of day, but I was way wrong," he said, sliding the phone across the table.

"I downloaded it to my laptop before I went to sleep so I could see it blown up. I also played around with the contrast and light so I could make her out better. I'm not afraid to admit I was a little creeped out."

Eddie popped an orange slice in his mouth, tilted back in his chair. A passing child bumped into him and pitched him forward. He scowled, but said nothing to the kid who was just eager to join his parents as they were leaving. "We were both there, about a foot away from her, and she looked as real as anyone around us. She interacted with the physical world just as any living person would. Proof of that is in the car she steamrolled. That picture just doesn't make sense."

"Of course it does. Eddie, we're human. We perceive what we want to perceive and when things appear in front of us that our brains can't comprehend, we just fill in the gaps so they fit with the paradigm we're comfortable with. Cameras don't have a mind or a soul. They only show us what was in front of the lens the moment the picture was taken. Doppelgangers have appeared to people in dozens of different ways, so this isn't that far of a stretch."

Eddie mulled her words over, then pointed an orange slice at her. "I understand that some people see doppelgangers as a living person with depth and dimension, while others have reported them to look pretty much like your average wispy ghost. What I'm having a hard time with is the discrepancy between what we saw and what the picture shows, even with your explanation."

"That aside, do you agree something odd, possibly paranormal, happened last night?"

He chewed on the top of a corn muffin. "Yes. And I'm also wondering why I'm not picking up a damn thing around the Leigh house or Selena's doppelganger. That could all be a personal problem and have nothing to do with them. I keep thinking that Edwin's EB screwed me up somehow. I never made contact with a spirit that drained me physically like that."

When they finished, they walked to the pool area. The gates had just been opened and children swarmed from every corner of the hotel to jump in, despite the water being chilly so early in the morning. They sat at a nearby picnic table and watched the controlled chaos.

Jessica said, "So, do we go pay a visit to Rita and Selena this morning? It's Tuesday, so I'm pretty sure Greg would be at work."

"I don't know if that's such a good idea. If Greg found out, and he will, that could be the end of it."

"As far as Greg is concerned, it *is* over. What happened last night changes things."

"Right, for *us* it changes things. Not so much for him. He'll think we're just making it up."

"What about when I show him the picture?"

"He'll assume you doctored up a picture of his daughter. It doesn't take much to fake a ghost picture nowadays. In fact, it's so easy that you almost have to throw out any photos taken over the past ten years."

A soaked girl wearing water wings scampered behind Jessica, giggling. Her older brother shot her with a water pistol and they ran back into the pool. Eddie laughed when he saw that the boy had gotten Jessica's hair wet in the process.

"Kind of hard to talk about something so weird and serious in this setting," Eddie said.

"You think? What do you want to do next?"

"You should call Rita and tell her what happened last night. Better that than an email or text that her husband can come across. While you do that, I'm going to call Dr. Froemer at The Rhine."

"Who's Dr. Froemer?"

"I was the prize lab ape when I was there and he was the head scientist." He saw the shocked look on Jessica's face and added, "It was more like a student-professor kind of relationship. He's as nice as he is smart, and that's saying a lot. I'm wondering if he knows anything about doppelgangers or could at least point me in the right direction."

Jessica smacked the table and stood. "Sounds like a plan. Knock on my door when you're done."

Eddie took one last look at the families having fun in the pool and tried to remember if his own family had ever had a moment like this. There was that one time they had gone to Disney Land, but then he remembered his father being separated from them, only to be found at the hotel pool later chatting up a pretty girl lounging in a bikini who was at least ten years younger than him. It was no wonder he turned out this way, talking to a dead man so he could find his ghost-hunting daughter and be accosted by poltergeists and doppelgangers. Dysfunctional childhoods led to dysfunctional adults.

He chuckled, then went to his room to call his mentor.

Dr. Froemer sounded distracted, which meant he was preparing the next day's tests with the subject du jour. Despite that, it was good to hear his voice. Eddie never thought he'd feel homesick for The Rhine, especially so soon after leaving.

"I know you're busy, but I was hoping you could help me out with a little situation I've stumbled upon here."

"Nonsense, I'm never too busy to talk to you." He heard a heavy *thunk*, as if the doctor had dropped a large book on his desk. "Now, where would *here* be?"

"I'm currently in New Hampshire."

"Live free or die!"

"What's that?"

"It's the state slogan. One of my favorites. I thought you had moved to New York."

Eddie turned on the air conditioner and sat at the small table beside the window. He put his feet up on the bed. "I did. I'm here for a few days. I'm with Jessica Backman. You know, *the girl*."

Dr. Froemer was silent.

"I mean I came with her on an investigation," Eddie clarified. "I'm not actually *with* her."

"I have to hand it to you, Eddie, you are a very resourceful man. I'm a little embarrassed to admit that we've had a few wagers over the probability of your successfully meeting this mystery girl of yours. It looks like I'm out ten dollars. Oh well, easy come, easy go. So, what's she like?"

Eddie paused and answered carefully. "She's tough as nails and passionate in her beliefs. She's not your average nineteen-year-old."

"If the stories are true, I suspect she grew up very fast. So, how can I be of assistance?"

"This is actually my second investigation with her. The first involved a very peeved spirit that had power beyond anything I've ever heard. It knocked me out. I'll tell you more about that another day. What we have here in sunny New England is not your typical haunting." He thought about Selena's doppelganger slamming into the car mirror, how it didn't even slow her down, and felt a cramp in the pit of his stomach. "What do you know about doppelgangers?"

Dr. Froemer exhaled into the phone. "Whew, when you said you had something rare, you weren't kidding. A doppelganger. Have you seen it?"

He told him about his suspicions when they pulled up to the Leighs' house and how they had stormed it like a couple of paratroopers. He tried not to leave a single detail out as he relayed the encounter just a few hours earlier and how the Leigh family members, house and doppelganger were all coming up as psychic black holes.

"I have to admit, this is a little out of my area of expertise. I've read papers on the doppelganger phenomenon and how it relates to artists and the workings of their overactive subconscious. Over the years, I've heard of the odd case here and there of a doppelganger appearing to an individual or a family, but I'm not entirely sure I trust the sources. With you, I don't doubt the source one bit."

"And we have proof," Eddie added, thinking about the photo captured on Jessica's phone.

"Give me a moment, I have something I want to look up."

Eddie heard his chair squeal and the doctor mumbling as he shuffled around his office. He could picture him, fingers resting on his chin, eyeballing the rows of books that surrounded his desk, his memory better than any card catalogue. There was a knock at Eddie's door, but this time it was only housekeeping. He opened the door and asked if she could come back later, then slipped the plastic Do Not Disturb sign over the door handle. By the time the maid, a pretty blonde girl with a Russian accent, had finished apologizing, the doctor was back on the line.

"I'm not the expert on this subject, but I do know a couple that have had an experience similar to yours. The man, Morgan Stern, wrote to me ten years ago describing his multiple run-ins with the doppelganger of his father. When his father, who had been in a nursing home at the time, passed on, the doppelganger vanished, but Mr. Stern swore that the ordeal had left him with psychic abilities he'd never had previous to the apparition's appearance. He was living with a woman, Gigi Staub, at the time, and it was through her urging that they came here to have him tested.

"They stayed here for one week and we put him through everything we could think of. He scored a remarkable above-average on several tests, high enough to pique my interest at the time. Whatever untapped powers that had been opened to him from the encounter with the doppelganger, if that was truly the catalyst, were sadly short-lived. Within a year, he reported back to me that he was no longer anticipating what people would say before they spoke or having visions of events moments before they occurred. It was as if it had given his brain a short-lived charge that could power his extra sensory abilities until it just fizzled out. That wasn't unique in and of itself, but the fact that he and his girlfriend had been seeing a doppelganger before it happened was."

Eddie wasn't sure where this was going or how this information was supposed to help him. Dr. Froemer didn't keep him hanging long.

"Morgan Stern and Gigi Staub lived in Massachusetts at the time, a little north of Boston. I could see if their phone number still works and ask if they could meet you. They're a nice couple, very sincere. Maybe talking to them could help shine a light on your situation."

"That would be fantastic. We're about an hour away from Boston, so we could meet them any time."

"Good. I'll call them later this morning, after my meeting. I'll let you know."

Eddie hung up and knocked on the connecting door to Jessica's room.

"Any luck?" she asked.

"There's a couple near Boston that had their own experience with a doppelganger. We may be able to meet them."

Jessica gave him a hard fist bump. "We're two for two. I just got off the phone with Rita Leigh. Greg is at work and she wants us there. We're going back now."

Chapter Twenty-Eight

After Rita Leigh had gotten off the phone with Jessica, she asked Selena if she could take Ricky out to the park so they could both get some air. Selena had eyed her suspiciously, but there were times when a mother had to protect her kids. Rita did not want either of them around when Jessica and Eddie returned. First, she wasn't sure how Selena would react to seeing a picture of her double. Second, she didn't want them to have to lie to their father. This way, they were none the wiser about the entire thing.

Jessica and Eddie rang her bell fifteen minutes after Selena had taken Ricky with great reluctance to the field several blocks away. Neither of the ghost hunters looked as if they had slept much. "Can I get you both some coffee?" she asked, showing them into the living room.

"Coffee would be great," Jessica said.

Rita couldn't help but notice her shaking hands as she stuffed the filter into the coffee maker and poured in the water. She was nervous as hell. Preparing coffee delayed the viewing of the picture, which would mean complete validation of everything that had been happening. It was a welcomed validation as much as it was terrifying. It meant they weren't all crazy, but it also meant they had a bigger issue to face.

She laid out some cookies and sat across from them.

"Believe me, Mrs. Leigh," Jessica began.

"Please, call me Rita."

Jessica fumbled with her phone, turning it over in her hands again and again. "Rita, we would never have come back here unless we thought it was absolutely necessary. I understand why your husband was upset and kicked us out. That was very unprofessional of us."

Rita slowly nodded and took a sip of her coffee.

"What I'm about to show you is pretty intense. It's the reason we're here now, and I hope you can convince your husband to let us stay. When you see it, you'll understand why I didn't even bother asking you if Selena had been home last night."

She pressed a button and made a few finger swipes across the screen. Rita felt her heart tap dance in her chest and she could hear the rush of blood in her ears. When Jessica handed the phone to her, she held it in both hands to keep it steady.

"It all started when Eddie heard knocking on his door at three a.m. At first, we thought it was Selena. But there was something about the way she looked and was acting that didn't seem right. When I tried to approach her, she ran off, bumping into and tearing off a car mirror. Eddie had been taking pictures and it was too dark in all but this one, the first one he took. Seeing it confirmed that it wasn't Selena that had found us at our hotel."

A rush of tears sprang to Rita's eyes as she looked at the grainy image on the phone.

Sweet mother of God, it can't be! How is such a thing even possible? But there was no denying it, not this time.

It showed something that looked like Selena, but pale, its features as waxen as a full moon. It had been in the process of turning away from the camera, though she could still see most of the face—Selena's high cheekbones framed by strands of her straight hair, her thin upper lip and the distinctive bump at the bridge of her nose, a result of having broken it while playing soccer when she was nine.

But the eyes!

They were just two black pits, at least four times the size of a normal person's eyes. They reminded Rita of pictures of gray aliens that she'd seen on TV shows and books.

And if she needed further proof that the being caught on camera was, in actuality, not her daughter, the diaphanous body, so insubstantial that she could see the car behind it through its gauzy form, settled things for good. She pushed the tears from her cheeks with a hasty swipe and gave the phone back to Jessica.

Eddie was the first to speak. "Despite what you just saw on the camera, to our eyes, she looked as real and solid as your daughter."

"It didn't take long for us to realize something was off. At first, I thought Selena was in shock, but there was just an odd feeling about her that didn't seem right," Jessica added.

For the first time since this entire madness had started, Rita felt true, stomach-clenching fear. She knew she had to show this to Greg, to get him to understand what was going on, and to let Jessica and Eddie help them. Her brain buzzed with differing scenarios on how her breaking the news to him would work out.

Jessica asked, "Would you mind if we stayed here for the afternoon? Just to get a feel for the house, learn its sounds so we know what's normal and what's not?"

Rita checked her watch. Greg wouldn't be home for another six hours.

"Yes, I would like that," she said, her voice shakier than she would have liked. She was about to ask if they preferred her in the house or not when Eddie's eyes flicked somewhere over her left shoulder. His body stiffened.

"Is everything all right?" Rita asked, snapping her head around in the direction of his gaze.

"Don't mind me," he assured her. "I thought I saw a spider on the wall. I have a thing about spiders. I'm happy to report it was just my eyes." He gave her the same kind of grin that she would give her kids when she lied to keep them from knowing something that wasn't meant for young minds. She decided to let it go, not ready to hear any more strangeness this morning.

"Well, I think I'll meet my kids at the park, maybe take them out to lunch in a little bit. The house is yours until four o'clock. I'll be back by then, and my husband gets home around five."

Jessica reached over the coffee table and clasped her hand. She could feel the tight muscles in the slight girl's hands.

"We won't change anything around in the house or make a mess, I promise. This is what I wanted to do last night, which is just sit still and absorb things. I'll make sure we wrap up before you get home."

Rita thanked them, got her purse from the kitchen table and left, eager to see her daughter. She needed to hold her and she didn't give a damn whether Selena wanted the public display of affection or not.

Once Rita closed the door behind her, Eddie jumped from the couch and strode toward the stairs. He pointed to the upstairs hallway.

"I've got some news that I think you, of all people, are going to like."

Jessica eyed him with growing suspicion. "I was looking that way, too, and I didn't see Selena's doppelganger."

"I didn't, either. No, what I did see, though not in the sense that I saw with my eyes, was something else entirely. Now I know why everything was coming up a blank. Remember when I said it felt like something was consciously blocking me?"

Jessica nodded as she turned on her audio recorder.

"It was because there *is* something in the house trying to keep itself hidden."

"Something else?"

"Jess, we're not alone right now. There's an entity, or EB, whatever you want to call it, in this house. It's powerful and it's not nice at all."

Chapter Twenty-Nine

Jessica joined Eddie at the bottom of the stairs and was about to make her way to the second floor when he tapped her arm.

"It's not up there, not now," he said.

"What is it? You said it was powerful, so that rules out a residual haunt. Is it a non-human EB?"

Jessica referred to these types of hauntings as demonic, but she wasn't sure of Eddie's personal religious philosophy. She didn't know if implying there was a demon would have him dismiss her outright. It had been proven to her that there were dark forces in the world, and demonic workings were at play, somewhere, every minute of the day. Whether they were demonic in the religious sense was still up for debate. Biblically based or not, evil was evil and forces of evil were best labeled as demonic.

Eddie shook his head. "No, this was definitely a person, and I stress the word *was*. It felt strongly like a male and he was very interested in our conversation. I think he was concentrating so hard on us that he forgot to conceal himself from me. Once he realized I had latched on to him, he slipped back into the void."

"Did you get anything like a name or the reason he's here?"

"It was just a quick impression, but it was enough to make me wince. There's some bad shit surrounding this EB. It makes that Edwin Esposito EB look like Casper."

Jessica was happy to see that he had adopted referring to ghosts as EBs, even if it was just to stay on her good side. A question popped into her head.

"Is there any chance this male EB is also masquerading as Selena's double?"

Eddie walked back into the living room and paced. It looked as if he was searching for something but had no idea where to start. Next, he went to the kitchen, stooping down to open cupboards.

He looked up at her. His hair had fallen across his face and he had to blow a lock out of his eyes. "To answer your question, I don't know. Like I said, I have zero experience with doppelgangers. I don't think we'd be going out on a limb by following that line of logic, though. The bigger question is, why is he here and then, why is he choosing to be seen as Selena's doppelganger? Until we get more information, we're just connecting the dots on a page where ninety percent of them have been erased. So, what's next? You're the expert on this part."

Jessica pulled a second audio recorder out of her pocket. "Your Spidey sense telling you the best place I should put this and let it run?"

Eddie rolled his eyes. "Spidey senses. Very original. Like I said, he just came and went. I have no idea where he is now, if he's even here at all."

"You're positive he's not hiding under the sink?"

"You'd be surprised where spirits hide out. Having zero mass makes it easy to find a spot where you won't be disturbed."

"Point taken. I guess I'll just put this in Selena's room and keep the other one down here in the living room." She jogged upstairs, placed it on Selena's desk and came back down. "Now for the fun part. This is where we get to sit quietly and just let the house come to us."

"Something tells me our nasty little EB isn't going to be back any time soon," he said, taking a seat around the kitchen table.

"I don't mean the EB. I...*we* need to understand the house better. That way, when something does happen, we can filter out the common from the uncommon. You comfortable down here by yourself?"

He crossed his hands behind his head. It reminded Jessica of Liam. He almost never sat without the back of his head cradled in his hands. "For the moment. It's getting hotter. Is it a rule to keep the fan off?"

"Yes, it is. The fan noise will ruin the audio."

She felt satisfied by the look of resignation on his face.

"You won't be suffering alone. I'll be upstairs sweating my ass off."

She spent the next several hours alternating between sitting in Selena's room and the hallway. A couple of times, she heard Eddie walking around, but overall he did a very good job of keeping as still and silent as could be expected. It was almost three when she stopped the recorder and came downstairs. It had been uneventful, but that was normal. Other than the Haunted Mansion in Disney, houses were typically pretty sedate, even the haunted ones.

"You can turn the fan on now," she said.

Eddie wasted no time switching on the ceiling fan and positioning himself under its cooling breeze.

"Anything else come to you?" she asked.

"Nada, other than a very strong personal feeling that we need to come back."

Jessica bit her upper lip. "Yeah, that's the part that worries me right now. I'm hoping that Rita can convince Greg that we need to be here. A doppelganger doesn't seek you out in the middle of the night without a damn good reason."

Rita returned at four on the dot with Selena and Ricky. The young boy was wearing a Red Sox cap rimmed with sweat and dirt. He barely gave them a second glance before running up to his room.

"He's having video game withdrawal," Rita explained. "When I saw your car outside, I told him that we had exterminators out to check on the house."

"I would have done the same thing," Eddie said.

Selena's face brightened when she saw them, a wave of relief softening her posture as her shoulders dropped, relieving the obvious tension she'd been carrying around all day.

"You're back!" she exclaimed.

"Yes, your mom was nice enough to let us in."

Standing behind her daughter, Rita motioned with her hands to keep it short, meaning she hadn't told Selena about last night. Jessica winked in acknowledgement.

"Mind if we talk to just your mom for a little bit?" she asked.

Eddie piped in, "You know what, I wouldn't mind talking to Selena while you two catch up. Is that okay with everyone?"

Rita at first looked reluctant, so Jessica added, "That sounds like a good idea." Eddie had broken her rule about interjecting himself but she realized it was a good idea to deal with them separately.

Rita nodded and Selena said, "You want to talk out in the yard? We can sit on the patio in the shade. I'm all sunned out today."

Eddie followed her out the back door. Once they were out of earshot, Jessica told Rita about the male EB that was in the house and her feeling that it may be the same thing posing as Selena. It was a difficult conversation because Rita looked as if she was about to pass out once she mentioned that the EB was giving off a negative impression. Jessica spied the clock in the kitchen, counting the minutes she had left before Greg Leigh came home and threw them out on their ears, again.

The air was much cooler in the yard. The patio was surrounded by two ash trees, providing plenty of shade. Cicadas chittered away. Eddie remembered calling them heat bugs when he was a kid and how their buzzing music always signaled the heart of summer.

Selena had brought out two bottles of cold water. He had to restrain himself from chugging it all at once.

"So, how long have you been doing this?" she asked.

Eddie almost choked on the water. "Me?"

"Both of you."

He was at a crossroads—did he lie and tell her he was a battle-tested expert, or admit that this was only his second investigation? She looked so tired, so desperate for answers. He couldn't bring himself to lie to her.

"But I thought Jessica had this big website and did all kinds of cases," she said when he told her this was his second time.

"Don't get me wrong. Jessica is younger than me, but she has a lot of experience. She's the pro here. I'm like the apprentice."

Selena narrowed her eyes at him. "I'm a girl and I can tell that Jessica isn't someone who needs or wants any help."

"How would you know that?"

"Call it female intuition."

Eddie recalled the various tests he'd seen performed at The Rhine, analyzing just that. When all was said and done, female intuition turned out to be no better than chance guessing. Lab tests aside, past experience with the fairer sex had taught him better.

"You're right, I'm not exactly an apprentice."

She sat back in the Adirondack chair and smiled, satisfied. Her yellow tank top pulled up to reveal her taut, tanned stomach. "I knew it. I've always been good at reading people. So, what are you to her?"

He knew that she needed something to give her strength, to make her realize that she was no longer in this alone, that help was here and her sleepless nights were coming to an end. Facing a doppelganger wasn't only terrifying, it was also intensely personal. Her core had been shaken and there were cracks in the foundation. What he said next had to help rebuild her.

He knocked back the rest of his water and placed the bottle on the table.

"Do me a favor and pick up that bottle," he said.

Selena's eyebrows knit. "Why?"

"Just humor me."

She shifted forward and took the bottle in her right hand.

"Now, hold on to it, but not so tight that you crush it."

Selena gripped the bottle, causing the plastic to crackle.

Eddie stared at the bottle, burning its image into his brain, willing it to come to him. Selena started to speak and he held up a finger to quiet her, adding a wry smile to allay any concern.

Closing his eyes, he had a vision of the bottle, a glowing effigy against the black backdrop of his conscious. The more he concentrated, the brighter it became until it was blinding in its brilliance.

Selena gasped when the bottle flew from her hands and landed, right side up, on the table in front of Eddie.

When he opened his eyes, he had to shade them with his hand to allow them time to adjust.

"How...how did you do that?" she gasped. He was relieved to see that she appeared more curious than afraid.

"I can tell you one thing. It wasn't magic. David Copperfield, I'm not."

Chapter Thirty

The following day was spent waiting. Jessica and Eddie had left with minutes to spare before Greg Leigh came home. Rita promised to talk to him that night and vowed that she would convince him to let them back in the house. When she had suggested that she and Eddie just come during the day, when he was at work, Jessica had told her that she much preferred working with total honesty. Hiding things from Greg was not the answer.

What she didn't tell Rita was that in some cases, deception or anything with a negative connotation could feed the presence in the house like milk bones to a hungry dog. Thanks to Eddie's sensitivity, she knew that there was at least one EB in the house that was antagonistic and highly deceptive. She didn't need to add to its power.

Because she had spent most of the night listening to the audio that she had downloaded onto her laptop, she was now going on two nights with barely any sleep. If things kept up this way, she was going to get mighty irritable. Sleep and hunger were her two triggers to becoming a bitch on wheels.

Eddie, on the other hand, had gone out after breakfast and bought a bathing suit at a nearby mom and pop store and was now sitting poolside. Jessica watched from under the awning of the hotel's back patio as a single mother took the lounge chair next to him. After applying sunscreen to her son, she proceeded to chat him up.

"Typical dog," Jess muttered.

The chemical odor of over-chlorinated water permeated the air around the pool. Jessica's stomach grumbled because it was lunch time, but she had to get away from that smell if she ever thought of eating. There was a little snack stand that sold burgers and hot dogs upwind from the pool. Walking there, she was run into by no less than three kids, all of them laughing and without a care in the world.

She envied them. She couldn't remember ever being like that. There had always been a dark specter hanging over her and her family, even before her father had passed away. He had never gotten over the death of her mother. It must have been so hard, to say good night to the one you love only to have them never say good morning again. Her mother had been perfectly healthy. It was just her time to go.

Carefree moments were few and far between in the Backman family.

"What'll it be?" asked a cute boy who looked to be just about Jessica's age. He was tall with shaggy, blond hair and the most intense blue eyes she'd ever seen. He spoke with a heavy eastern European accent, as did most of the people who worked at the hotel. She assumed they must all have been part of some Russian exchange program.

"I think I'll have two chili cheese dogs, fries and a large Coke," she said, fishing her money out of her purse. The boy eyed her up and down, no doubt wondering where she planned to put all that food. He wasn't the first, wouldn't be the last. When she tried to think of some small talk, she came up blank. She didn't even realize he was still talking to her.

"Would you like ketchup or mustard?" he asked.

"Oh, no, thank you." Her mouth opened to say something else, but nothing came out. He leaned forward on his elbows, waiting. A heavy-set man that had been waiting behind her stepped to the counter and started spouting his order. Jessica moved over to the pickup window, embarrassed that she had stood there catching flies.

Why did she even care? She wasn't here on vacation or to find a man, especially a kid in high school.

She looked back at Eddie who had put his newspaper down and was leaning close to the mature but pretty woman at his side. She wore a bikini top with black shorts and was leaning close to him, angling her chest so he could get a good look at her ample cleavage. Guys were so easy to manipulate.

"Now you're being stupid," she said to herself.

"Excuse me?" the girl at the pickup window said. She was holding a basket of food.

"I'm sorry. Just talking to myself. Thanks."

Sitting at a wooden picnic table under a stand of fir trees, Jessica devoured her food. Speed eating was a tendency of hers whenever she was worried or upset. Right now, she couldn't tell which emotion held sway, much to the utter demolition of her chili dogs and fries. Her stomach was bloated and sour when she was done. She lay back on the bench, just taking in the fresh air and appreciating the shade. Sun had never been her friend.

She made a mental note to go to City Hall after she had digested. It was high time she looked through the records to see if she could find anything on the house, its history and even the geography of the land. It was said that certain types of minerals were conducive to spirit activity. Underground, running water was also said to enhance EB power. She wasn't a huge believer in that, but it was part of her job to leave no stone unturned.

When her cell phone went off she bolted upright and answered on the first ring.

It was Rita Leigh, and she sounded distressed. "Jessica, can you come over now? Please?"

"Is everything all right?" Jessica felt the hairs at the back of her neck prickle with expectation.

"Just, please, come here."

Jessica ran to the gate surrounding the pool and waved Eddie over. She must have looked as if she was in no-nonsense mode, because he broke off his conversation without hesitation and jogged to the white fence. "What's up?"

"I just got a call from Rita and she sounded weirded out. She wants us to come to the house ASAP."

Eddie hopped over the fence. "I'll just need a couple of minutes to change."

"I'll grab some of my equipment. Meet you at the car."

Jessica could feel the daggers the woman by Eddie's now-empty chair was throwing at her back, but she couldn't give a damn. From the sound of things, Rita needed help, and at the moment, that was all that mattered.

They made it to the house in less than ten minutes, thanks to Jessica's lead foot and bob-and-weave driving skills. When Rita answered the door, she looked a decade older than the day before. Jessica could tell by her puffy eyes that she had been crying. Rita ushered them in and quickly closed the door. Selena was holding her brother on the couch. His head was pressed against her chest. Greg sat in his easy chair, elbows propped on his knees, his head in his hands.

Jessica decided to get right to the point. "Okay, what happened?"

"It's *still* happening," Selena said before burying her face in Rick's crew cut hair. She looked as if she was ready to rabbit out of the house. Her grip on her brother was the only thing keeping her from doing so. It was apparent little Ricky knew they were not exterminators.

Rita was about to speak when Greg said, softly at first, "Do what you have to do. I don't care what it takes. Just...do it."

Greg wore an expression she had seen a few times over the past couple of years. It was defeat. He could no longer fight the crumbling of what he believed to be reality, the certainties of life and death. Everything he had known had been stripped away. This was beyond his control, beyond his comprehension and well beyond his ability to handle.

The waves of fear coming off all four members of the family were so thick, so strong, it was practically tactile.

Eddie moved onto the couch and sat next to Selena and Rick. When he asked her why she was so upset, her face brightened.

"After you guys left, things got pretty heated. My dad, well, he was angry that we let you in without telling him and we all got in an argument."

Jessica looked toward Greg, but he avoided her gaze.

"I...I got mad because he didn't believe me. When I asked him if he would at least look at the printout of the picture you took, he told me to go to my room. I was so upset, I didn't even stop to think that I hadn't been in my room in weeks."

She had to stop as her breath hitched in her chest like someone winding down from a good, long cry. Jessica turned on her audio recorder and pointed it toward the couch.

Eddie gently prodded her. "It's okay, Selena. We're all here. Did anything happen to you in your room?"

Her head snapped up and her eyes were wild, almost feral.

"It was a bad night, she's worn out," her mother said.

"I can do this, Mom." Selena patted Rick on the head and he held her tighter. "My parents were still fighting and I just wanted to block it out, so I stuffed some tissues in my ears and cried. I don't know for how long, because next thing I knew, I was asleep. It was one of those deep sleeps, you know, the kind where you don't even dream. I was just out, exhausted. At one point, I must have pulled the sheet over myself. It got cold last night. When I felt the sheet being pulled off me towards the foot of the bed, I woke up."

Greg held his hand up for Rita who took it in both of her hands. They watched their daughter recount her experience, willing her the courage to continue, ready to come to her side if she couldn't.

Jessica asked, "You're positive at this point you were awake?" She knew that the moments between sleep and waking could be filled with all kinds of sensations, thoughts, smells and visions that had nothing to do with reality. Sometimes it took the brain a bit to shake off the after-effects of its dream world.

"I'm positive," Selena shot back with undeniable certainty.

"I apologize, it's just something I have to ask. Please, tell us what happened next."

Selena took a stuttering breath. "I was too afraid to move, so I just lay there, feeling the sheet pull down past my shoulders, then my stomach and hips. I was on my side, and I could see out my window that it must have been late in the morning. I didn't need to look at the end of the bed to know something was there. Aside from my sheet being pulled, I could *feel* that I wasn't alone, that there was someone else in the room with me and it was…it was *hungry*. I don't know any other way to describe it.

"When the sheet was down around my knees, I knew I had to do something. In my mind, I thought that if I was on the bed, exposed, something bad was going to happen to me. But I was so scared, I wasn't sure if I could even lift my head off the pillow. It was like I was paralyzed. Then, I felt the sheet slide past my ankle and I knew I had a few seconds to make a move. So, I pulled my legs up as far as I could, rolled onto my back and sat up. As soon as I did that, I saw the remainder of the sheet fly off the bed, like it had been yanked off. It landed by the door on the other side of the room. I tried to scream, but, nothing came out."

Selena started shivering and Eddie put an arm over her shoulder.

"And then I saw it, and I did scream, and it…it…it didn't even move!"

Chapter Thirty-One

They had to wait several minutes for Selena to calm down. Greg and Rita moved to either side of the shaking teen. Eddie was amazed by the sudden turn of events. Everyone in the Leigh family looked shattered.

Jessica took the time to pull her camcorder out of the case and turn it on. She had two digital cameras strapped around her left wrist and an audio recorder in her right hand.

Eddie still wasn't sure what Selena had seen, so when it seemed she had settled down enough, he asked.

"It was that thing that looks like me. It was sitting on the chair by my desk, watching me. Even when I was shouting for my parents, it didn't blink, didn't flinch."

She bolted from the couch and grabbed his arms.

"It's still there."

Eddie glanced at Jessica, saw the fervid look in her eyes. She was anxious to get to Selena's room, but she also didn't want to crash through the house like the other night, no matter how desperate the Leighs seemed at the moment.

Greg confirmed his daughter's claim.

"Just before you got here, I went up to her room to see and it's still sitting in the chair, looking at the bed. What is it? Why won't it leave?"

It's still there? It didn't seem possible, but here was Greg, a man who had to hold himself back from physically throwing them out a couple of nights earlier, now desperate for their help. It was as if the doppelganger was going out of its way to clear any hurdles they had to remaining at the house and doing what Jessica did best. It was discomforting, to say the least.

"That's what we're going to find out," Jessica said. "Why don't you all go into the yard for a bit? Some distance and fresh air will do you good. Eddie and I will take it from here."

Rita gathered her children to her side and walked into the kitchen. Greg stood, contemplating his next move. He looked like a man on the precipice of a life-defining moment. On the one hand, he must have wanted to be with his family, to give them comfort. On the other hand, he was also the man of the house and would want to be with Eddie and Jessica to confront what had invaded his home.

Eddie put a hand on his shoulder, said, "Your family needs you with them. You've seen enough for today."

Greg's shoulders slumped and he nodded. "I don't care how you do it, just make it go away."

Outside on the patio, they pulled the heavy wooden chairs close to each other and sat holding one another's hands. It was heartbreaking to see.

Jessica held a digital camera out to him, refocused his attention. "Can you feel anything now? Is it still here?"

He didn't have to probe deep to know they were not alone in the house. It was a welcome relief to finally regain his sixth sense, though it was a bit dull around the edges at the moment. The presence in the house was strong, embracing, like a golden retriever jumping at your chest, hungry for attention. "Yes, but I don't think it will be for long. Let's go."

Jessica took the stairs three at a time. Eddie nearly slammed into her back when she stopped at the door to Selena's room.

"Holy mother of God," she murmured.

He looked over her shoulder and gasped.

It was Selena, or her exact duplicate, as real in appearance as the frightened girl sitting outside with her family. The sole difference was in the eyes. Its irises were twice the diameter of a normal eye and black as tar.

The doppelganger continued to stare at the empty bed, ignoring their slow entrance into the room. It was wearing a light pink sun dress and sat cross-legged, its hands resting on one thigh. Eddie noticed that it was barefoot. Its skin was a healthy pink and looked even healthier and better rested than Selena. It was as if it had drained her life force, building its own in return until it could swap places with her.

Jessica inched closer to the bed, filming the specter. She spoke to it, "Selena? Can you hear me?"

The air in the room felt heavy, dull, absorbing sound, numbing senses. The sensory deprivation worried him, made his arms break out in gooseflesh.

Jessica continued trying to communicate with it, taking small, steady steps.

"Do you think it knows it's not Selena?" she asked him, her eyes and camera trained on the doppelganger. Then she shouted, "Hey!"

She startled only Eddie.

Eddie felt nauseous and lightheaded. It couldn't be fear. He'd spent his life talking to the dead, living in their world as much as his own. What the hell was going on here?

He had to grip the dresser to keep upright.

When Jessica was a foot away, she stopped and took a series of pictures. The doppelganger didn't so much as twitch a muscle. He knew he had to make himself more useful than backup cameraman, but he was beginning to worry that he was about to pass out.

He called out, "Jess, don't touch it."

She turned to look at him, and mouthed, *why not?*

"Let me try to make a connection first. I don't want you to scare it off," he said, his breathing ragged.

"You have one minute."

He put the camera on the bed, nodded, then closed his eyes, retaining the image of Selena's double sitting vigil, eyes unblinking, chest devoid of the normal in and out motion of breathing. Reaching out to it was like swimming against the current at the lip of a tall waterfall. Subtlety wouldn't work here. Jessica had been on the right track when she shouted. She just needed to know how to do it without actually verbalizing.

Eddie targeted all of his waning energy at the doppelganger and bellowed within his mind until it reached a howling pitch. His eyes snapped open when he was hit by a psychic reverberation. That did it!

The doppelganger jerked its head to face them, its eyes dark, fathomless, yet still very real, almost superhuman. Jessica took a tentative step back, jolted by the unexpected movement.

The nexus between Eddie and the doppelganger was as fine and fragile as a string of cotton candy. He opened up to it, hoping, in computer terms, to pull in an information dump so he'd have enough to sift through later, maybe find out why it was here and seeking Selena, and now them, out.

Jessica fired off a series of questions, pausing between each, hoping for an answer. "Can you hear me? Who are you? Can you tell us why you're scaring Selena? *What* are you?"

A sharp pain knifed down the center of Eddie's skull and he was sure his knees were going to give out. The pain obscured any images or feelings he might have picked up. He saw Jessica standing firm, the doppelganger staring past her, at him, curious.

When Jessica leaned forward and reached out, it leaped from the chair and jumped onto the bed, desperate to avoid contact, just like the night at the hotel. The chair clattered against the desk and turned over. Jessica shouted, "Wait! We won't hurt you! We just want to know how to help you!"

The doppelganger focused on the open closet and took two steps toward it. It wanted desperately to be there. Eddie could feel its anguish, despite the blinding agony that had iced its way down his neck and into his shoulders.

Jessica ran around the bed in an attempt to cut it off.

Pushing outward, Eddie used his telekinetic ability to slam the door shut. It stopped Jessica and the doppelganger in their tracks, but only for an instant. The mimicking wraith lunged at the closed door, plunging through it as if it weren't there, had never been solid wood. He heard Jessica let loose with a string of profanities, more in amazement and shock than anger. She dropped her camera on the bed and yanked the door open.

As they both suspected, it was empty.

"Can I pass out now?" Eddie groaned.

"What?" Jessica was in the closet tapping walls and the floor.

He positioned himself so he would fall face first on the bed and let the darkness overtake him.

Chapter Thirty-Two

When Jessica heard Eddie collapse, she forgot about finding the doppelganger and ran to him, scooping his head into her arms. Though his breathing was regular and steady, his coloring was cadaver gray.

"Eddie, wake up. Eddie, can you hear me?" She tapped his cheek with her fingers.

She'd never had someone pass out around her before and had no idea what to do. It seemed the best thing would be to try to snap him out of it, but how? Had he had a seizure? Did she have to stick something in his mouth to keep him from biting his tongue, or did that only apply as the seizure was happening?

"For such a smart girl, you really are a dummy," she hissed at herself, feeling her heart gallop in her chest, all thoughts of the doppelganger forgotten.

Complete panic was seconds from taking over when Eddie's eyelids fluttered, then opened wide. He looked into her worried eyes, uncomprehending, empty.

"It's me, Jessica. Can you hear me?" She stroked his hair back. His neck was clammy.

Relief washed over her when he mumbled, "I told you I was going to hit the deck." He tried to smile, but it came out as a grimace. When he attempted to sit up, she pulled him back onto her lap.

"Maybe you should wait a little before you move. I don't want you fainting again."

"Women faint. Men pass out."

"Is this really the time to be a chauvinistic pig?"

This time he did smile. "I'm better now. Honest."

He sat with his back against the bed, rubbing his temples. The glassiness in his eyes had started to fade.

"Does your head hurt?"

"A little."

"You might have whacked it when you slipped off the bed and fell on the floor."

"It was hurting before then, but much worse than now. Wow, that wasn't fun at all. Maybe you should check the house, see if it went somewhere else. I promise I'll stay put."

She was reluctant to leave him, but he did have a point. She grabbed her camcorder and headed to the other rooms. "I'll bring you back some water."

He nodded, then shooed her out of the room.

The Leighs' house wasn't very big, so it didn't take long to realize that Selena's phantom double was nowhere to be seen. The family picked their heads up when they saw her go into the kitchen. She opened the sliding door and asked them if they could sit tight for a few more minutes.

"Did you see it?" Greg asked.

She had to restrain her enthusiasm. What had happened upstairs was incredible, maybe a first in the paranormal field of investigation.

"Yes, for a little bit. It's gone now."

Rita, Greg and Selena looked as if they had a hundred questions they wanted to ask, but she had to get back up to Eddie. She noticed that little Ricky was throwing a ball high in the air and catching it in the middle of the yard. She worried about how he was processing everything most of all. Jessica knew full well how something like this could affect a young child.

True to his word, Eddie was still sitting on the floor. He gratefully accepted the cold bottle of water.

"Feeling better?" she asked.

"Much. I guess you didn't find it."

She cocked her head at the dark, empty closet. "Not unless I could find the dimensional portal in there. That was frigging weird. I never saw something that looked that solid pass through a door before. You think it could be a projection coming from Selena? She *is* a teen girl. We have a tendency to tap into mental abilities at that age without knowing it."

"Not this time. No, whatever it is, it's definitely not originating within Selena's mind. I managed to bond with it for a couple of seconds. It has emotions, with concern overriding everything else. I left myself open to it, and that's when the pain in my head started and I felt all of my senses go numb. Selena's doppelganger was as confused as I was. I think that's what chased it off, though I suspect your attempt at touching it didn't help."

Jessica felt her temper flare, but checked herself. Eddie had just woken up from a dead faint and he *was* giving her some insight into the doppelganger. The more she thought about it, the more she realized he may be right. There was something about the doppelganger that compelled her to reach out to it, to fully experience its presence with all of her senses, that she could barely control herself. It was like fighting a primal urge.

"But it looked so damn real. If I didn't try, I'd spend the rest of my life regretting the chance at knowing what it felt like."

Eddie stood up. His color had returned and he looked none the worse for wear. "Trust me, I'm not blaming you. If I wasn't feeling like I had been lanced in the skull, I would have been right alongside you." He pointed at the camera in her hand. "You want to see what you recorded, while it's all still fresh?"

"We'll just check out a minute or so. I don't want to leave the Leighs hanging much longer."

He moved to her side so he could see the tiny screen. Jessica tapped a few buttons, rewound to the moment just before she entered the room and hit Play.

The adrenaline high she had experienced from the rush of seeing the doppelganger, then tending to Eddie, evaporated as quickly as a girl's innocence at the prom. There was nothing but static. She fast-forwarded through and saw the same black-and-white fuzz.

"No. No way," she said, tightening her grip on the camera. She stopped it, rewound to the very beginning. It showed her ascent up the stairs, the hallway, and dissolved into snow just before she turned to enter Selena's room.

She snapped the camera shut, barked, "Pass me the digital camera!"

Eddie found it on the bed and handed it to her. He was smart to not say anything. She was bound to blow at the slightest provocation.

It was the same thing with the still images.

Nothing.

She checked the battery. It still had a full charge. She snapped a couple of pictures of the room, hit the Back button and saw that they had come out perfect. No distortion.

"I know this kind of stuff happens, but this is ridiculous. Not even one lousy picture."

She slumped onto the bed, defeated.

Eddie waited a while before speaking. "Mind if I say one thing?"

"No."

"The pictures and the video aren't important at all. The Leighs have seen it multiple times. They don't need proof. We have to help them now."

He was right...again. What was it about this house that made her lose all sense of perspective? Was it an after-effect of close contact with a doppelganger? She was very much aware of her age and lack of experience, but she wasn't a total neophyte either. She'd been off her game from the moment she had pulled into their driveway two days ago.

"You're becoming handier than a pocket on a shirt," she said to him. "Thank you."

He extended his hand to her. "I know this is exciting, but we both need to keep our cool. There's more going on here than what we've experienced so far."

Jessica couldn't imagine what, besides the presence of the doppelganger, was active in the house. So much of this was shades of her father's trip to Alaska. The big difference here was her experience and Eddie's abilities. She had to put her faith in him if she desired to get through this in one piece, and she very much wanted that.

"You think you can ask your doctor friend to get you a meeting with that couple in Massachusetts today or tomorrow?"

"I'll call and ask while you talk to Greg and Rita."

"Good. I'm going to see if I can move in for the next few days. I hope it will make them feel better knowing I'm right here in case something comes up again."

Before she went to the back patio, she turned to him and said, "Nice work with the door."

Now that things had settled down, she began to process everything that had happened in just a few short minutes. *A psychic-medium with telekinetic powers. The intrigue of Eddie Home continues to grow.*

He looked at her, quizzical.

Jessica said, "That was you, right? You did hint on the ride up here that you could move objects. Not that I believed you at the time. But, I don't think the doppelganger would throw an obstacle in its own way."

"Oh, that. Guilty as charged. It seemed like the only thing to do at the moment."

He walked out the front door, already on the phone and talking to the doctor. Her estimation of him grew while her skepticism of psi abilities shattered like a thin pane of glass.

Chapter Thirty-Three

Eddie was grateful that Jessica wanted to talk to the Leigh family alone and try to assuage their fears. It took a good deal of the afternoon, and in the end, Greg, Rita and the kids decided to spend the night at a hotel. They agreed that they would all return to the house after a good night's sleep. Jessica would stay with them the following night while Eddie made a trip to Massachusetts to visit the quasi doppelganger experts.

The Leighs packed overnight bags and headed to the next town over to stay at a hotel a cut above the Best Western.

It wasn't until he and Jessica had returned to their rooms after dinner at a nearby Pizza Hut that Eddie realized he was not going to be getting back to work any time soon. In all the excitement, he had forgotten about the health food store, not to mention his need to pay rent, buy food and gas. Knowing Jessica's past, and the fact that she was one of the least assuming multi-millionaires in the world, he thought it best to keep his sudden concerns to himself. He didn't want her to think he had sought her out so he could sponge off her.

The way things were going, he wasn't sure when he'd be back, but decided it was best to at least call his manager and apologize. Ted was a decent guy. Maybe he'd understand. When he phoned the store, Adelle, the night supervisor, told him Ted had left for the day but would pass along the message. *Well, at least I tried,* he thought.

That night, he slept like the peaceful dead, not waking up until ten o'clock, missing out on the free breakfast. His phone showed one missed call, so he checked his voicemail. It was exactly what he needed to hear.

He knocked on Jessica's door but there was no answer, so he sauntered a few blocks to a Dunkin Donuts and grabbed a semi-stale croissant and coffee. By the time he returned to the hotel, Jessica was back, sitting on the hood of her car, listening to her iPod.

"I'm surprised you're not in your bathing suit," she said, pulling the ear buds out.

"Not today. I'm here awaiting orders."

"Did you hear from that couple?"

"As a matter of fact, I did. I guess Dr. Froemer called them back to let them know how urgent the situation is here. I'm supposed to meet them at six tonight. As luck would have it, they both still live together in a town called Framingham. I never heard of it, but I do have an address. I'll map it later online."

Jessica slid off the hood and opened the passenger door, rummaging around in the glove compartment. She handed him a palm-sized GPS device. "Just plug the address in here. It'll do the rest."

"This brings up another question. How am I supposed to get there? We only have one car between us and I think a taxi would cost me a year's salary."

She shook her head at him. "You sure you graduated from Duke? I'm not going to need the car, because I'm staying with Selena tonight. You can drop me off and then head down to Massachusetts."

Eddie slapped his forehead with the palm of his hand. "I knew I shouldn't have dropped that course on common sense."

Her laugh pumped him up, gave him hope that he was breaking down the five-foot-thick wall she had erected around herself. "What time are you expected there?" he asked.

"Any time this afternoon. If you want, you can drop me off in an hour and come back here to get cozy with one of the MILFs until it's time to go."

He was about to ask her where that came from when he remembered talking to the cute mother at the pool. It seemed so long ago, yet it had just been twenty-four hours. It was amazing how much had changed in such a short amount of time. He felt his cheeks redden and said, "Har-har. I think I'll read up on doppelgangers on the Internet instead so I don't sound like a total idiot later."

"Your call," Jessica said over her shoulder as she walked into her room. "I just need an hour to do a couple of things and we'll get this show on the road."

The older woman at the front desk of the hotel was happy to give Jessica directions to the nearest church.

"Best you should go to St. Matthew's," she said. She pulled a pencil out from her tightly braided gray hair and drew a little map. "They keep their doors unlocked all day. It's only a couple of miles from here and they have a nice little lot right next to the church."

Jessica thanked her for the help and got a "Bless your heart," in return.

St. Matthew's was an old, small church that had no neighboring houses or buildings. It looked as if it had just grown up out of the surrounding fields many decades ago. The doors creaked when she entered and the air was hot and stagnant. All of the windows were shut tight.

I'll have to make this a quick visit, she thought. Beads of sweat broke out on her forehead.

She entered a pew by the front of the church and pulled out the kneeler.

Since there was no one inside with her, she spoke out loud as she prayed, first an Our Father, then a Hail Mary, followed by the reason for her visit.

"God, I'm never sure if you approve of what I do, but I could really use your strength right now. I have to admit, I'm a little scared. Not of the entities I'm facing. This family needs my help and I can't stop thinking that I'm in over my head, even with Eddie at my side. I don't want to fail them. I *can't* fail them.

"So, please watch over the Leigh family and if you can, maybe give a little hand to me and Eddie so we can end their nightmare. I'm not sure why things are always so crazy around me, but I know it's all part of your plan."

Jessica let the silence of the church comfort her, despite the cloying heat.

She was about to silently thank God for the things she'd been given when she felt a slight tap on her shoulder.

"I'm sorry for talking out loud. I promise I'll—"

She opened her eyes and turned to apologize but there was no one there.

Her breath caught in her throat when the sound of the metal latch on the doors clicked. One door slowly opened, the hinges crying in protest.

A chill ran through her that made the sweat along her hairline feel like tiny icicles.

Looking back at the open door, there was a flicker, like a reel of film fading in and out of a movie screen. For the briefest of moments, Selena's doppelganger, its eyes wide and black as the night sky, stood beside the door, one pale hand on the handle.

In the blink of an eye, it was gone.

The door closed, this time without making a sound.

Still staring at the doors, Jessica said, "See, God, that's what I'm talking about."

Having a little time to kill, Eddie took a walk and called his friend Tobi.

"Hey, you better be calling me to tell me what day is good for me to visit your ass," Tobi answered.

"You have a one-track mind."

"You're my ticket to seeing New York without having to pay for a hotel. Of course I do, man."

"I actually called to ask you something. You ever hear of a doppelganger?"

"I've heard of them, sure. I know it's German for something, like a twin, right?"

"Kinda, yeah."

Eddie spied a little pond and walked to its edge. Dozens of fat bumblebees dipped from flower to flower, paying him no mind.

Tobi said, "So, tell me, what's going on? You sound more morose than usual."

"I take offense to that," Eddie replied. "I like to consider myself moody and introspective, not morose."

He told his friend everything, from Jessica's strange ability to the doppelganger and the other presence around the family. It felt good to talk to him. Tobi was the one person he could lay it all out to that wouldn't say he was crazy. Well, his father would be in that category, too, but they weren't on the best of terms.

"Dude, that sounds trippy," Tobi said. "That's the kind of stuff my Uncle Jack would eat up."

"How is Jack?" Spilling the beans to Tobi made him feel lighter. He even felt the tension in his shoulders ease.

"He's cool. He wants me to come down to Florida on some business trip with him so we can visit a couple of haunted lighthouses. I don't know about Florida in the summer, though. That's when people fly out, not in."

They laughed and Tobi told him about The Rhine's newest recruits. "No one like you, though," he added.

Eddie checked his watch. "Thanks for the talk, Tobes. I gotta get going. Jessica will be back any minute."

"You take care of yourself. If you get lost in the weeds, you call me. Remember, two psychics are better than one."

Eddie got back to his room just as Jessica pulled up in her Jeep. Showtime.

Chapter Thirty-Four

They didn't speak much on the way to the Leighs', both lost in the thoughts of what lay ahead. To his surprise, Jessica didn't make any death threats about her car. He was sure she would extract a limb if he so much as scratched it, but she just gave him the keys and said to call her after his meeting. She also shocked him by leaving most of her equipment back at the hotel. Tonight, it was all about making Selena feel safe and gaining some control over the situation.

He read what little credible information there was on doppelgangers back in his room and set out for Framingham at four. It was about sixty miles away, but he gave an extra hour cushion for rush hour traffic. The sun felt as strong as ever, pushing the temperature up to a balmy ninety. He drove with the windows wide open, listening to Jessica's CD collection. Traffic was as bad as he had anticipated, so he was able to make it through discs of Metallica, Overkill, Enuff Z'Nuff, Celtic Frost and a few others he'd never heard of. When a convertible filled with girls with high, over-teased hair and shirts that fell off their shoulders pulled up next to him on I90, he thought for sure he had entered a time warp and was now in 1988.

Thanks to the GPS telling him where to go, he only made three wrong turns, finding Morgan Stern's house ten minutes before six. Framingham was a quaint suburb just outside Boston. The house was a bright yellow Colonial complete with porch swing, filling him with a terminal case of house envy. Now this was a place he could settle into. It sure as hell beat his apartment in the Bronx.

Morgan Stern answered the door, his tall, broad-shouldered frame filling the doorway. He had long hair flecked with strands of gray and a beard to match. Eddie couldn't help thinking he looked like a towering Moses.

"Eddie Home, I presume," he said with a disarming smile. His voice was soft, inviting, in complete contrast with his physical appearance.

"Mr. Stern?"

"Morgan to you. Come on in. Gigi is just cleaning up dinner."

The smell of meatloaf and roasted potatoes made Eddie's stomach protest. In his eagerness to get here, he had forgotten to grab something to eat. Morgan showed him to a comfortable living room. The chairs and sofa were all soft, brown leather. A pair of tiffany lamps provided a cozy glow. The central air conditioning brought much-needed relief from the summer heat.

"Can I get you something to drink?"

"Water would be fine."

As Morgan went to the kitchen, his girlfriend Gigi came in to greet him, wearing a dish towel over her shoulder. She was at least ten years younger than Morgan with long, blonde hair and lively eyes that reminded him of some of the surfer girls he'd met when he used to go to Los Angeles to visit his cousins for the summer.

"Thank you for letting me come here," he said as they shook hands.

"Please, we're happy to help, though I don't know how much we can actually do for you. I'm just glad Dr. Froemer referred you to us. We know how difficult something like this can be."

Morgan came back with three glasses of water and three bowls of ice cream on a tray. "It's dessert time, so I figured why not share it with us."

"Much appreciated," Eddie said, hoping that some sweets would calm his stomach's whining.

As they ate, they went through the obligatory small talk between strangers. Eddie didn't want to hit them over the head with his dilemma or seem overanxious. He knew this was a tricky subject. Sometimes the long, meandering road was the best way to get to where you were going. He learned that Morgan was an English teacher at a nearby high school and Gigi, true to his gut reaction, was a West Coast transplant. She was an engineer at a pharmaceutical company. They had met at a book signing event fifteen years earlier and had been inseparable ever since. He could feel the warmth radiate from them. They were living proof that you didn't need a marriage certificate to be a happy, committed couple. He got the feeling they must be a blast to be around at a backyard barbecue.

After the ice cream bowls were cleared, Morgan said, "Dr. Froemer tells me you worked with him at the center. He said you've come across something similar to what Gigi and I experienced with my father."

Eddie was grateful that Morgan had been the first to dive in. "Yes. My partner and I were called in by a family in New Hampshire because they repeatedly saw their daughter when she wasn't around. Things got kind of hairy when she saw herself one night."

Gigi frowned, clasping Morgan's arm. "The poor girl. She must be scared to death."

"You could say that. How often did you see the double of your father?"

Morgan stopped to think a moment. "It had to be at least ten times."

"It was twelve," Gigi reminded him.

"I defer to the little lady. The first time was when I had just come home from work. He was sitting in the same chair you're in now, reading the paper."

Eddie suddenly felt a strong desire to stand.

"I was shocked, because we had just placed him in a nursing home two months earlier. He had Alzheimer's and it had gotten past the point where we could effectively care for him. At first, I assumed he must have just walked out and come to the one place he knew. The nursing home is just a half mile away, you see. I said, 'Dad, you scared me half to death. How did you get here?' He just kept reading the paper, acted like I wasn't there, which wasn't so unusual at that point. I figured I'd let him stay for dinner, then take him back afterwards. I knew the nursing home had to be wondering where he was, so I went to the kitchen to call them. The line was busy, and when I popped in to check on him, he was gone.

"Now I was in a panic. I searched the house, running like a madman. I even went through the neighborhood shouting his name. I was worried he had wandered off and could get hurt. I went back and called the nursing home and told them what happened. The attendant was confused, and asked me to hold. When she came back, she said he was in his room, sleeping. He'd been there all day. Now, I knew there was no way he could make the walk back to the nursing home that fast, but he had to have done it somehow. Maybe he got a ride or something. The attendant was wrong, but as long as he was safe, I was fine."

Gigi said, "It wasn't until a week later that I saw him. I was out shopping for groceries and spotted him pushing a cart two aisles away. I thought, 'Oh my God, he got out again,' and rushed over to get him, except by the time I got there, which could have been no more than five seconds, he was gone. I went up and down every aisle of that supermarket four times looking for him, but it was as if he'd never been there."

Morgan continued, "When Gigi got home, she was very upset. After calming her down, I called the nursing home and was told again that he was in his room, safe and sound. Now things were starting to get crazy."

Gigi took a long sip of water and leaned forward, resting her arms across her thighs. "The next day, we both saw him when we pulled up to the garage after a night with friends at the movies. He just stood there in the glare of our headlights, staring at us. When Morgan stopped the car to get out, he was gone. Poof!" She snapped her fingers for emphasis.

"We saw him six more times, briefly, over the next week," Morgan said. "Another time in the house, then by the mailbox, walking past the window when we were eating in a restaurant. Each time, I called the nursing home to the point where I'm sure they thought I had become unglued."

Curious, Eddie asked, "Did you ever have a moment where you were able to confront it, I mean *him*?"

Morgan raised a reassuring hand. "It's fine by me, now that I know what we saw was not really my father. And yes, the last two times, and they were both out in the yard, we did get to see him for more than just a few seconds. That's when we knew we were dealing with something out of this world."

Gigi shivered and Morgan reached over to massage her upper arms and back.

"When I think about what it said," she said, her gaze drifting back to ten years earlier.

"Excuse me, did you say you spoke to it?" Eddie asked, his interest heightened exponentially.

"Oh yes, we talked," Morgan said. "We talked for a long time. I don't think I'll ever forget it."

Chapter Thirty-Five

Greg and Rita had decided to go all out for dinner, lighting up the grill in the yard and barbecuing everything from hot dogs to filet mignon lathered in garlic and butter sauce. The whole family looked well rested, thanks to the previous night spent away from the house, but Jessica could see the expectant fear take hold of them from time to time.

"Where's your dog?" Jessica asked. It seemed like a dog playing fetch in the yard was the only thing missing from the scene of Americana.

"We're having a good friend watch him. I thought you might want to keep him from being underfoot," Rita said.

"Not that he's done much good. All this stuff going on and not so much as a growl," Greg said, flipping a steak.

"Believe it or not, not all animals are sensitive to this kind of stuff," Jessica said. "Some of them can be as obtuse as people."

Greg huffed and went back to grilling. Jessica hoped he didn't think she was trying to compare him to the dog. One more miscue to add to the pile.

She was a little surprised when they were joined by two of Selena's friends, Julie and Crissy.

When they arrived, Rita pulled her to the side of the house and explained that Selena had asked if she could have them sleep over for the first night. Jessica wasn't keen on the idea.

"My daughter needs her friends right now," Rita said. "It's only for tonight, but there's no way I'm not going to give her whatever she needs to feel secure. I hope you understand."

The look in her eyes told Jessica it didn't really matter how she felt about the wrinkle in the night's plans. A mother's concern overrode the wishes of a stranger.

Jessica did understand the concept of safety in numbers. She just hoped the girls didn't experience something that would scar them mentally, although Crissy looked like the type of kid who sought stuff like this out for kicks. Julie, on the other hand, despite her tough talk, seemed as scared as Selena. She must be one good friend to swallow that unease and spend the night here.

By the time they had finished dessert, Jessica caught Rita alone in the kitchen and said, "I'll need you and Greg to do me a favor."

Rita put down the load of dishes in the sink and wiped her hands on a paper towel. "Sure. Anything."

"If I call you into Selena's room, I need you to get all of the girls out as quickly as possible. I know Crissy and Julie want to give her moral support, but I'm worried about how they'll react if something happens tonight. It's bad enough that the four of you are going through this."

For the first time she could remember, Jessica wished she were older so she could have the weight of experience and authority on her side and insist to Rita that the sleepover wasn't a good idea and couldn't happen. Being just a few years older than Selena, she found it hard to tell the teen's parents what they could do in their own home. She would just have to make the best of it.

"I understand," Rita said.

"I'll give you a walkie-talkie because I don't want to shout across the house and frighten it off, if it shows. If you hear me beep three times, that'll mean I need you in her room right away."

"I'm sure we won't be sleeping much tonight, so no need to worry. Ricky will be sleeping with us."

"How has he been taking it?"

"He's scared, but he's still at that age where he believes mom and dad can protect him from anything. I wish that was true."

They watched a couple of Adam Sandler movies after dinner, in need of a mindless diversion. There was very little laughter, but at least his movies didn't add to the tension.

While they were in the living room, Jessica stayed upstairs, primarily in Selena's room. It was just big enough to accommodate two sleeping bags. Jessica would sit in the desk chair, watching over them. She'd made it clear that when they came to the room, they had to sleep, so they needed to make sure they were good and tired before coming upstairs. It wouldn't work if they treated it like a regular slumber party. It was her one demand and they willingly obliged.

She called Aunt Eve to let her know she was still very much alive and no worse for wear.

"We're having a slumber party," she said, dripping with mock enthusiasm.

"That's a first," Eve said, sounding amused. "Did you bring a sleeping bag?"

"I'm the one who gets to stay up all night and watch them. The girl, Selena, requested it so she would feel more comfortable and her mother kind of insinuated that it was non-negotiable."

"I can understand that. And where does Eddie fit in with a slumber party full of girls?"

"He's down in Boston meeting with a couple that had their own doppelganger experience years ago. It's kinda nice to have another person do some of the legwork."

"Sounds like you have things in hand."

"Everything is locked and loaded."

"Well, you call me any time, let me know you're okay. Even if you just want to talk. You know I love you."

"I love you, too. And I will. Talk to you soon."

Jessica knew she made things sound rosier than they were, but she didn't think there was any need to get her aunt upset or nervous.

Everyone came up around eleven. Jessica's cell phone vibrated on the desk but she didn't notice it as the girls walked into the room with pillows in hand. Selena and Julie looked as if they were stepping onto a terrifying ride at an amusement park while Crissy seemed almost excited.

"How were the movies?" Jessica asked.

"Okay, I guess," Selena said.

"Adam Sandler is mad stupid," Julie added with a weak smile.

"Yeah, he is stupid," Crissy added. "I'll go get changed."

The girls took turns changing and getting ready in the bathroom. Selena settled into her bed while the girls slipped into their sleeping bags on either side of the bed. Jessica sat in the chair at their feet.

Selena sat up and said, "I don't like the word doppelganger."

That took Jessica by surprise. She was prepared to have to answer a few questions, but this wasn't in the script.

"I don't know, it just sounds creepy, and seeing it is bad enough."

Crissy piped up, "Did you know that doppelganger is a German word?"

Jessica shook her head. "I wasn't aware of it, though it does sound Germanic. So, how would you like us to refer to it?"

"Crissy said that the word means double walker. I like that much better. It kind of makes it sound, well, Native American or something, like it's more spiritual," Selena said.

"You think you could trap it in a dream catcher?" Julie asked.

"That's even dumber than Adam Sandler," Crissy countered.

Jessica could see things getting out of hand fast. She interjected, "You know what, I think I like double walker better, too. It's a deal. I'll tell Eddie and your parents tomorrow. And, Julie, I'm not sure if that would work or not. No one's ever tried to trap one before. My goal is to find out why it's here and help it go away."

She saw Crissy roll her eyes but was happy with Julie's and Selena's reactions.

"It's getting late. Time to shut out the lights and try to get some sleep," she said. She turned off the overhead light and settled into the chair.

In the dark, Selena asked, "Won't you get bored and fall asleep just sitting watching us all night?"

"Not me. You forget, I do this for a living. I'm used to it. Good night, girls."

To their credit, they snuggled into their pillows and remained silent, feigning sleep long enough to actually fall asleep. She knew they were all down for the count by the sound of their light snores and shallow breathing.

The doppelganger, or double walker now, appeared to gravitate to Selena and her, so it was her hope that two beacons would be impossible for it to ignore. She'd left the closet door open a crack, not that an inch and a half of wood could stop it from coming and going. That lesson had been learned yesterday. Shielding the light from her cell display, she saw that Eddie had left a message over an hour ago. The house was too quiet to check it now. It would have to wait until morning.

Time inched by like it always did when night draped over a house she was sitting vigil within and there were no distractions to mar the silence or divert her concentration. Twice she crept out of the room to walk through the house, spending several minutes in each room, listening for anything out of the ordinary. The house had its share of creaks and groans, just like any other, but because she hadn't had time to get more acquainted with it, she was on high alert. With so much adrenaline rocketing through her system on a steady basis, she knew she was in for one hell of a crash come morning. Thank God the bed at the hotel was a king and comfortable.

She checked her watch, saw that it was several minutes before three, right around the time the double walker had visited them at the hotel. Three a.m. was the true witching hour, not midnight, the time when the veil between the living and the dead was at its finest. Never a big proponent of spirits working on a schedule, she still felt that it might have some importance to this particular paranormal entity.

The girls were still asleep and didn't stir when she came back, settling into the chair, wincing when the faux-leather protested. Soft shafts of moonlight bathed the room in a dull, blue light. Selena had kicked off her covers, which were now draped across Julie's sleeping bag. She lay on her side, legs tucked together and bent at the knees. Her dark hair fanned out across her pillow. *If nothing happens tonight,* Jessica thought, *at least she'll have gotten a good night's rest.*

It was going on three fifteen when Jessica felt the temperature in the room plummet.

She jerked her attention to the ceiling fan to see if it had kicked into a higher gear. That sometimes happened with the ones that had a wireless remote control. It still spun at a moderate speed, as it had since earlier that evening.

Something was about to happen. She knew as much from the tingling at the base of her scalp as the chill that now permeated the small room.

Jessica waited, breathing slowly through her mouth to keep the amount of ambient noise in the room and in her head as low as possible. She sat forward in the chair, vigilant. Her gaze darted to Selena when she shifted in her sleep, pulling her legs up closer to her midsection until she was in a tight fetal position.

She reached for the ceiling fan remote on the desk and pressed the button to turn it off.

The silence was so perfect that her ears buzzed with a dull whine.

Selena moaned softly, drawing Jessica's attention again. It was now as cold as a meat locker. Jessica could see the vaporous exhalations of all three girls. When Selena started shivering, she had to stop herself from covering her with a blanket. This entire tableau was being set by the unknown entity that had decided to take up residence in the house. The last thing she needed to do was upset even the smallest element.

She wanted it to feel comfortable. To feel as if it had the upper hand. To show itself.

Jessica stared into the dark closet, waiting for the double walker to emerge, preparing herself for its normal yet otherworldly appearance. It was the most unsettling thing she had witnessed in her short time of working in this field, but far from enough to scare her off. She doubted there was anything that could do that.

While she was concentrating on the closet, she heard Selena's mattress crinkle as if a heavy weight had settled onto it. She saw a depression, about the size of a hand, form just inches below Selena's feet.

It was here.

"Come on, show yourself," Jessica whispered.

The depression filled back in, and was replaced by a new one next to her knees.

Jessica waited for the doppelganger to take shape, but there was only the steady progression of a phantom creeper in the bed with Selena.

"Who are you?" Jessica asked, low enough not to wake the girls. She held her digital recorder toward the bed. "What's your name? I know you're not Selena, no matter how much you want to look like her."

She rose from the chair when she saw deep depressions simultaneously form in four corners around Selena. The force on the mattress had to be intense to push down as low as it had. It was as if it had boxed Selena in and was about to draw itself over her.

"I'm Jessica," she said, louder. "Can you tell me your name?"

She knew it wasn't going to be that easy but it was worth a try.

The bed frame creaked from the extra weight being exerted upon it. It was time to get the other girls out, now!

When Jessica reached for her walkie on the desk, it was nowhere to be found. *Did I leave it downstairs?* she thought, cursing herself.

It was time to break this up. Things were taking a dark turn. Selena whimpered in her sleep as if she was being hurt. The wood frame of the bed sounded stressed to the point of breaking.

Subtlety had to be thrown out the window. She had to shout for Rita and Greg to get the girls. She opened her mouth, but nothing came out. Her lungs felt as if they had snapped shut and she was locked in a silent scream.

Selena muffled a desperate, "No!"

But like Jessica, she was meshed in place, trapped in her dream world while her body was pinned under the weight of a presence that had sinister intentions. She knew that now. Something was very wrong here. The game had changed.

165

Chapter Thirty-Six

Morgan Stern had asked for and received Eddie's permission to smoke in front of him. He was surprised when the high school teacher opened a small drawer and extracted a pipe. All he needed was the tweed jacket with patches at the elbows to complete the stereotype.

"It's a shame your generation is being robbed of the simple pleasures in life, like a good after-dinner smoke. I never did see the sense of going into the ground with a bunch of healthy parts. Might as well use them up while you have them."

Gigi gave his arm a light slap. "Don't go encouraging him to take up smoking. Lord, the things he comes out with. He used to smoke cigarettes. This is his way of quitting."

"I went from two packs of cigarettes a day to one pipe an evening. Not a bad trade-off. I have one of my colleagues at school to thank for it. He thought he was getting me a gag gift for my fortieth birthday. The joke's on him."

The tobacco smoke carried an aroma of cherry with hints of vanilla. If it tasted as good as it smelled, Eddie could see why Morgan took up the habit.

But, he wasn't here to talk about the pleasures of a post-repast pipe. He steered the conversation back to the interaction between Morgan, Gigi and his father's doppelganger in the yard. It seemed as if Morgan had used the pipe as a small diversion, delaying the recitation of a painful memory. He had to let them take their time, not push things.

"Eddie, how much do you know about the myth of the doppelganger?"

"Not a whole lot. And would you call it a myth, when we have three people in this room who have seen one?"

"Absolutely. Not all myths are unfounded or stories based on false perceptions. Some myths are quite the opposite, though we as a species try our damnedest to relegate them to the world of fantasy. And do you know why we do that?"

"Because we can't apply scientific standards to prove their

existence?" Eddie answered.

Morgan drew on his pipe, allowing a moment to savor the sweet tobacco. "Not entirely. It's because it scares the hell out of us. When the stuff of nightmares follows us into the daylight, we do anything we can to banish it back to the realm of impossibility. If you ask me, I think people see doppelgangers far more than we know. The problem is, the unmitigated fear that comes with such an experience is so terrifying, so perplexing, that our brains automatically sever the neural pathway the event navigates and deletes the source. It's powerful stuff."

Now Eddie was beginning to feel creeped out, despite the warm surroundings and pleasant company. Morgan was making him realize the full weight of the situation he and Jessica had blindly taken on, and it didn't look like things were going to get any easier.

"When you said you spoke to your father's doppelganger, was it just the one time?"

Gigi answered, "It happened the last two times, both out back. The first time, he didn't say much, just 'You startled me' when we came outside to do some yard work. I remember at the time thinking that he didn't look the least bit startled. It was as if he had consulted a book of proper phrases and decided that was the one to use when someone suddenly came upon you. We knew by then that it wasn't Morgan's dad, so we just stopped and stared at one another for a few seconds. Then he walked down the alley between our house and the one next door and disappeared."

Morgan picked things up. "We didn't have an actual back and forth conversation until a few days later. Gigi and I were sitting in the yard one night, having a glass of wine and unwinding from a long day. We jumped when we heard our gate open, then froze when we saw my father walk in and take a seat right across from us."

"So, he was able to interact with objects around him that time?" Eddie asked.

"Just as easily as you or I," Morgan answered. "It was then that I decided enough was enough, I had to find out what he, what *it*, wanted. So I just came right out and asked it."

Gigi nodded and her shoulders bunched as if she had a chill pass through her. "I have to be honest, I almost died when it smiled and answered him."

"Do you mind telling me what it said?" Eddie asked.

Morgan said, "Before I do, I need to ask if you know what most people associate doppelgangers with."

Eddie thought, but nothing came to him. Everything he had read was a jumbled mess in his brain. He was so wrapped up in Morgan and Gigi's recounting of their experiences that he couldn't concentrate on anything else. "To tell you the truth, I'm at a loss."

"*Death omens*. It's believed that when you see a doppelganger, it means the person the entity has chosen to represent in this world is about to die, or has already passed on. I did a little research on the subject after everything had happened and had I known then, I would have thought for sure my father was telling me goodbye the only way he could, him being ensconced in a nursing home and all. In a way, I'm glad I was ignorant of the theories because I'm not sure I would have had the courage to talk to it so freely."

Before he could continue, Gigi said, "I think what Morgan is trying to say is that you can't go by predominant theories when dealing with a doppelganger. In our case, it was far from a death omen. Morgan's father lived for another year after the last appearance."

"How long did you talk to it?"

"About five minutes or so, right?" Morgan said, looking to Gigi, who confirmed.

"After I asked him why he was here, why he kept coming to us, he looked at me and said, 'Don't go to Florida.' I nearly dropped my wineglass," Morgan said.

"What was in Florida?"

Morgan said, "Nothing, at the time. But, I was scheduled to take a six-month sabbatical after the new year. I had been toying with the idea of spending that time in Fort Myers. Gigi's parents had recently passed away and left us a condo there. She had a ton of vacation time saved up and I thought we could spend a few months in the sun and I could work on learning to sail. It had become a new obsession of mine."

"Had you told your father about your plans?" Eddie asked, putting to test one of the theories that doppelgangers were a type of astral projection, carrying all the knowledge of the person who inadvertently created them.

Morgan shook his head. "That's just the thing. The only person I had discussed it with was Gigi. My father no longer even recognized me, and when I did visit, I would read books to him, all of his favorites, but there was no reason to talk about my tenuous plans."

"Then it told him that Arizona was nice that time of year and he should take that trip to Sedona," Gigi said.

"Another interest that no one else knew about," Morgan said.

"It talked on and on about Arizona, places to stay, what to see, like it was a travel agent selling us on a trip. I can't even begin to tell you how strange the whole thing was. I would have been less freaked out if it just started talking in Latin or repeating a phrase over and over again like in some horror movie."

"So, did you go to Florida or Arizona?" Eddie asked, knowing there was still more to the story.

"That's just it," Morgan said. "We didn't go anywhere. I'm not ashamed to admit, I was tripped out. After it made us promise not to go to Florida, it just got up, closed the gate behind it and left. At the time, I decided I wouldn't go to either place. I was too afraid to take a chance. And it's a good thing we didn't. The condo in Fort Myers burned down in the middle of the night on Valentine's Day. There was a gas leak, then a spark from God knows what, and the whole house went up. We would have been in the house at that time."

Gigi leaned forward and placed a small hand on Eddie's knee. "It saved us. I don't know how, but it did. And for months afterwards, Morgan kept having these lifelike dreams that would sometimes come true. Little things, like knowing when one of his students was going to cut school or that my sister was pregnant with her first. That's when we went to the Rhine Research Center, using some of that sabbatical time we had saved by not going to Fort Myers."

"I have to admit, it was fun being the one tested instead of giving the tests. Dr. Froemer was very thorough and very understanding. Sadly, I never did turn out to be a star pupil."

Something had just locked into place in Eddie's mind and for the first time since coming into Jessica Backman's crazy life, he felt as if he was on the verge of gaining the upper hand, something he had been very accustomed to thanks to his multiple gifts. Ever since the night at the McCammon house, it had been like treading water but getting nowhere. First, the EB nearly blew out his skull, then they arrived at the Leighs' and he was thrown into a dark box where no light or sound could enter.

"For you both, then, seeing your father's doppelganger was a positive experience," he said.

Morgan tapped out his pipe in the ashtray. "Absolutely. Thanks to it, the fates were denied our souls, at least for the time being, to put things poetically. As a sort of epilogue, Gigi and I did eventually go to Sedona four years ago, six years after we had last seen my father's doppelganger. We were on a tour of one of the vortexes, you know, those places in Sedona where dimensions are said to overlap, and as we were leaving, I could have sworn I saw my father entering the small tour bus. Needless to say, I jostled a few people out of my way and almost tripped getting onto the bus. He wasn't there, but I think him, or his doppelganger, guided me to that place so my father's true spirit could see me, and I could see him, one last time."

Eddie thanked them both, promising to call them with the outcome of his particular doppelganger situation.

When he got back inside the Jeep, it was late. It seemed impossible, but he'd been with Morgan and Gigi for nearly five hours. The information they had shared with him was invaluable. He called Jessica and got her voicemail.

He turned on the GPS and headed back to New Hampshire. When he flipped the radio on, a traffic report said there was major night construction on I90. He slammed his palm on the wheel and hoped the delays weren't as bad as they sounded. Pushing the Jeep faster than he normally would, he navigated through side streets, jumping on the highway and offering up a prayer to the traffic gods.

A sea of bright red brake lights and immobile cars and trucks stretched on for miles.

Chapter Thirty-Seven

When Selena awoke, her wild eyes and tight grimace made her look like someone buried alive, which was very close to what she was experiencing. A deep indentation had formed around her body on the mattress, as if a moat had been dug around her. She tried to move her arms to no avail.

"Help me!"

Crissy and Julie jolted awake, both scampering away from the bed when they saw what was happening. They looked to Jessica for help.

The mute oppression that had overtaken her broke, and she shouted, "Girls, I need you out of the room, now!"

The two girls ran into Rita, Ricky and Greg as they entered the room. Rita yelped, covering her mouth with quivering hands. Jessica held her arm out to stop them from moving any closer. Selena whimpered, paralyzed as the unseen presence pushed down on her.

Jessica reached out to touch Selena's leg and was staggered by an electric shock that was so intense, the spark momentarily lit up the room, filling it with a gut-tightening whiff of spent ozone. Everyone in the doorway shrieked with unbridled horror. Greg, no longer able to watch his daughter suffer, strode into the room.

"It's okay, baby, I'll get you out."

As he went to grab her off the bed, he was hit by another shock so intense, it blew him off his feet. Selena wailed, "Daddy!"

Greg landed in a heap on the side of the bed, unconscious. Pandemonium was in full swing in the cramped room.

Holy shit, get ahold of the situation, Jessica commanded herself. Unlike everyone around her, she wasn't frightened. She was confused, concerned and angry. This was *not* the work of a doppelganger. Everything happening in the room was a grim reminder of what she had seen as a small girl, and she was not going to let it go one step further.

"Let her go, now!" she said, her tone piercing, yet controlled. "Tell me who you are. What do you want with Selena? If you tell me your name, maybe I can help you."

She hoped that the EB couldn't detect her subterfuge. If she was lucky, it was saying its name right now, just not in a register that could be detected with the human ear. Once it left, and *it would leave*, she would check her digital recorder and maybe have what she needed to put an end to this.

"I'm not afraid of you," she continued. "I'm taking Selena, right now, and there's nothing you can do to stop me. You're going to leave this house. You're going to let her go and leave. Do you understand?"

She plunged her hands onto the bed and under Selena's midsection. She felt spidery nips of electricity dance up her arms and knew that her hair, as long as it was, was standing on end. But the EB's power had diminished greatly, and she was able to scoop a frantic Selena into her arms. The teen threw her arms around Jessica's neck, sobbing. Jessica carried her past the crowd in the doorway and down the stairs, as far away from the room as she could get. Greg had recovered and followed everyone else into the living room. He held his head as if it might break.

After placing a teary Selena onto the couch, the girl was immediately surrounded by her mother, Julie and Ricky. The four of them heaved with sobs while casting terrified glances at the stairs. Greg remained in the middle of the room, a perplexed look on his face. Crissy was the most together, but it was plain to see that the past several minutes had jangled her.

Greg reached out to Jessica's shoulder. "What the hell was that?" he asked, his voice raw and confused.

"I'm not sure. Whatever it was, it didn't want any of us to get to Selena. Are you okay? Let me get you something to drink."

She rushed to the refrigerator, not concerned that she was treating it as her own. She grabbed bottles of water and juice for everyone.

When Greg regained some of his composure, she continued, "I'm pretty sure that the entity, or EB as I call them, thought that by shocking you the way it did, the rest of us would be scared off. That's why the energy field it had built around her was so weak when I grabbed her. When an EB is negative, it uses everything in its arsenal to induce fear. Most times, that works." She approached Selena. "You feeling a little better, honey?"

She could only nod as she hiccupped, holding back a fresh wave of tears. Selena had every right to be scared out of her mind. What they had all witnessed was a flat-out assault, not just on her, but her father and Jessica as well.

"Rita, do you think you could take Selena to the bathroom and check her for any marks? I need to know if there are any bruises, burns or scratches. Take my camera with you and if you both agree to it, take pictures of anything abnormal. This has gotten serious and I need to document everything."

Rita agreed and, holding Selena by her shoulders, walked her to the bathroom.

"Why does the ghost want to hurt my sister?" Ricky said. He now sat close to Julie who had placed a protective arm around him. The question broke her heart.

She was at a loss. What could she say to this little boy who had just witnessed one of the more personal violations that a person could endure by an EB? As much as she wanted to reassure him that everything would be all right, she also didn't want to lie to him. Everything had been turned on its ass and she no longer knew which end was up.

The doorbell saved her from stammering through a lame explanation.

Greg answered, opening the door wide to allow Eddie inside.

"I'm sorry to ring the bell in the middle of the night, but I saw the lights on," he started to say, then stopped when he saw everyone in the living room. "Is everyone okay?"

"Physically, yes, I think," Jessica answered, looking at Greg who still appeared stunned.

"You missed some dumb scary shit," Julie said, then clamped her hand over her mouth when she realized she had cursed in front of Selena's parents.

"It was totally freaky," Crissy said. "Something attacked Selena and made people fly around the room!"

A dark cloud passed over Eddie's face and he raced up the stairs. Jessica's first instinct was to join him but she realized she was needed more down here. The floorboards creaked as Eddie went from room to room.

Rita and Selena emerged from the bathroom. "She has bruises on her shins and shoulders. I took a picture of each." Her hand shook as she passed the camera back to Jessica.

"I think it's best I get you all out of the house now. Why don't you follow me to the Best Western? I'll phone ahead and get you a couple of rooms."

Greg protested at first, insisting *he* get the rooms, but she stood firm. He was too drained to argue. Eddie came back down five minutes later, his complexion ashen.

They were all on the road a minute later, the Leighs and Selena's friends bundled into their minivan.

"There's another presence around Selena," Eddie said.

"So that wasn't the doppelganger, right? I knew it."

"Not even close. And it doesn't want to scare her."

Jessica navigated her Jeep through the dark, empty streets, the passing streetlights stabbing through her tired eyes. She slammed on the brakes when he spoke next.

"It wants to rape her."

Chapter Thirty-Eight

The next day, Greg and Rita drove Crissy and a shaken Julie back to their homes, leaving their kids with Jessica and Eddie. It was important to at least try to get Rick's mind off the horror of the night before, so they brought him to the game room and gave him two rolls of quarters. While he played a game that required his shooting a continual onslaught of zombies, Selena sat on the small pool table and stared into the distance.

"We have to get to the house as soon as Greg and Rita get back," Jessica said, whispering in Eddie's ear. They were both afraid to mention anything in front of Selena. She looked as fragile as a crystal needle.

"Time is not on our side," he said. "The entity isn't tied to the house, but I felt that it is nearby. It's trying to bond with Selena so it's free to go anywhere she goes, and have access to her any time it's built up enough strength." He led Jessica by the arm to the door. "We'll be right outside, guys. You'll be able to see us through the window. Okay?"

Ricky was lost in battle. Selena gave a soft nod, though with obvious trepidation.

The air outside the cramped, stuffy game room was a nice relief. Dark clouds were gathering to the west. It already smelled like rain.

Jessica asked him, "So the haunting isn't necessarily part of the house?"

"No, it's entirely centered on Selena. Jess, the thing I sensed in there last night is bad. If I could have washed my body, mind and soul in acid to cleanse myself, I would have. I was just catching the residual emotions it left behind and I was hit with desires and intentions so twisted, I'm almost afraid to think about them, much less talk about them."

Jessica looked him square in the eyes. "I need you to be one-hundred-percent positive about this. I haven't known you long enough to get a good sense of what you can and can't do, but what I've witnessed so far has me seeing things in a different way. Is Selena in danger?"

"Oh, yes," he exhaled.

"And what about her double walker? Where does that fit in?"

"Double walker?"

"It's what Selena requested we call it. She says the word doppelganger sounds too frightening."

"After last night, the doppelganger is her best friend. I had a long talk with Morgan and Gigi last night and I realized their experience is very similar to Selena's. Most times, people equate the appearance of a...a double walker, with impending disaster or, at best, a bit of bad news to come. In Morgan's case, he kept seeing his father because the doppelganger was trying to warn him. Turns out, the advice it gave him saved his and Gigi's lives."

"They spoke to it?" Jessica was flabbergasted.

"Just the same way I'm talking to you now. This was the last time they saw it. I think it had been gathering enough energy, establishing its place in the here and now, to keep them from making a decision that could have killed them. And I think that's the same thing with Selena's double walker. It's trying to warn her, or protect her, I'm not sure yet, from the other entity that's been circling her, waiting for its moment."

"Then is it even wise to leave her alone if we go to the house? Should one of us stay here?" She checked in on the kids and waved. Selena returned with a half smile that never reached her eyes.

She opened the door for another theory that had been formulating in the recesses of his mind ever since the night they had sent the poltergeist-like EB packing. He was worried how she would take it, but it had to be said.

"Can I be blunt with you?" he said, tensing, waiting for her to hit him with a roundhouse.

"You have to be," she replied.

"It's about you. I think we need to keep some distance between you and Selena."

Jessica stared at him with a mix of bewilderment and the beginning sparks of anger. "You said I've proven myself somewhat to you in the short time we've been together. You have to realize, I don't say this lightly, because I think what you do is heroic. I've been involved in this world, and when I say *world* I mean communing with spirits, for as long as I can remember. Being a psychic-medium with PK abilities has made for a very interesting life, and I've seen and heard things that would send most people running. Except you, and I can't say that about anyone else I've ever met. And as much as I bring to the table with faculties that extend into the paranormal, I've come to realize that you have your own powers, ones that I'm sure you're not even aware of, aside from realizing that you can send EBs away just by saying their name. Do you know how or why that works?"

"No, but the end result is all that matters when I'm asked to help someone. What are you getting at? I hope you're not trying to tell me I'm psychic."

"There's a big similarity to what you can do to an EB with the Catholic rites of exorcism, only without the holy incantations. In the rites, the priest commands the demon to tell him its name, and when it does, the end of the ordeal is near. Now, what you deal with isn't necessarily demonic, but you've instinctively tapped into a process that's been around for millennia."

The first rumble of thunder rolled overhead and the small sliver of sun dipped behind a massive rain cloud.

Eddie continued, "Look, I'm not sure how your *banishing* thing works, but I do know that when spirits are around you, they get an extra boost of energy. It's kind of like you're a generator, doling out power without even knowing it. Haven't you ever wondered why so many of the cases you've worked on have been so intense?"

Jessica bent down to pick up a small rock, tossing it across the parking lot and into a stand of trees. She said, "To tell you the truth, everything I've ever experienced has been held up to what happened to my family when I was young. Anything less than that has been normal to me. I never once thought that I was making things worse."

Eddie was relieved that she hadn't thrown any punches, verbal or otherwise. He dared to hold her hand and gave a gentle squeeze. "You're not the bad guy in all of this. You bring the storm, but you also bring the calm. Let me take the lead today and I can show you what I can do and together, we can see how both of our talents can work as a team. We just need to do it all *away* from Selena."

Jessica paced between a pair of parked cars. He allowed her as much time as she needed to absorb everything. Selena and Ricky were now playing pool, though neither seemed to be deriving much fun from it.

Finally, Jessica came to a stop and said, "Tell me what to do."

Chapter Thirty-Nine

Greg Leigh sat in their hotel room nursing the whiskey he had poured in one of the plastic cups that had been placed by the bathroom sink. When he stared at himself in the mirror, he was shocked by his reflection. He looked plagued, like a man who was no longer sure about anything or even his place in the world. Maybe a stiff drink would help put things in perspective. At the very least, it would quiet the running questions in his mind.

Rita came up behind him, rubbing his shoulders, pressing her cheek against the top of his head. Together, they watched Selena and Rick sleeping in the double bed. The kids had passed out, exhausted from the level of panic that had ridden hard through them over the past couple of days. Selena lay with a protective arm over her brother, snoring softly.

"I should go there," Greg said, his lips pulled tight against his teeth from the bite of the whiskey.

"We all need you here, Greg," Rita said, taking the chair next to him. Her hair was wrapped up in a white towel and she smelled like soap and body lotion. He'd wanted to join her in the shower, needed to feel her touch, to ground himself back into the reality that had suited him just fine for the past forty-four years. With the kids so close, he had to find another way, which was why he went out to buy the bottle of Maker's Mark.

"I don't even know if we can trust Jessica and Eddie. We don't really know them. In fact, the only thing I *do know* is that ever since they arrived, things have gotten worse. This whole circus could be a setup and they're robbing us blind while we sit here in a room smaller than our kitchen." He knocked back the rest of the whiskey and crushed the cup, a macho move that lost a lot of its luster when he realized the plastic was about as thin as a sheet of paper.

Rita pulled his face close to hers, caressing his tense jaw with her fingertips. "It's perfectly normal to try to rationalize what's been happening. I'm no more comfortable than you with accepting the fact that a ghost or whatever you could call it is in our house and tried to attack our daughter. Jesus, we just saw it hours ago and saying it out loud makes it sound impossible. But it *did happen,* Greg, and we should be thankful that we have people who are willing to face it."

I'm willing to face it, he grumbled to himself. The shock from the entity that had tried to smother his daughter had strengthened his resolve to confront whatever had insinuated itself into their lives and spun them out of control. Everyone had pleaded with him to go to the emergency room to make sure he didn't sustain any damage that they couldn't see, but he refused. What was he supposed to tell the doctor? *Well, while my daughter was pinned down by a ghost, I tried to rescue her and was tasered by Boo Berry.*

"Why don't you take a nap, too, hon?" he said.

"I think you should join me. You got as little sleep as the rest of us, and then some."

He kissed her. "I will. I just need another round, then I'll be good and tired."

Rita adjusted the air conditioning and settled under the covers. Greg poured another drink, waiting.

The house had a different feel to it now that it was empty and in the daytime, though the gray skies provided very little light. It felt hollow, like going to a wake and viewing a loved one, surprised by the absence of a soul in the cool body in the coffin. It was why wakes were a necessary function for so many. It gave the grieving the opportunity to realize that the deceased was no longer in their body. They had moved on.

What had been in the house last night had moved on as well. Jessica had followed Eddie throughout every corner of the house, doing something she normally hated, which was giving someone else the lead.

"Nothing," he said when they finished in Selena's room. The residue of the night before, rumpled sleeping bags and scattered pillows, lay everywhere. "It's gone for now, partly because I think we removed its reason for being here."

Jessica concentrated on the closet, waiting for Selena's double walker to appear. She asked, "What about the doppelganger? Is that gone, too?"

"*That* is always with Selena. I'm convinced that doppelgangers are nothing more than extensions of the person they appear to be, even if they're deceased. If my hunch is correct, it's completed the task it came into being to do. It got help for Selena. Now that I know there's something else at play here, I doubt it will come back."

"Well, that's one piece of good news at least. I don't know if Selena could handle seeing it again, even if it has good intentions."

The wood of the roof popped and they both froze, straining to hear any follow up noises.

"That was just the house," Jessica said. The wind had picked up outside, causing the wood joints to shift. She pulled her Guns N' Roses T-shirt away from her chest to let some fresh air against her damp skin. The humidity from the coming storm was peaking and unpleasant.

"So, what do we do now? I have no problem camping here for the week if I have to."

Eddie chuckled. "I know you wouldn't. I'm pretty sure it won't come to that. The EB might not be here now, but I'll bring it back. Can you close the blinds while I gather up all these blankets?"

"Please don't tell me you're going to do some Ganzfeld procedure or anything like that," she said.

The Ganzfeld procedure was a once popular parapsychology experiment where people with reported psychic abilities were given two white discs to place over their eyes while wearing headphones piping in white noise. Sometimes, strobe lights were added to the mix. It was supposed to heighten a psychic's abilities. She thought it looked nice and creepy for movies and TV shows, but couldn't for the life of her understand why it would help someone who was a true psychic. If you had a gift, you had a gift. What was the point of all the external nonsense?

He tossed all of the blankets and pillows into the closet. "Not for me, thank you. I had to go through a few of those while I was at The Rhine. I found it to be distracting. I prefer au naturale, just like my old great grandpa. Now my father, he did some odd things to communicate with the dead like soaking in an ice bath or covering his head with a heavy cloth to block out any ambient noise. I think that's part of the reason he burned out so early. He tried too hard, though maybe he had to in order to make things work. We don't talk much about it."

She was about to ask him more about his father, but something in his tone told her it was best to leave it alone, for now.

"Okay, the room is clean and dark. What's next?"

"Now we get on the bed and lie down," he said with a smirk.

"Ha-ha, very funny. Seriously, what are you going to do?"

"I am serious. We both need to lie down on the bed." His expression had turned somber. "I promise, this is not some ploy to get you in the sheets. I'm going to do something that you don't read about in any books or see in any movies. It's something I can do that, so far, is unique to me."

Jessica had to keep her swirling doubts about the world of psychic phenomena at bay. Plus, curiosity was getting the better of her. Eddie propped his head on two pillows and stretched out. As she settled in next to him, she said, "Just a warning, I am a kickboxer, and not just some chick who goes through the motions to get a bitchin' workout."

"That doesn't surprise me. So it's in my own personal safety and interest to tell you up front that our hands will need to touch. I'm just going to rest the back of mine against yours, like that. Okay?"

She wanted to tell him it was very far from okay, but she had agreed to go along with him and if a little hand-to-hand contact was necessary, she would let it slide.

"This better be amazing," she said, staring at the ceiling. A chip of plaster hung down in the far corner.

Eddie exhaled heavily through his mouth. "If it works, it will be. Now, the one thing I do know about this EB is that it's fixated on Selena. I got the perception that it's been hanging on the periphery for a while now, biding its time. When we first came here looking for the doppelganger, this other presence was using its power to cloak itself from me, which is why I felt nothing. That was its first mistake, because I knew right away that something was off here. Every house has a kind of soul, especially one with people living in it. This house was so devoid of one that I knew there had to be another force jamming my frequency. The EB was right in doing it if it doesn't want to be found, because ninety-nine-point-nine percent of the population would have never picked up on that."

"Show off," Jessica said low.

"I'll let that slide. I know what you saw last night was intense, but I can assure you that its ultimate intentions are way more vile than simply scaring her, which is why we have to find it fast."

"And we do that by taking a nap? I don't know if you've realized this, but I kind of like to take action."

"You're going to get more action than you realize. I'm going to entice the EB back into the room now, using your latent capacity to attract it so it can pull more power from you."

Jessica moved to her side to face him. He looked at peace. His eyes were closed without so much as a flutter under his lids. "And how will you entice an EB to come to you when it wants Selena?"

"I'm going to make it think I *am* Selena."

Chapter Forty

Eddie was pleasantly surprised that Jessica didn't pepper him with a million questions and doubt. The whole process could take some time and he didn't want to waste what little they had.

"So, here's the last important thing," he said. She had rolled onto her back and moved her hand next to his. "When it gets here, I'm going to funnel as much as I can to you. That's why it helps to have our hands touch. You won't need to just take my word for what this EB is all about. We'll both experience it together. I need you to tell me you're willing to do it, because it can get pretty intense for me, and I've been doing it all my life. Plus, this EB is about as nasty as they come."

Jessica didn't hesitate to answer. "Do it. I want to see."

"All right. Just stay still. You'll know when it's here."

They took deep breaths. He could feel the heat of her body resting just inches from his own. The rain came down in earnest, peppering the window with hundreds of tiny taps while the heavy, comforting scent of the storm carried itself throughout the room, riding on the wave of escalating winds.

Eddie had been around Selena enough now to conjure up a perfect image of her in his mind. He imagined her on the bed, sleeping peacefully, and superimposed it over his and Jessica's forms, using it to mask their presence. To make it more enticing, her image was dressed in a small, tight night shirt and panties. The covers were pulled back, revealing the olive skin of her legs, hips, exposed belly and arms.

He built a cocoon around them, projecting a softly breathing Serena over it to bring the EB out of hiding.

That was the easy part. What most people didn't realize was that ghosts didn't always see the world of the living the same as they had with their eyes when they had been alive. Jessica was right in calling them Energy Beings, because they lived on as pure energy, seeing and reacting to the emanating vitality of the world they had left behind but couldn't entirely escape from.

Infusing that image of Selena with a replication of her life-force was the harder part, but not impossible. He had quietly absorbed enough of her essence over the past few days to give power to the mirage. It was very much like an impressionist donning makeup and adopting the speech and mannerisms of a celebrity for a play, except everything was done within his strange and unique psyche.

Like all girls her age, Selena was at times invincible and fragile, eager to grasp the infinite possibilities of the world yet afraid of leaving the comfort of her home, her family, behind. She was young and beautiful and possessed a charisma that drew people to her. It was that same charisma that had attracted the EB, igniting its twisted fascination.

The sounds and smells of the storm faded into the ether as Eddie concentrated. He didn't feel the sweat as it poured from his scalp and down his neck. The light touch of Jessica's hand was his only tether to his true self.

He *was* Selena now.

There was one more thing to add.

Fear.

He made the image of her sleep fitful, imbuing the atmosphere of the room with a sense of hopelessness. The EB liked her scared. It fed off her terror. He knew it had cultivated its taste for trembling awe during the course of its life. It had done bad things and was held prisoner to its vices. Death hadn't stopped it at all. It simply gave it free reign to find more victims without the threat of being seen.

When he had made brief contact earlier, he had felt its desire to be in the shadows. To wait and watch and plot. To build excitement until it literally exploded.

He channeled Selena's fear and heard Jessica gasp. Her fingers twitched, lacing within his own.

Eddie was afraid. There was no way to separate his own internal doppelganger of Selena from his true self. The transformation had to be total in order to work. His heartbeat galloped and his mouth became dry as if he had taken a mouthful of sand.

The skin on his arms burned with the start of pins and needles and his hairs rose as if pointing to the source of the impending doom that had set off his body's claxons.

It was close. Not in the room just yet, but cautiously approaching like a predatory animal. He increased the pressure on Jessica's hand, could feel it grow cold as the blood retreated to her core.

His eyes were closed, but he could see the EB melt into the room with perfect clarity, its hunger savage and thick, infusing the atmosphere with its unholy animus.

Keep coming, you son of a bitch, Eddie thought within the small part of himself that he kept locked from the invading beast.

The EB hovered over them, watching, debating what to do first. It absorbed the fear Eddie generated like a vampire, sating its need.

It was new to the spirit world, having crossed over very recently, still unsure of its powers, shocked that it could interact with the object of its obsession with such ease. Eddie couldn't get a sense of what it had looked like in life. This spirit wanted no connection with its former self. All it wanted to retain was its demented lust.

The EB didn't know how it had transformed from watcher to participant, but it was delighted with its newfound ability. It intended to use it to finish what had started...when? Eddie struggled to grasp on to its history without breaking the trap he had set. There was something more here. This was far bigger than either of them thought.

The EB growled, a soft ululation of almost demonic pleasure. Eddie prayed that Jessica wouldn't react and break the spell.

It came closer, hovering just centimeters above their faces, exploring the depths of what it thought was a discomfited Selena.

The spirit had no form, no phantom mask that would betray its characteristics when it was alive. It had lost its humanity far before the last beat of its heart, so long ago that it could no longer resemble what it once was—a living being.

An icy, ethereal appendage extended outward, dragging across Eddie's neck, lingering around Jessica's mouth.

Eddie felt it pull back in confusion. His impression of Selena faltered for just a split second, but it was enough.

An angry moan reverberated within the room. It dove into them with terrific intensity.

Oh my God, make it stop. Eddie tried to shut his totemic barn doors but it was no use. The flood of emotions and images was too strong to resist.

Dark, horrid pictures flashed through his brain. Twisted fantasies with Selena as the star attraction, the center of its obsession. Her naked flesh tantalized. Her moans turned into screams, terror scratching her throat raw.

Eddie felt the EB's desire as his own. Shame flushed through him as his cock grew hard. There was no way to control it. He wanted to look away, but visions of a breathless, wanton, tortured Selena were everywhere.

You sick fuck! Eddie spat at the terrible darkness that had hijacked his soul.

He struggled to shield Jessica from the EB's baser aspects. She didn't need to see this, to feel this...filth. No one did.

Using every ounce of strength he had, he conjured a gale force wind, pushing the EB out beyond the door of his subconscious. It tumbled back, pealing with wicked laughter.

He slammed the doors shut.

A burst of energy exploded in the room.

Eddie was catapulted off the bed, smashing into the wall, narrowly missing the window.

Jessica was raised up onto her feet as if she had been attached to a well-oiled pulley. Her eyes were wide and wild and she fought for control of her arms.

"That's right, you bastard, we tricked you! Now you're toast!" she bellowed.

Her bravado angered the EB. It lifted her higher, until her toes dangled above the bed. Eddie could see the fabric of her shirt bunch up as invisible hands pushed her up higher and higher until her head hit the ceiling. Jessica continued to fight.

"Show yourself, you coward!"

Eddie stared at her with astonishment. She had no fear of death, was almost reckless in her abandonment of self-preservation. She knew that death wasn't the end.

But she had no idea what she was up against. Death was only the beginning.

He rose to his feet on legs that felt as if he had just come home from a month's tour at sea. Between the pounding his back had taken when he hit the wall and the strength he had used up to get the EB here, then out of his head, he wasn't sure how long he would be able to remain erect.

Leaping onto the bed, he passed through the crackling field of static that surrounded the EB and grabbed Jessica around the waist, pulling them both into a heap on the bed.

"Get back!" he shouted at it. Jessica squirmed under him.

"Let it take me on," she protested. "I can handle it!"

"No...you can't!"

It was a matter of seconds before the EB retreated. Lashing out at

Jessica had drained it considerably.

"Oh shit," Eddie murmured. He felt the blow a moment before it hammered into him.

A blast of white-hot light buried itself into the center of his brain. He recoiled with a pained grunt. Jessica rolled out from under him and pushed herself up on his chest.

They both turned their heads when they heard someone yell, "What the hell is going on here?"

Chapter Forty-One

Eddie could only groan in reply. Jessica saw the drained look on his face and awkwardly slipped off of him and onto the floor.

Greg Leigh stood in the doorway, his eyes half-closed with the telltale, faraway look that said he had had a few drinks too many. He gripped the frame for support.

"This is what you two do when I give you the run of my house?" he blurted, his words running together in a sloppy bunch.

"It's nothing like you're thinking," Jessica said in protest. She bent over Eddie to make sure he was all right.

He grabbed his skull with both hands and his eyes were pinched shut. He stammered, "Oh, this is bad, Jess," before turning to his side, away from Greg's angry stare.

"You have one minute to explain yourselves," Greg said.

"Greg, I need you to calm down, please. We just made contact with the entity that's been in your house."

"I'm sure you made plenty of contact," he mocked.

Jessica rushed to his side. "Look, I know what you must be thinking, but you're way off base. We just had an intense experience with a male presence that has been stalking your daughter. It assaulted me. You came in right after Eddie broke its grip on me."

Greg eyed them both, saw that Eddie was in obvious pain. He stepped into the room, collapsing into the desk chair. It seemed like an hour before he said, "Go on."

Jessica returned to Eddie's side on the bed. He had maneuvered himself so he was on all fours, attempting to get right-side up. "We've got trouble," he said through gritted teeth. "It's nearby. It's always been close." He seemed to be talking more to himself than anyone in the room.

After helping him into a sitting position, she said to Greg, "I think I need to start with Eddie. He's more than just my assistant. Eddie is also a psychic-medium."

She waited for Greg to say something negative, but he only stared at them with withering patience.

She continued, "Until I met Eddie, I didn't believe in psychics myself, but he's proven me wrong on more than one occasion. He just introduced me to a special technique of his where I was able to see and experience what he could see. There's a male Energy Being that's attached itself to Selena. Something is very wrong with it, both in life and now in death. I think it knew her in some way when it was alive."

Greg closed his eyes and stretched his neck like a prizefighter before stepping into the ring. He buried his head in his hands and said, "How am I supposed to believe all of this? First there's some *thing* in my house that looks like my daughter, and now you're telling me there's an evil male ghost too? I hope you can understand why I feel you're stretching the limits of credibility here."

Jessica said, "Trust me, I do. Confronting situations like this is something I face all the time and even I'm having a hard time wrapping my head around this one. All I know for sure is that Selena is in danger and we need to do everything we can to eliminate this threat."

That's when Eddie finally spoke. "That won't be so easy." His face was drawn and he looked as if he were short two pints of blood. "The spirit found my weak spot, went right for it. While I was connected to you, you were vulnerable. It knows all about you, Jess. More importantly, it knows your gift now, which means there's no chance in hell it's about to give you what you need."

Jessica felt the walls closing in. It seemed no matter what she did, the multiple EBs were one step ahead of her. To make it worse, now she knew that her mere presence only increased its destructive energy. She was beginning to regret ever thinking she could help this poor family, but stopped herself from saying that to Greg. There had to be another way. Her father wouldn't have sent Eddie into her life without good reason. She needed time to figure out what to do next.

"You both sound nuts," Greg said, staggering to get up. She wondered how he managed driving to the house without killing anyone. Now that things had settled down, her nose twitched at the sour scent of alcohol coming off him in waves. "You're going to have to give me more than just crazy talk to keep me from sending you back to New York, again."

Eddie said, "You can't deny what you all saw the other day in this room. Even though you didn't see what just happened here, there's no way you can explain away what you and your family experienced."

Greg opened his mouth to speak, but nothing came out.

"And you saw Selena's doppelganger in your garage. None of that was imagined. We're telling you the truth, and we have nothing to gain. There's a real threat to Selena, and it's not from the doppelganger. In fact, I doubt you'll see it again. It fulfilled its purpose, which was to get help. If you don't want us to be the ones, fine, but you can't ignore this. We can't let you do that."

Jessica cringed inside, hoping he hadn't pressed too far. Greg's pride as the protector of his family had been dashed to tiny bits. Taking orders from a couple of kids wasn't going to make things any better. She needed to step in, fast.

"We're not asking anything of you other than your permission to do whatever we can to help Selena. In fact, you may be able to lend us a hand." She caught her image in the mirror behind his head and stiffened. Gingerly, she pulled the sides of her shirt down past her collar bones and saw the deep bruises in the shape of fingerprints on either side. In her struggle, she hadn't felt any physical sensation other than a hot desire to break free from the EB's grasp. The purpling marks on her body were proof that it had considerable power and malicious intent.

Greg saw the bruises as well, sobering at the reality of the situation. That derailed his train of thought. He pointed at her, paused and said, "What do you need me to do?"

The tension that had built within Jessica finally eased and the thick atmosphere in the room deflated.

Eddie preempted her, saying, "This spirit, or EB, knew Selena very well when it was alive. It hasn't been dead very long, but with each passing day, it's learning how to adapt to its new incarnation, getting more substantial. If we're going to find it, we'll need your help. Do you know of anyone close to the family that recently passed away?"

Jessica hoped it wasn't a family member. What she had sensed was putrid. It was hard to imagine a relative or friend wanting to do things to a teenager like this EB.

"Her grandmother, Rita's mom, died a year ago."

"This is definitely a male," Jessica said. "Is there anyone else you can think of?"

Greg shook his head. "No one. Not even any distant family or friends."

"Anyone in the school or neighborhood?" Eddie asked.

"I...I'm not sure. I know a few of my immediate neighbors, but that's about it, and they're all alive and well."

Eddie prodded him. "There has to be some connection, a passing that meant nothing to you when it happened but left some unresolved issues in its wake. We're going to have to talk to Selena, too, but if there's anything you can think of to spare her that... I got a very strong impression that the answer is very, very close to your home. Every neighborhood has a person who knows everyone's business. Growing up, we appointed the old woman next door, Marnie, the unofficial mayor of our block. If someone farted in their sleep, she somehow knew about it. You have to have someone like that here."

Sighing, Greg looked like a man about to break. A burst of thunder shook the house in tandem with a flash of lightning. The storm was as much outside the house as it was within.

Greg bumpd the wall with his fist and said, "Wait, I know exactly who you mean. Come with me."

Selena was the first to wake up and notice her father was gone. Assuming he was out at a store or getting an early dinner for them, she stretched, put on her sneakers and walked outside. The narrow awning was no match for the rain that blew sideways, drenching her in seconds. She'd wanted some fresh air and a chance to escape the cooped-up hotel room, but this was too much.

The wind caught hold of the door and slammed it shut behind her when she jumped back into the room. Her mother snapped wide awake at the sound, relaxing when she saw Selena, dripping wet.

"Did you just take a dip in the pool?" she asked.

Selena ran her hands through her sodden, stringy hair. "I only stepped out the door for two seconds. I need a towel."

"I'll get it for you."

"I've got it, Mom. It's like seven feet to the bathroom."

She vigorously rubbed the towel through her hair, worried by the girl looking back at her in the mirror. Even after a two-hour nap, she looked like hell. This whole experience was a drain not just on her, but now the whole family. She'd been reading up on ghosts the day before Jessica and Eddie had arrived and one of the things she came across had stuck with her. Negative hauntings were often made worse because of the reactions of those being haunted. Some spirits fed on fear, preferring to prey on terrified victims, gaining strength by siphoning off emotional energy.

"What the hell has happened to you?" she asked her reflection, relieved that it wasn't a double walker mimicking her on the other side of the glass.

"Did you see your father?" her mother asked.

She emerged from the bathroom with her hair wrapped in the towel. Ricky was still out like a light.

"Nope. I was hoping he was out getting us something to eat. I'm starving."

She followed her mother's gaze as she eyed the half-empty bottle of whiskey and plastic cup on the small table. She saw the lines of worry etch across her brow.

Now what? she thought. Something had happened between her mother and father while she was asleep. Her mother was doing a poor job of hiding her concern, but for what?

Selena decided she was no longer going to play the victim. It seemed as if everything had started with her, and she was going to do whatever she could to make it stop.

Chapter Forty-Two

Jessica and Eddie slogged across the muddy lawn to Greg's neighbor's house. They were soaked to the skin in an instant. He had a large wraparound porch that held the storm at bay and gave them momentary shelter. Whatever effects Greg had been suffering from his drinking binge were long gone now. Adrenaline had flushed it all out of his system.

He explained, "Mr. Murphy has lived here all his life. He knows everything about everybody. I figure he's as good a place to start as anyone."

Jessica stepped back when he swung the screen door wide and knocked heavily, if not frantically, on the front door. "Mr. Murphy, it's me, Greg Leigh. Mr. Murphy."

A round, gray-haired man wearing a Hawaiian shirt and tan slacks answered the door. He held a can of Piels Beer and eyed them all warily.

"Is something wrong, Greg? You look like you've just seen the ghost of Christmas Future. Who are your friends?"

"Can we come in and talk?" Greg said, having no patience for formalities.

"Sure, sure, come on in. Go on back to the kitchen where you can drip dry."

Eddie pulled close to her and said, "We need to pay attention to this guy. He's going to help us without realizing it."

She nodded. Eddie looked wet and tired, but there was a newfound burning in his eyes that told her he wasn't about to let up until they got to the bottom of things.

Mr. Murphy's kitchen must have been brand spanking new in 1970. It didn't look like much had changed since then. The walls were covered in pale green tiles with black trim and the linoleum floor was scuffed and cracked in more places than she could count. They sat around an aluminum table with a faux Formica top.

"Can I interest anyone in a beer? I was just about to have my one can of suds for the day and heat up some soup."

"Next time," Greg said.

Jessica and Eddie introduced themselves, but didn't say why they were there. That was better left to Greg.

"You relatives of Greg and Rita?" he asked.

"Just friends of the family," Greg replied. "I was wondering if you could help us out with something."

Mr. Murphy lowered himself into a chair. He pulled a pack of Kool cigarettes from his shirt pocket, ripped the filter off one and lit it. A thick cloud of gray smoke filled the air between them. "I'll do the best I can. Judging by the look on your faces, it must be serious."

"It could be," Greg said. "I was wondering if you knew of anyone in the area that died recently."

Mr. Murphy smiled and wagged a finger at them. "Ah, you must be in the market for some real estate on the cheap. I can tell by your accents that you're not from around here. It's an odd way going about looking for a house, but I can't say that I blame you. The cost of a house today astounds me, even with the depressed market."

Jessica hated to lie, but Greg did produce a gem of an excuse for their being here. She said, "You have to find an angle any way you can."

"You don't look like you're even old enough to smoke, young lady. You one of those cradle robbers, Eddie?" He winked at them both. "Now, let me think. I know there's a house for sale over on Alexander Street, but that's because the Langes moved out a few months back. Rose Hutchins passed away over on Forte, but that had to be a year ago. A young couple like yourselves bought it from her sons. Heard they got a pretty good deal."

Greg cut into his rumination. "Setting aside any houses that may or may not be for sale, can you think of anyone in the neighborhood that passed away recently?"

That got Mr. Murphy suspicious. Jessica willed Greg to cool down but had little hope. She was about to make a preemptive strike when Eddie said, "I'll be straight with you, Mr. Murphy. We're not actually looking to buy a house. Jessica and I are here to help Greg and his family with a little something they're going through."

Jessica added, "We just want to ask a few questions that I know are going to sound strange, but anything you can give us might be just what we're looking for."

Mr. Murphy took a sip of his beer with a shaky hand. He eyed Greg and said, "Is that so?"

"Yes. If you want us to leave, I understand."

Mr. Murphy waved a hand. "I could tell from the second I saw you that there had to be some kind of trouble. An old man like me doesn't get asked by many folks to help them out of a jam. Fire away." He took a last drag on his cigarette, smashed the small remains in an ashtray, took the filter off another and brought it to his lips. *He must have damn good genes to smoke like that and look this healthy,* Jessica thought.

She smiled, relieved, and asked him again if he could remember any deaths in the surrounding area over the past year. He spent half a can of beer thinking out loud, but could come up with nothing.

"I'm real sorry," he said and paused. "That *does* sound kind of strange, being sorry that no one around me has died. Greg, I've known you and your family since your girl was knee high to a grasshopper and little Ricky was only a wish you and Rita both shared. Maybe if you can tell me what kind of trouble you're in, I can help in some way, other than being a walking, talking obit page."

"You wouldn't believe me if I did," Greg said.

"How do you know unless you try?" Mr. Murphy countered.

Greg rose from his chair, pacing between the table and the refrigerator. "Because I'm living it and I'm not one-hundred-percent sure *I* believe what I'm seeing."

Eddie said, "Greg, I think you should give it a try."

Jessica was curious to see if Eddie was right and Mr. Murphy did have a clue locked away within his still-sharp mind. She decided to help press Greg a little further.

"If it can help Selena," she said somberly.

Greg stopped, looked toward the ceiling with resignation and pulled a seat close to Mr. Murphy.

"I hope you have an open mind," he said.

"I supported the hippies in the sixties and voted for Ross Perot. You could say that I'm open to new things."

Jessica and Eddie let Greg spill the entire story out to his neighbor, adding small bits of information when asked. To his credit, Mr. Murphy didn't recoil or look the least bit skeptical. He nodded in all the right places, asked a question here and there and at one point placed a reassuring hand over Greg's. When he was done, Greg slumped in his chair and said, "So, are you going to call the psych ward on us now?"

Mr. Murphy tottered to his fridge and got out another can of Piels. "I think this calls for doubling up on my daily meds." The top popped with a foamy hiss and he took a quick sip. "I'll be right back."

He walked off into the living room. They heard him open a few drawers and mutter a curse when he jammed his knee against an end table. When he returned, he was holding an old photo album, the kind you could have found in discount department stores a couple of decades ago, with little pockets for each picture. He carefully placed it on the table.

"You know, my wife Celia used to love taking pictures. I would tell her she was more Japanese tourist than New Englander."

Jessica and Eddie both gave a reluctant laugh.

"Whenever we went away for at least a week or two, which we did every single summer of our marriage, she had that camera glued to her hand. We'd send bulging envelopes of rolls of film to be developed and she would go out and buy these albums by the gross."

He flipped through the pages, passing snapshots at Gettysburg, the middle-aged Murphys standing side by side outside the National Military Park, then through what looked to be a spring in the Florida Keys. They looked close, happy, enjoying their travels together. "Here we go," he said, pointing at a page of eight pictures, all landscape shots.

"We were in Cape May, must have been the summer of eighty-five. Another couple came with us, the Cranstons. Good people, used to live in the house next to you, Greg. Well, Celia went out one early morning with her camera, said she wanted to take in the scenery. She stopped by this sand dune right here because she said at the time that she saw a beautiful sea bird that she wanted to get a picture of. Except when the film was developed, this is what she got instead."

Their three heads pushed close to one another as they looked at the picture of the sand dune. Sitting in front of it was a small girl, or the faded image of a small girl. She was smiling for the camera, wearing a one-piece bathing suit that stopped mid-thigh and a bathing cap. You could see right through her to the tall sea grass that sprouted behind her. Jessica felt a chill run down her back. No matter how many EB pictures and videos she'd seen, ones involving children still disturbed her.

"It was the damnedest thing, but Celia believed right away that the ghost of that little girl made itself look like that bird so she would take her picture and not be scared. My Celia was a wonderful woman, but she had all the creativity of a block of wood. I guess that's why she took so many pictures, so she could at least appreciate the creativity of the people and places around her. If she believed it was a ghost, and it sure as hell looks like one, well, it kind of opened my eyes. You see, Greg, if you live long enough, I think everyone will have their own ghost story."

Greg had taken control of the album and ran his finger along the picture.

"We know for a fact that the spirit's attraction for Selena was formed before it crossed over. Did you ever notice anyone take a special interest in her? It had to have been a man, late thirties, early forties," Eddie said.

Jessica saw that the rain had finally stopped and the late afternoon sun was trying to break through the departing clouds. She hoped they hadn't dumped too much on Mr. Murphy but she was betting on Eddie at this point. After being a loner for so long, it seemed odd even to her to put so much trust in him. His connecting her to the horrid EB shattered any lapses in faith she might have had in him and his abilities. The things she'd felt made her stomach knot. Despite that, she also sensed she somehow didn't get the whole picture. There were moments when it seemed the flow of images and feelings was cut short. Maybe Eddie was running interference. She wasn't over the moon with the thought. But then, maybe he did it for a reason.

She added, "Selena is a very pretty girl who looks older than she really is. Did you ever notice anyone paying extra attention to her?"

The effect was instant. Mr. Murphy's eyes brightened and he tapped the beer can on the table. "Yes, yes, I have. I think I might know who you're looking for."

Chapter Forty-Three

When the rain let up, Selena asked her mother if she could go to the convenience mart across the street for an iced tea and some snacks. Ricky perked up at the promise of food. Her mother, who was looking more worried, drawing into herself a little more with each passing minute, nodded and said, "Just grab what you need from my wallet."

They hadn't heard from her father since they woke up. No one knew where he was, but her mother kept assuring them he was out blowing off some steam and would be back any minute. He'd looked pretty shaken up last night and she wouldn't be surprised if he found the closest bar to try and drown out what he saw, at least for the afternoon. Odds were he called one of his friends so he'd have someone to talk to. Selena wasn't freaked out by his absence. Right now, she had other things on her mind.

"Can I come?" Ricky asked, donning his baseball cap.

"Stay here. I'll only be a few minutes."

He sneered at her. "No fair. Why should you be the one to pick out what I eat? You'll get something gross like a granola bar. Mom, tell her I can go."

"I can't see why not."

Selena whirled on her brother. "I know you don't understand this, but I need some space! I promise I'll get you a snack that's orange and salty and nasty, just the way you like it."

"Mom!"

"Selena," her mother pleaded.

"I said no!"

She slammed the door behind her before the argument could escalate any further. Sleeping by her twelve-year-old, snot-nosed brother for the past few weeks, and now sharing a bed, was too much. If she didn't get out of that room, she was going to scream.

The first step out the door landed her in a puddle that went up to her ankle. Disgusted, she trudged over to the gas station. But once she was there, she didn't go inside to find food. Instead, she pulled her cell phone out of her shorts pocket and dialed Crissy's number.

"Hey, Sel," Crissy said, answering on the first ring. She'd been afraid that Crissy may have been too freaked out to even talk to her. She knew Julie would have been. Poor Julie. She'd have to think of a way to make things up to her. But that would have to come later.

"Do you have your driver's license yet?" Selena asked.

"I came close the second time I took the test. I fucking can't stand parallel parking. You all right, you know, after everything at the house?"

"Yeah, I'm fine. I was hoping you could borrow your mom's car and come over and pick me up. Guess I'm stuck here." A pair of guys in their early twenties came out of the store, each with a case of Bud under his arms. They almost knocked into each other when they saw her, their eyes taking her in from top to bottom like a couple of jewelers appraising a diamond. She smiled and gave them the finger. She wasn't in the mood for typical male stupidity at the moment.

Crissy said, "Why didn't you just say that? I don't need my license to drive over and get you."

"But what about your mom? I doubt she'll give you the car without a license."

"She's zoned out in her room. She hit the wine earlier than usual today. Where should I pick you up?"

"At the Mobil station across from the hotel. I'll wait outside."

She figured it would take Crissy about ten minutes to get there, which left her time to buy an iced tea, guzzle it down and follow it with a Red Bull. By the time she was done, and let loose with a tremendous burp when she made sure no one was around, Crissy was pulling up in her mother's Outback, hitting the brakes too hard and causing the car to come to a screeching halt.

"See, I told you it wouldn't be a problem. Where to?"

Selena slid into the car and said, "First, I need to go to Target."

"Target it is." Crissy ground the shifter and sped out of the station.

On the way there, Selena kept staring at her cell phone, deciding when would be the right time to call her mother. She'd start to freak out in about ten or fifteen more minutes. That gave her enough time to do what she needed to do.

Mr. Murphy scratched his head, thinking. "Now, this may amount to a hill of beans, but I did see something a little odd a few months back. Didn't think much of it at the time."

Greg leaned in closer to his neighbor. "Please, anything could help."

Eddie felt a prickling at the back of his skull, as if a fine-toothed comb were being dragged across his brain. It was his body's reaction to what his psyche already knew—the answer was ready to pop.

"I remember back in the spring, I was sitting on the porch reading the paper when I saw your girl walking down the street after school. There was a car driving kind of slow, just a few feet behind her. I remember the car because it was pretty distinctive. Kind of like your car, Greg. It was a bright red Thunderbird, must have been a late seventies model, looked newly restored. Well, it stayed behind her for just a moment, then took off. No big deal. But then I saw it again about a week later, only this time I noticed her say a few words to the person inside."

"Did you get a good look at the driver?" Jessica asked. She had quietly taken her audio recorder out and placed it on the table.

"Can't say that I did. I assumed it was one of the boys at school because she didn't look the least bit worried about it. Both incidents got put into the old storage unit I call my brain, and I only recalled them when I saw the same car drive past her another time going maybe half the speed limit. Again, I assumed it was one of the boys out cruising and trying to impress a pretty girl. Hell, that's all my boy Andy used to do when he was that age."

"How many times in all did you see the car near Selena?" Jessica asked.

Mr. Murphy's brow crinkled, then he replied, "Just the three. Like I said, it's probably nothing."

The tingle in Eddie's skull had turned to a winter chill that permeated his entire head and cascaded down his neck and into his shoulders. A picture was forming, hazy, disjointed, but he could feel it weave itself like a sentient tapestry, and the more he concentrated on it, the less he felt as if he was in the room with the others. Their voices became hollow, distant. Jessica and Greg pressed Mr. Murphy for more details, but most of what he needed was already here, hovering, unseen, in the atmosphere around them. He just had to tap into it, absorb it, concatenate the images until they coalesced into the face of the EB that refused to let go of its earthly craving for Selena.

He interrupted Jessica's line of questioning. "Thank you, Mr.

Murphy. You may have given us something to go on. For now, I think it's best we get Greg back to his family. Would it be all right with you if I needed to come back at a later time, just to pick your brain a little?"

They all rose from their chairs and headed toward the front door with Mr. Murphy at the rear. He said, "That's not a problem at all. Like I said, I'm happy to help in any way I can. You all be careful. I don't pretend to understand what you're in the middle of, but it sounds like it has a nasty side. The best way not to get bit by a junkyard dog is to stay out of the junkyard. But if you have to go in, make sure you're wearing good shoes and you know where the exits are."

Mr. Murphy watched them go from behind his screen door, sipping on his beer.

As they crossed into his yard, Greg asked, "What do we do now?" The time spent in his neighbor's house had calmed him somewhat, but he still looked ready for a fight.

"Eddie was right, we need to get you back to Rita and the kids first. Maybe we should all head back to regroup."

"I don't think that's the best way to go," Eddie said. Jessica raised a finger in protest, so he decided to head things off at the pass. "I'll go back to the hotel with Greg. I can get anything we need from your room and bring it back here. Jess, you should stay at the house in case something happens while we're gone."

Greg ran his hands through his hair, tugging on the ends in frustration. "Jesus, I bet Rita's flipping out right now. I didn't exactly tell her where I was going. Then again, I hadn't planned on all of this. I thought I'd be back in a half hour, tops. Do you think what Mr. Murphy said about the red Thunderbird really means anything?"

"I'm not entirely sure," Eddie replied. "Why don't you start the car up while I get the list of things that Jessica needs and her room key."

"Yeah. I can drop you back off when you're ready."

When he got Jessica alone by her Jeep she whirled on him. "What are you up to? I don't like being left in the dark."

He held up his hands. "Hold on a sec. I don't want to push Greg to DEFCON one. Mr. Murphy was right on about the car. It has something to do with our rogue EB. I can feel its energy all around here, like it's rooted to this local area. I don't want to risk it attaching itself to you as a power source and leading it right to Selena. It's better if you stay here. I'll reunite Greg with his family, then I plan to get them out of the hotel and as far from the EB as I can. I'll know they're at a safe distance when I feel the break in its, for lack of a better word, pulse. Right now, it's sending out waves all over this place, and I think I've gotten familiar enough with it now to distinguish it from the usual spiritual white noise that I see and feel every day."

"I can't believe I'm the one making things worse," she said, kicking a tire with a dull grunt. "Well, I can't just sit here. I think I'll drive around while we still have some light, see if I can find any vintage Thunderbirds on the street or in a driveway."

"If you do, just note where it is and get the hell away. I don't want you too close to the source. It could be bad for you as much as Selena. It knows you know, and it doesn't want you in the way." There was more he wanted to tell her, *needed* to tell her, but it had to wait. If he did, he worried how she would react, and he needed her to remain strong and convinced they could end this.

"Got it. See you back here in about an hour?" Jessica said.

"That should be enough time. Remember, if you see the car, write down the address it's near and haul ass."

She gave him a mock salute. "Aye-aye, Captain."

He knew she wasn't used to taking orders and was encouraged that she seemed to have enough confidence in him to not fight him every step of the way. He whispered, "John Backman, what did you get me into?" as he walked to Greg's car. All the way back to the hotel, he could feel the EB's life-force as it cast a wide net, searching for its prey.

Chapter Forty-Four

Moments after Jessica's Jeep pulled down the street in search of the car Mr. Murphy had described, Selena and Crissy rolled into the driveway with a suspension-groaning stop.

"Good, no one's here," Selena said, grabbing the plastic bag from the back seat.

Crissy followed her into the house. "Don't you think you should call your mother now?"

"I thought all you goths were anti-authority?"

"Yeah, we are when our moms are emotional wrecks that think the sky is pink. Your mom is actually nice and I'm sure ready to call the cops."

Selena turned the phone over and over in her hands, pondering. On the one hand, she didn't want her mother or father to interfere. This was something she had to handle on her own. Jessica and Eddie were nice and seemed super concerned, but she had a strong feeling that she was the only one that could put an end to this. The ghost had attacked her in her sleep. Now it was her turn to *attack it.*

On the other hand, she was terrified, and she wasn't too old to crave the strength and comfort of her parents at a time like this.

She grumbled in exasperation, and hit speed dial for her mother. At the very least, she could assure her that she was fine and would be back soon.

"Smart decision," Crissy reassured her.

The phone rang until voicemail clicked on. "Hi, Mom, it's me. I just wanted to let you know not to worry. I had to get out of that hotel room, so I decided to call Julie. Her sister picked me up and I'm at her house now. I'm gonna stay for dinner, but I'll come back right after. Love you."

Crissy rolled her eyes, "Oh, that'll make things way better."

"If she listens to my message soon, at least it'll buy us some time. I'm a big girl. I can deal with the consequences. Come on, let's go to my room and get this started."

She was at first taken aback by the state of her room, especially her bed. It looked as if people had been dancing on it. She hoped those people were the living kind, like Jessica and Eddie, and not her double walker or the other thing that they were going to try to communicate with.

Selena unwrapped and laid out the Ouija board she had purchased in the toy section at Target. She placed the plastic planchette in the center of the board.

"You're sure you know how to work this?" she asked Crissy.

"I used to do it all the time with my cousin Dee when we would visit them in Bridgton. We talked to all kinds of crazy spirits."

"And you're positive it wasn't just your cousin messing with you?"

"No way. There was this one time we tapped into the spirit of some dude who said he had died in one of the mills that used to be all over the town. He wanted to know if we could tell him where his wife was. Dee was so freaked out, she started crying. She may be a drama queen, but even she can't act that well."

Selena nodded. "Okay, you're the expert. What do we do first?"

Crissy reached out and held Selena's hands. "First, we need to get real quiet and think positive thoughts. We have to prepare ourselves so the spirit knows we're ready to talk."

Earlier, Selena had asked Crissy if she was worried about the ghost attacking them again. Remarkably, Crissy found the entire thing too cool to pass up. She had assured her that the Ouija board, in giving the spirit a channel to communicate with them, would focus its energy on that, rather than lashing out physically. Selena assumed that goths knew more about these things than anyone else, maybe even more than Jessica who seemed pretty normal (at least for someone who looked for ghosts for fun), and she was very glad for the company. As much as she wanted to confront this ghost, she wasn't sure she would have the guts to do it alone.

When they were younger, Crissy had always been the strong one, the first one to seek out adventure, like the time they explored the abandoned house on Verner Street and the floor gave way under their feet. They'd ended up in the basement, shaken but not hurt. Crissy had laughed her head off and continued to explore the house as if nothing had happened.

Selena had always admired that in Crissy, and she was hoping to steal a bit of courage from her today.

"We'll just sit here for a few minutes and stay as silent as possible," Crissy continued. "When I let go of your hands, place just your fingertips on the planchette. I'll start asking questions and if we make contact, you can jump in any time. You ready for this?"

Selena took a deep breath, as if she were about to dive into the deep end of the pool. "Not really, but let's get this done."

They closed their eyes and turned inward. For her part, Selena thought of her grandmother who had passed away when she was ten. She used to love helping her make cookies from scratch. Crissy said to think positive thoughts. She couldn't imagine anything more positive than visiting her grandma's kitchen on a sunny afternoon, laughing while they mixed a batch of Boston drop cookies and listened to salsa music on her old radio perched on the windowsill. She could almost smell them baking in the oven.

The vision was as real as the mattress beneath her. For the moment, she was in that kitchen and felt the warm softness of her grandma as they danced and laughed. She looked up at her grandma and said, "You'll watch out for me forever, right?"

Before she could answer, Crissy's hands fell away and she opened her eyes, gently placing her fingers atop the planchette.

"Just keep your hands and arms loose. When we make contact, it'll start to move a little, then build up steam until it starts pointing to different letters. We should both pay attention to the order it goes in so we know what it's trying to say."

A hard gust of wind came whistling into her window, blowing some loose papers off her desk. It startled them both, but they regained their composure.

"Hello, my name is Crissy, this is my friend Selena. We'd like to make contact with the ghost that keeps coming here to this room. We don't mean you any harm. We just want to talk to you. Can you please let us know if you can hear my voice?"

The planchette didn't move. Selena stared at it, biting her lip. Crissy persisted.

"I know that you've been trying to connect with Selena. She wants to know who you are and what you want. Don't be afraid. We've opened ourselves to you and only ask the same of you. Please follow my voice and move the planchette to the 'yes' on the board to confirm that you understand."

They waited ten seconds.

Thirty.

Then several minutes. Nothing happened.

In fact, Selena was beginning to feel comfortable in her room for the first time since seeing her double walker in the closet. Maybe Jessica and Eddie had come back and done something to send the ghost to the light.

"Maybe you should try asking it something," Crissy suggested.

Selena swallowed to clear her throat. "Um, if it's me you really have been wanting to talk to, I'm here to listen and I'm not afraid this time."

She drew in a sharp breath when she heard, rather than saw, the planchette begin to move. It slowly scratched along the board, tilting to one side, then moving with more force as it settled into a counter-clockwise rotation, stopping at nothing in particular.

Crissy's eyes were wide and sparkled with the thrill of opening communication with a spirit. Selena's heart was racing so hard, she found it hard to breathe.

The planchette settled into a steady figure-eight motion, now moving with incredible ease. Even when Selena decreased the pressure her fingers exacted on the planchette until it was just a feathery connection, it continued as if it had a will of its own.

It tilted to the right, zeroing in on the first letter.

"W," Crissy said.

It moved up the next row and to the left, settling on the letter H.

Then back down to Y.

"Why what?" Crissy asked.

The planchette slid across to the letter N, followed by the O and T.

It moved back to the center of the board and stopped.

"Why not?" Selena whispered. She looked at Crissy. "What does that mean?"

"I forgot to warn you. Sometimes, they talk in riddles or half thoughts. It takes a while to decipher what they mean."

Selena asked aloud, "I don't know what you mean by 'why not'. Can you explain?"

This time, the planchette moved to the YES on the upper left corner of the board so fast that she had to dive toward Crissy to keep from losing all contact with it.

Crissy started calling out the letters again.

"A...F...R..."

The planchette stalled for a moment, and before Selena could ask if it was still with them, it glided to the letter A.

Then I, and settling on D.

"Why not afraid?" Crissy said.

It circled back to the *YES*.

"Holy crap, I started by saying I *wasn't* afraid," Selena said. Was it asking her why she wasn't afraid? Could it see into her soul and know it was just false bravado?

"Maybe because we're alive and you're not," Crissy said. "We don't even know who you are. Can you confirm that you're the one that keeps coming here?"

The planchette jerked hard to the right, then circled back onto the *YES*.

Selena was no longer sure that she wanted to talk to this ghost. This was all too much. From seeing her double to being attacked by something in her sleep and now talking to a ghost that wondered why she wasn't afraid was more than she could handle.

"Crissy, I think we should stop."

"Don't you want to know for sure? Maybe we can get it to cross over or at least get the point that you want to be left alone."

"I really don't—"

Both girls recoiled as an electric charge shot from the center of the planchette. They stared in horror as it began to move without the need of their touch.

This time, it shifted with incredible speed, lingering on a letter only long enough for them to say it aloud in fear-struck tones before darting to the next.

"Y...O...U...B...E...M...I...N...E," Crissy read the letters aloud.

Selena's hands flew to her open mouth. "Oh my God!"

The planchette continued to move while Crissy backed off the bed.

"M...I...N...E."

Selena screamed. "No! You can't have me! I won't let you!"

It veered back over to *YES*, backing off and landing back on it over and over, as if to emphasize its malevolent promise. She shouted when Crissy pulled her off the bed and onto her feet. The room smelled like freshly struck matches and the air felt as if it had been vacuumed out of the room. It was difficult to draw a solid breath.

Crissy yelled, "We have to get out of here, now!"

Selena's legs shook, but she willed her feet to move as fast as they could.

She stumbled against the bedpost and stifled a cry when she felt a cold hand pull at her shirt. The fabric was taut against her chest.

Selena watched in horror as a dent the size and shape of a fingertip moved from her belly to between her breasts.

"Crissy, help," she whimpered. She couldn't move if she wanted to.

Something was holding her in place.

A deep, malevolent cackle rumbled from every corner of the room.

The finger made a slow circle around her right breast, moving closer and closer to her nipple.

Crissy let out a cry and slammed into Selena with a sharp hip check. It hurt like hell, but it also broke the entity's grip.

Selena grabbed hold of Crissy's hand and they struggled to remain upright. Her legs had never felt so leaden.

"Run!" Crissy ordered.

One simple word was enough to send up the last bits of adrenaline left in her body.

As they sprinted toward the door, the planchette shot forward, missing Selena's arm and burying itself two inches deep into the thick wood. They jumped when it snapped with a loud crack.

The floor buckled, like the vinyl of a loaded bouncy castle. It almost made them fall headfirst down the stairs. Selena's body swiveled into the stairway wall as she gripped the banister. Somehow, she managed to hold on to Crissy and keep her from pitching into a deadly plunge.

They fled from the house, their voices paralyzed. Neither heard the resonant laughter that chased their heels to the front door.

Chapter Forty-Five

"Holy shit, Jessica, do you want me to come up there?" Angela Bastiani said after Jessica unloaded the details of their New Hampshire insanity. She'd decided to use the time cruising the neighborhood to make a few calls and let her friend know she was still alive, but definitely in the weeds with the investigation.

"Ange, if you were here for this, you would go running right back to Long Island." She laughed for the first time in days. It felt good.

"How are things with Eddie? It sounds like he's been a pretty big help."

"I have to admit, I'm kinda glad he's here. I think I may be learning some things about myself, and you know how much I hate introspection."

"It's not one of your stronger points. From what you tell me, I'm surprised you've let him take the reins. That is so totally not your style."

Jessica had to slow to look down a driveway, past a parked Toyota. There was a red car in front of it, pressed against the tan garage door. It turned out to be another Toyota. Not what she was looking for.

"You could say that again. He's earning his stripes. If he can help get this family out of this mess, I may promote him to full-time partner. That is, if he would even want to do this again. Contact really takes a physical toll on him. I would understand if he opted for a quieter life."

"There has to be a bigger reason why your father reached out to him and brought him to your door, so to speak. Right?"

Jessica turned another corner, noted that the gray skies were now turning a darker shade of purple. Pretty soon, she would have to head back to the house and wait for Eddie to return.

"I think that's part of the reason why I've let him break my house rules. I keep thinking that somehow, my father is the one calling the shots. I know that sounds weird."

"Jess, if it came from anyone else, it would, but I've known you too long. I have a strong feeling you're right."

They talked for a few more minutes, with Jessica promising to call the next day to keep her up to date. It was now too dark to see, what with so many streets without working streetlights, a sign of the faltering economy. She drove back to the Leighs' house. Then, she called home.

Eve answered after the first ring. "Jessica, I've been worried sick."

"I know. Things have been a little crazy here. I've barely slept the past couple of nights and this investigation seems to be on a twenty-four-hour-a-day cycle."

She recounted the events of the past few days, just as she had with Angela, with one exception. She didn't tell her about Eddie's earlier contact with her dad. That was something best left for another time. She wasn't sure Eve could handle it.

"So when do you think you'll be coming home?" Eve asked.

"I really don't know. Soon, I hope. I have a feeling Eddie is on to something."

"He's the real deal, huh?"

"I think so, yeah."

"Then you should tell him."

Eve didn't need to expand on her sentence. The meaning was crystal clear.

Angela was the only other living person who knew what had happened in the cabin in Alaska when she was six. Eve's parents had known, of course, but they had passed away several years ago. And the others, those from the small town left behind, well, they had never been able to cope with what they had experienced.

Eddie knew some details about it, but she was sure most of them were false. In the paranormal field, what had happened to her family was the stuff of rumor. Eve had to spend a good deal of money keeping things out of the paper, not that that area of Alaska was a media hotbed. Still, tiny bits did get out, though most of it fabricated. But no matter how wild the false stories were, none came close to the high strangeness and sheer terror of the truth.

If her father had sought Eddie out, then he must have wanted him to know the truth, *her truth*, as well. And now here was Aunt Eve, still on the same page with her father just as they had been when he was alive.

Eve said, "You know, kiddo, Liam and I can always come up to New Hampshire and offer some moral support. The last time I was there I must have been nine or ten. We stopped there for a couple of days on our way to Maine. It would be nice to see it again."

Jess knew this wasn't a question. Eve was coming, whether she wanted her to or not.

"How about this? As soon as this is over, I'll call and you and Liam pack your bags. We can all use a nice vacation. Maybe we'll explore here a little bit, then find a nice island or something off the coast of Maine." As soon as she said it, she was flushed with a sense of anticipation, coming to the realization that she needed some time to recharge. Between college and her paranormal investigations, this one especially, the past couple of years had been a whirlwind of nonstop motion. She needed a break before she broke.

"I like that. I'll look for places to go, if you promise you can do two whole weeks without looking at your laptop or searching for ghosts."

"EBs," she corrected her.

"Fine, EBs. And don't forget to talk to Eddie. At this point, he deserves to know."

"I will."

She disconnected the call feeling a little lighter.

Then she looked at the Leighs' house, now shrouded in night, and the smile dissolved from her face. An evil pall had possessed the fibers of the house, the upper windows staring back at her like a pair of soulless eyes. She hoped she wasn't giving strength to the EB now, and silently urged Eddie to return.

"This isn't good," Greg said as they pulled up to the space just outside their hotel room. Rita and Ricky stood by the open door. Rita was wringing her hands and looked as if she was about to scream.

"What's the matter? Did something happen to Selena?" Greg asked, jumping out of the car before turning off the ignition.

"Where were you?" Rita asked, her harsh tone leaving no room for hesitation on his part.

Ricky attached himself to Greg's side, relieved to see his father. He said, "Selena disappeared, Dad. She said she was going to bring back something to drink and eat, but she never came back."

"What?"

Rita regarded him with pursed lips. "I was hoping she was with you, but I can see that's not the case."

"Oh Christ," Greg hissed, walking in a tight circle, his nervous energy returning and going at NASCAR speed. "When did she leave the room?"

"Over an hour ago. I couldn't call you because you left your phone here and you took our goddamn car!"

Eddie didn't need to be a psychic to realize that things were about to blow. The Leighs had had it tough when they were acting as one solid unit. Now things were fracturing, in every way possible. It felt as if they were playing right into a pre-determined plan set in motion around the time of his and Jessica's arrival.

"Has she tried calling you?" Eddie asked.

"I wouldn't know. My cell is dead and I left the charger back at the house." He noticed her take a step back when Greg tried to place his hand on her shoulder.

"Do you have any idea where she might have gone?" Eddie asked.

"She was getting antsy and irritable before she left, so at first I assumed she needed to walk a bit. Now I'm just hoping she called one of her friends and went to their house. I couldn't even use your phone because your damn job put that goddamn password on it."

"I'll call Julie's dad," Greg said. He walked a few feet away to make the call.

Acting on a feeling that had started to build in intensity since they had arrived, Eddie asked Rita, "Is there a chance she went back to the house?"

Rita shook her head. "She's terrified of it. That's the last place she'd go."

Greg came back to them, his face grave. "Julie's father said she's not there. I also called Ashley and Wendy's parents. Nothing."

"Do you have Crissy's number?" Eddie asked, wondering why he wouldn't call the girl who had been close enough to sleep over the night before.

"No. Their friendship is relatively new, in a manner of speaking. They hadn't talked to one another much since they got to high school," Rita said.

"All right, everyone in the car. We'll drive over to Crissy's house," Greg said as he opened the passenger side doors.

Rita ran back into the room. "Wait! I'll leave a note for her just in case she comes back before we do."

Greg tore out of the parking lot as if the Grim Reaper were in hot pursuit. Eddie apologized to Ricky when he slid over and crushed him against the door.

He knew they wouldn't find Selena at Crissy's, but he had to let Greg and Rita find out for themselves. Despite the desire to white knuckle the drive, he closed his eyes and searched for Selena and the EB. Sooner or later, one of them would turn up. If they were lucky, Selena would be free and clear from the spirit's range.

Chapter Forty-Six

It was moments before the stars began to blink their way into existence in the sky when Greg's car came to a screeching halt in front of Jessica's Jeep. Greg jumped out of the car and ran to the house, fumbling with his keys.

"What happened?" Jessica asked Eddie.

"Selena's missing. We just came back from Crissy's house. Her mother's car and Crissy are both gone, so we assume they're together. Have you seen them at all?"

This was bad. The last thing they needed was the target of the EB's infatuation on the loose and with no one to protect her, not that they had done an admirable job to this point.

"I've been in the car waiting for you for the past twenty minutes and didn't see them. Maybe they're in the house?"

"Let's see."

Rita and Ricky were now inside as well, all calling Selena's name. By the time they walked through the door, Rita was close to tears. "She's not here."

Greg entered the room and stormed past them. "I'm going to drive to the beach, see if they parked there with the other kids. I'll call you and let you know if I find her or not."

Rita nodded. "I'll plug my phone in now."

Eddie looked up toward the stairs and motioned for Jessica to join him. "Do you mind if we check her room, just to make sure nothing else has happened there?"

Rita nodded and grabbed hold of her son. With each heartbreaking scene Jessica witnessed with this family, she became angrier and angrier with the EB that was torturing them, and with herself for being the source of its increasing power.

"What do you sense?" she said in a low voice to Eddie.

"Whatever it is, it's residual, but it might point us in the right direction."

The first thing they noticed was the plastic planchette half-embedded in the door. A Ouija board lay on the floor. It looked as if the shiny surface had been scorched with a match.

Eddie muttered, "Fucking Ouija boards. Why does it always come down to ignorant kids messing around with these damn things? They have to take this shit out of the toy aisles."

Jessica picked up the Ouija board and examined the burn marks. It looked as if the planchette had taken off on the board like a jet tearing down a runway.

"They made contact with him," Eddie said. He tried to pull the planchette free, succeeding in breaking off the end. "I'm guessing they didn't like what he had to say. They were scared as hell, I can tell you that. I can taste it, like bad cologne left in someone's wake. They ran out of the house, took off in Crissy's car. We can hope they went back to the hotel and saw the note her mother left."

Jessica broke the board over her knee and tucked the pieces under her arm. The theory that using a Ouija board opened up portals best left untouched was a hotly debated one in the paranormal field. Some swore to the positive validity of their use, while others warned against it, like telling your child not to do drugs. A third camp thought it was all nonsense and its place in toy stores as a novelty was fitting. She had heard enough stories about Ouija boards gone wrong to adopt a stance that they should be avoided at all costs.

But Selena and Crissy were just kids, and not exposed to ongoing debates. One thing Jessica had to give them was credit for balls. Not many girls, or men for that matter, would have returned to the scene of a horrific paranormal event to make contact with the EB that had just scared the life out of you. Maybe that trait was the very thing that attracted it to her in the first place.

"So now what do we do?"

Eddie shrugged. "I guess we wait and see if Greg can find Selena, or if she comes back here. I can feel that she's not far, but that's about it. I'm assuming you didn't see any red Thunderbirds sitting out in the open?"

"No. I knew I wouldn't get that lucky. Think of it. If someone takes the time to restore a T-Bird, wouldn't they store it in a garage and not leave it out in the elements?"

Eddie looked around the room, lingering on the window. "I know he's close."

"I'll go down with Rita, try to keep her calm. You can stay up here and read vibrations or whatever it is you can do if you want."

He stopped her by lightly grabbing her wrist. "There's something I have to tell you."

Her heart sank. If he had more bad news, she didn't know what she would do. Things were getting out of control in a hurry, and for the first time ever, she was beginning to feel she was in over her head. She wondered if this was how her father felt during their last days in Alaska, and most especially in the hours leading up to their final night.

Dad, if you can hear me, I need your help. No one knows what's going on here better than you. Please, tell me what to do.

"Do I get a choice between good and bad news?"

"I wish it was that easy. I know that at this moment, he, *it's*, back to its hiding place, the one area it feels safe, building up its strength for another go at Selena. It's had a taste of her, and it's been driven mad with desire. If we don't find her soon, *it will*, and when she walks away from all of this, she'll never be the same. The EB will make sure of that."

Jessica had to restrain herself from punching the wall. The twisted EB had been playing them like a handful of toy figures.

"The only thing we have going for us now is that Selena's not close to you, and neither is the EB at the moment."

"How much time do you think we have to find this damn thing before it goes apocalyptic?"

Eddie looked at his watch. "A few hours, tops. The charge of fear that Selena gave off when she and Crissy were here with the Ouija board was enough to put it over the edge."

"Then let's get in my car and have you lead us to it. Do you think you've made enough of a connection so you can find it?"

"I'm pretty sure I have, but there's more. I need to be with Selena. I know how this thing works and I know I can protect her when it makes another try at her. If I go looking for it with Selena, I'm delivering her to it on a silver platter, and if I'm wrong and can't keep her safe, I don't know how I can live with that."

Jessica said, "And we both know you can't leave her with me. So what do I do? Drive to Boston and wait it out until you give me the all-clear?"

The thought of backing out made her blood boil, but if she had to do it for Selena's sake, she'd tear ass down I495 right away.

"Look, I can communicate with it, but I'm not the kind of TV psychic that can make a spirit walk into the light and cross over. To tell you the truth, after talking with spirits all my life, I'm still not sure what goes on when we die and what the rules are. When a spirit truly moves on, I can see them no better than you can talk to Jesus. It's only the ones that linger for one reason or another that communicate with me, and they don't have a clue about what lies next, either.

"You're the one that has the gift to send this thing away, whether it's heaven, hell or the Arby's in Worcester. Without you, there's no telling when this will end."

"Yeah, but you said it knows what I can do and won't play into it. What good am I then?"

He was about to answer when the front door flew open downstairs and Rita screamed.

Chapter Forty-Seven

Eddie was relieved to see the mini family reunion in the living room. Rita had Selena in a bear hug and kept repeating, "Please don't do that ever again. I love you so much."

Selena was barely able to return the hug because her arms were pinned to her sides. Even her little brother had come up behind her and buried his face in her back.

When Rita broke her embrace, still holding on to her daughter's arms, she said, "When this is all over, we'll figure out what the punishment will be for making us worry. Your father is still out looking for you and Crissy."

"So, I guess you know that she borrowed her mom's car to get me." Selena could hardly bring herself to look her mother in the eye.

"You say borrowed, she says stole. Don't worry about Crissy. She has her own music to face. What on earth were you thinking?"

Eddie saw Selena steal a glance at the broken board tucked under Jessica's arm and her eyes widened just enough for him to take note of her fear of discovery. Jessica saw it too and put her finger to her mouth, letting her know this particular secret was better left unsaid for now.

"I...I just needed to get away for a little bit and clear my head," Selena said weakly.

Rita frowned. "I can't even begin to tell you how dumb that was."

"I know," she answered, just above a whisper, and Eddie knew she was sincere. Her bravery had exposed her to a harsh reality and it had rocked her. That she was even back in the house was a credit to her resolve. She was one tough kid.

"We were just driving around, and then I asked Crissy to take me back to the hotel and I saw your note. I realized that I need to be with you and dad and even Ricky. I can't face this alone, even though I thought for a little bit that I could. Please don't be mad at me."

Rita pulled her in for another hug, and this time there were tears for both.

Ricky walked over to Eddie and Jessica and said, "Can you make it stop now?"

Jessica leaned down so her face was level with the boy. "I promise that tonight, Eddie and I are going to do everything we can to put an end to this."

Rita called Greg and told him the good news. He said he was just a few miles away and would be back in a few minutes.

Eddie felt a building tension in the house ever since Selena's return, and it had nothing to do with the emotional outburst between her and her mother. His head felt like a heavy burlap sack that was slowly being filled with wet cement.

Jessica flashed the broken Ouija board to him and said, "I'm going to throw this in the garbage outside. When I get back, maybe you can tell me what the best plan of attack should be."

"In the kitchen, away from Rita and the kids."

She gave him a thumbs-up and went out the back door.

Greg walked in the front door at almost the exact same moment, and the smile on his face brought Selena running to his outstretched arms. "You trying to give your old man a heart attack?" he said into her mussed hair. "My life insurance policy isn't the best, so you might want to try and keep me around a little longer."

"I'm so sorry, Daddy."

They talked and hugged in a way that told Eddie it had been some time since they had shared a close moment. It happened all the time when daddy's little girl transformed into a young woman. Most fathers hadn't a clue how to adapt to the brave new world a teenage girl brought them kicking and screaming into. Sometimes, it took a crisis to restore their special bond. He'd spoken to many mournful spirits over the years that lamented not having the chance to hold their grown-up daughters one more time. Their experience, their knowledge, the wisdom of the dead, in turn made Eddie an old soul.

Lessons from the dead. He could teach a four-year class on the wealth of material he'd been given from the other side.

He jumped when he felt a hand on his shoulder.

Jessica said, close to his ear, "Great, they're all here, but so am I. What should I do now so I don't put them in any more danger?"

They walked into the kitchen. They could have set off a cherry bomb and none of the Leighs would have noticed their presence. At its essence, that was a good thing.

Eddie said, low enough so his voice didn't carry into the living room, "I need to make one more connection with the EB so I can pinpoint its ground zero. Once I do, and if it's as close as I think it is, we can jump in the car and get it before it gets her. It's not ready yet, but it's building like a tsunami. The key is that I need you there, right where it lives, so to speak."

"And what about Selena?"

"Like I said, we need to strike right now. I'm going to go to her room and do my damnedest to get into its head. You stay here and keep them together. It should take me five, ten minutes, tops. It's like driving. Once you've been to a certain place, getting there the next time is that much easier. Just be ready to dash when I come back down."

"That I can do." She patted the car keys in her pocket.

Before he headed back up to Selena's room, she said, "Hey, be careful."

He smirked. "I didn't know you cared."

She rolled her eyes and shooed him out of the kitchen.

He was glad she couldn't detect the dread he felt about the prospect of connecting with the EB again. This time he would have to go deeper, and there were things in its soul better left unseen. He kept an image of Selena and Jessica in his mind to keep him strong, to push him further than he would ever want to go, and with that, settled into the lotus position on her bed in the dark room and closed his eyes.

Selena told her parents she needed a drink so she could go to the kitchen and speak to Jessica.

"Thank you," she said. It was difficult to keep her voice from fluttering. She'd screwed up big time and Jessica was her only hope now. Every time she thought things couldn't get worse, they did.

Jessica leaned in close and whispered, "Promise me right here and now that you'll never, ever mess with a Ouija board again. You may have just made things worse."

Hearing that from Jessica made her knees weak. She nodded. "I promise." She looked back to make sure her parents weren't listening in and added, "It said that I should be afraid and I would belong to it. Then the planchette-thingy went crazy and smashed into the door like a dart. We weren't even touching it when it did that. I wanted to face it down, tell it I wasn't afraid, and now I'm more scared than ever."

Jessica lightly touched her face. "I know. You didn't ask for any of this to happen and to tell you the truth, I may have done the same thing if I was your age and in your shoes. I never was one for taking things lying down. For the rest of the night, though, I need you to do exactly what we say, you got it?"

"Got it."

"Good. Now get something to drink or your parents will be suspicious. Your little secret is safe with me."

Selena felt an ache in her bladder that had started when she was in Crissy's car, both girls driving nowhere in particular and frantically recounting what had happened with the Ouija board.

Jessica said, "I also have to ask you a couple of questions that may help us pinpoint the source of the EB that's attached itself to you. We think we can track it down tonight."

Relief swept through her body. They could track it down...tonight! She was starting to feel as if she would be trapped forever between an entity that wanted to attack her and a double walker that wanted to scare her.

Jessica asked, "Do you remember someone in a red classic car driving next to you, maybe even stopping to talk to you, when you walked home from school? Can you recall that person's face?"

Selena twisted a bottle of water in her hands and thought. Guys stopped to hit on her all the time, and it wasn't always unappreciated.

Then she remembered the old guy.

"Yes, I do. There was this guy, maybe a little older than my dad. A couple of times he pulled up to ask me directions. The first time it happened, I didn't think anything of it. When he asked the second time, I just figured he was an old creep. I didn't see him after that, though, so I kinda forgot about him."

"Can you tell me what he looked like?"

Selena shook her head. "Not really. I remember he had tinted windows and the interior of the car was dark, so it was hard to make out his face."

Jessica was about to ask another question when she cut in.

"Can I go to the bathroom? I gotta pee."

Jessica took a moment to mull over her request. Considering all that had happened, Selena couldn't blame her for the hesitation. With obvious reluctance, she said, "Yes, but you have to use the bathroom down here. I don't want you any farther from us."

"Will do."

The small bathroom was just off the kitchen and was her father's sanctuary. A magazine basket filled with well-thumbed copies of *Sports Illustrated* and *Newsweek* sat between the toilet and sink. She took a moment to lean against the sink and calm her nerves. Even if Jessica and Eddie somehow managed to make everything go away, she wasn't sure she could ever spend another night in this house.

Being scared or anxious always made her have to pee, and she was surprised she had lasted this long without letting off the mounting pressure on her bladder. She unbuttoned her shorts and pulled them down with her panties.

"Oh my God that feels good."

It felt as if she hadn't gone to the bathroom in weeks and the stream came out in a never-ending rush.

As she went to pick up a *Newsweek*, the light suddenly went out, immersing her in total darkness. The bathroom had no window, so she didn't even have the weak glow of twilight to see by.

There was a soft tap on the tile floor, and she gasped when air in the cramped room changed, becoming icy and thick. It was like trying to draw a breath through a cold, wet towel. Her heartbeat burst into high gear until she could hear the pounding of its overworked valves in her ears.

She bent down to pull up her shorts and shrieked when a pair of arctic hands clutched her wrists, pinning them to her sides.

She barely managed to cry out, "No!"

The rest of her words were cut off. She was being suffocated. Something blocked her nose and mouth and she struggled to draw a breath while the cold, invisible hands moved to her thighs, slowly creeping inward.

Chapter Forty-Eight

This time around, finding the EB was much easier for Eddie. It was as simple as a bloodhound tracking the scent of a ripe, decomposing body. That's how strong and repugnant the essence of this EB was, and in its growing confidence, it no longer felt the need to exert its efforts to mask its presence.

He had managed to yank the planchette free from the door and used the psychic residue left on it to amplify his own abilities at locating spirits beyond the veil. The broken triangle of plastic sat in his upturned hands.

In his mind, he sat atop an old milk crate within the doorway of the open barn, his psychic talisman. He felt like a farmer, waiting for the cows to come home, except this would be no ordinary night on the farm. Even the flies on the wall would shriek by what they saw. Groping for the tether that had fabricated between them from their brief encounters, he merely had to pull, dragging it into his realm.

It came, and it was awful beyond measure.

"Got you," he said aloud, keeping his body still, his eyes closed.

The EB was startled at first, much as a rat would be when disturbed in its lair, gnawing on a stolen scrap of food. It appeared to him as a dark, purple blob where occasional sparks lit up within like firing neurons. Eddie tried again to get a sense of what it had looked like in life. It was impossible. What it had become could no longer remember the contours and facets of its earthbound shell. When the man had died, his soul had exploded from his body, reveling in the freedom from limitations and the overall weakness of the human condition. In death, it had, for the first time, found true life.

Everything about this EB made him recoil, but he had to stay focused. This wasn't an experiment in The Rhine, or the cry of a helpless spirit in the night when he was alone in his room. For once, he had been the seeker, and he didn't like what he'd found.

He felt the EB turn its full attention on him.

"You'll never get me," it said in a low, scratchy tone. It was like listening to an old, worn record.

"I guess that's why you keep running from us." As much as it repulsed him to do it, he needed to maintain contact as long as he could. Each passing second would bring him closer to the EB's source.

The EB laughed. *"You're the one who should be running now."*

The planchette jumped from Eddie's hand and smacked into the opposite wall. Eddie didn't flinch. He knew it could see what he could see, so he opened his eyes and found the plastic piece on the floor.

It began to vibrate like a ball bearing on a drum skin, then lifting until it was balanced on one corner. With an outward push from his mind, Eddie made the planchette go airborne, drifting across the room until it was nestled back in his hands.

"See, I can do it, too, and I didn't have to die to make it happen."

The EB reacted by emitting a pulse of fury that washed over him like low tide in a diseased ocean. Again, he didn't react, which only added to the EB's anger.

Its defenses were crumbling. He needed to prod it just a little bit more, like Jessica had done with the EB back in New York. This was new territory for him. He'd always been passive, open, understanding. Prodding a spirit to make it angry could be dangerous, but it had to be done.

"Do you have any other tricks? I love magic shows."

"I can show you what I want as a treat."

Eddie's mind was overpowered with a burst of images along with a painful thrumming of emotions and impulses, each one more horrifying than the next. He saw the undefined shadow of a man, hiding in a darkened room by a solitary window. The shadow wore women's clothes. It moved about the room, mimicking the walk of a woman. Eddie delved deeper, until he could see through the EB's eyes. *Dear God, no.* It was watching Selena, blissfully unaware that a predator watched her every move as she walked home from school. He experienced the abominable impulses that had controlled it when it was alive.

"Ungh!"

Eddie reeled back on the bed. His back arched and his arms and legs were splayed as if tied to stakes. The shard of the planchette dropped to the floor. Every pore in his body opened up, releasing a torrent of cold sweat on his clammy skin.

It was worse than he could have imagined.

The man, though monster would have been more appropriate, had lived in another country until his forties. Eddie saw snow and close city streets, heard people speaking in English and French, and knew it had been Montreal when he saw the deep emerald dome of St. Joseph's Oratory. Eddie had stayed with a friend in Montreal one spring break and remembered clearly the magnificent holy sanctuary.

Images melted into one another until they formed a pattern. A parade of young, underage girls, some walking home from school without a care in the world, others in darkened rooms, reduced to quivering balls of terror and confusion.

He had stalked them. The lucky ones only became part of the menagerie of his sick, masturbatory fantasies. But there were others, so many, where he could not be satisfied by mere stolen glances or surreptitious photos. He had to feel their perfect, unblemished skin, taste their tears, and so much worse.

Eddie shook his head back and forth, fighting now to break their connection. He couldn't stand the perverted pleasure the man took from their pain, the innocence he claimed and devoured like a force of nature.

Still, the portraits of a demon in human form came. In his struggle to free himself, Eddie's telekinetic abilities were let loose, and small objects throughout Selena's room hovered in the air, waiting for his cue where to go.

"Get...the fuck...out of my head!" he shouted.

The reply was chilling. *"Better to be in the house."*

With a heavy *whoosh* that could be felt, not heard, everything turned off at once. Eddie's body relaxed as pens, a hair brush, papers, loose change and a pair of headphones crashed to the floor.

He sat up quickly, despite his mental and physical fatigue, because there was screaming coming from downstairs, followed by loud banging. The room was pitch-black and the hallway light had been turned off. His body protested as he forced himself to stand up, and he had to lunge and grab the door handle to keep from falling.

Cries of desperation rang throughout the house. He fumbled to the stairs as fast as he could.

Jessica was in the midst of telling Greg and Rita that they should remain in the house, together in the same room, once she and Eddie left when she felt a cold jab at the base of her spine. The jolt of pain was like being stabbed with an icicle. The sudden, shocked expression on Greg's, Rita's and Ricky's faces told her they had felt it, too.

Jessica looked up and scanned the room. "It's here."

Greg pulled Rita's and Ricky's hands into his own. They jumped when they heard Eddie shouting.

"What's going on?" Greg said.

"I don't know," she replied. Then it hit her. "Selena!"

As she ran to the bathroom, all of the lights in the house were extinguished. Two quick steps in the dark brought her crashing headlong over a kitchen chair. She spilled onto her stomach, her breath knocked out of her. Struggling for air, she brought herself to her knees. Greg brushed past her as he charged the bathroom door. They heard Selena shout, "No!" and nothing more.

"Selena, unlock the door!" Greg demanded, on the verge of panic.

Even though she was woozy, Jessica joined him at the door.

"Selena, are you all right?" she said. Her lungs ached from the effort.

The sounds of a struggle were their only reply.

Greg pounded on the door with his fists. He and Jessica both knew there was no way Selena could let them in.

"Hold on," she said to him, taking a step back. She raised her leg and kicked as hard as she could at the door, right near the handle. Her leg jarred painfully into her hip. It felt as if the door had been reinforced with steel. She tried again, gaining nothing more than a sore leg.

Greg joined her, throwing his body into the door. The wood didn't so much as creak.

"What the hell? The door is hollow. It should break just by blowing on it," Greg said, breathless. "Selena, we're coming!"

Jessica picked up her pace, interspersing her kicks with his body blows, and she would keep it up until her leg fell off. She knew with sickening dread what Selena was going through on the other side, and she would do everything she could to stop it.

"Let's try it at the same time," she said.

Deep down, she doubted they could break it if they had a steel battering ram. It wasn't the door that was keeping them out. It was the EB. Fighting the metaphysical with the physical was like bringing a water pistol to a duel, but it was all she had.

A muffled cry escaped from Selena.

Don't you dare touch her, she thought with panicked desperation.

Jessica reared back, then let loose with a war cry.

Now that his eyes had adjusted to the dark, Eddie motioned for Rita and Ricky to stay where they were on the couch. A dull sliver of moonlight parted the curtains, haloing their terrified faces. He tried his best not to show the fatigue that ran through his body like white water rapids. As he turned the corner of the kitchen, he saw Greg nursing his shoulder while Jessica repeatedly rammed her body against the bathroom door.

"What's going on?"

His voice startled them both. Greg brushed past him without saying a word.

"Selena's locked inside and the EB's in with her. It's doing something to make the door unbreakable."

She gave the doorknob a vicious kick that should have sent it spiraling into the air. In reality, nothing happened to it at all.

He stopped her from making another attempt by grabbing her shoulders. "You have to get out of here."

He couldn't make out her expression in the weak light, but he could feel her studying him, sense the desperation that had overtaken her reluctance to give way to calm rationalization. Then she drew in a sharp breath, and he felt her shoulders relax.

"Crap, I'm making it worse, aren't I?"

"I think so. I need you to—"

Greg came running back, snapping on a flashlight. The sharp beam of light made Eddie and Jessica throw up their hands to protect their eyes. He was also holding a hammer and pry bar in his other hand.

"I need one of you to hold the flashlight while I try to...to..."

The light wavered to their left and began to tremble. When Eddie and Jessica turned, they saw Selena approaching from the closed corridor.

Except, it wasn't Selena at all.

The doppelganger's cold, fathomless eyes looked through them, to the depths of their souls or the vastness of the infinity that lay beyond life. It stopped just short of touching Jessica, then turned to the door.

Its appearance stunned them all into paralysis. Jessica didn't dare to come any closer to it, lest she chase it away again. Eddie held his breath.

Slowly, it brought its arm up and placed its hand flat against the door. There was a sudden change in the ambience of the entire house. It was as if it had been electrified with a wild, untamable current that set invisible fires in the ozone, raising the hairs on their bodies and pricking their skin like a tattoo artist's needle. Now, with the appearance of the doppelganger, that surge of unchecked energy had been cut off, the breaker closed, the source of the surge contained, though still a danger.

There was a loud *thump*, as if something heavy had landed on the floor in the bathroom, followed by a piercing wail that sounded like a silent scream finally set free.

When they heard Selena's scream, Greg dropped the flashlight. He bent down to snatch it back up. When he shined it back near the door, his daughter's spirit double was gone.

Chapter Forty-Nine

Selena had resigned herself to endure whatever horrors the invisible entity had planned for her. She felt it envelop her body, could see the depression of fat, strong fingers on her skin as it kneaded and pinched her arms, thighs, belly and breasts. An uncomfortable, barbed heat pressed between her legs, seeking entry to the one place she feared the most. When she tried to close her legs, pain shot through her hips as they were forced apart.

She was still sitting on the toilet, exposed, helpless, gagging from the effort of trying to draw a solid breath. Her shirt had been ripped down the middle and she was forced to watch the inexorable progress of the ghost as it worked its way down her chest, focusing all of its attention below.

Her father and Jessica yelled and pounded against the door and she couldn't understand why it hadn't smashed to splinters. Hot tears ran down her face and she desperately wanted to beg aloud for her parents to save her.

She stiffened even more when she felt a gush of hot breath blow against her inner thighs.

Please, God, no, no, no, don't let this happen to me! Help me, God, please!

Her legs were pulled farther apart, bending up toward her chest. She struggled to break its grip, rocking from side to side, frantic to stop the growing heat between her legs before it entered her, where she was sure she would burn to death from the inside out.

The toilet seat slipped, snapping off the bolts that held it in place, and she fell sideways onto the floor. For an instant, she was free. She screamed so hard, she thought for sure she had severed her vocal cords. When she tried to pull herself up using the side of the tub, the ghost pounced on her, driving her to the cold tile floor. It pressed hard on her face, grinding her cheek until she tasted blood as her teeth shredded the tender flesh within.

Her eyes were blinded by a fresh wave of tears, but not enough to block the vision of a pair of luminous legs standing before her. For a moment, she thought her father and Jessica had broken through. Her terror escalated when she saw the door behind the legs very much intact. Straining against the pressure on her head, she managed to look upward, settling on her own face staring back at her with an expression of unbridled anger.

In that moment, she knew its ire wasn't directed at her. It was as if she had entered the soul of her mirror image. For the first time, she was grateful to see her double walker. It wasn't here to scare her. It had never intended to do that. Selena had just never known how to process the experiences.

"Help...me," she pleaded with her double walker.

It reached into the space around her, stopping inches from her back. She felt relief from the malicious weight that had pinned her to the floor.

There was a flash of light, white and hot as if it had come from the quick snapping on and off of an aerial spotlight. Both the ghost and the double walker disappeared in the brief flicker between dark and light, and dark again.

She scrambled to a sitting position, drawing her legs close to her and sobbing.

The door split in half as her father drove the pry bar down its center. He pushed through the shattered remains of the door and rushed to her.

"Daddy!"

She held out her arms to him and he gathered her up like he used to do when she was just a small girl. Her mother and Ricky were waiting right outside the door. There was a lot of commotion as he carried her into the living room. Her sobs made it hard for her to talk or even swallow and her mother, to her credit, kept a brave face and did her best to calm her down. Even her little brother kept his cool, running to get her a glass of water and a blanket.

"We have to get out of here, now!" her father snapped.

Eddie tried to talk low, but she heard him say, "If you do, it will just follow you. We have a perfect window to get it now."

The rest was lost to her as she fought to regain her composure, but every time she tried, she felt the cold, determined hands roughly fondle her body, and all was lost.

Jessica knew she had to get away from the Leighs as fast and far as she could, but first she and Eddie had to talk Greg down, convince him that his running was not the answer.

They went into the yard, where the cooling night air sent a shiver across her shoulders.

Eddie said, "I know where he is."

"He? What do you mean he?" Greg said, his patience visibly short.

"The man who's doing this to your family...to Selena. I made a solid connection with him upstairs."

Greg walked away a few steps, then came back sharply, stopping close to Eddie's face. "Then tell me where he is. I'll kill the mother fucker."

Jessica stepped forward, trying to wedge herself between them. "Greg, the man he's talking about is dead already."

Eddie added, "We need to find his body."

Greg swayed, looking like a man just coming out of a dream after a late night sleepwalk. "Find his body?"

"I'm going to stay with you while Jessica goes out to find it," Eddie said. "His body isn't buried. I could feel it above ground, for lack of a better term."

"No offense, Jessica, but it sounds a little crazy, sending a kid like you out to find some dead body," Greg said. She knew he also wanted to add that she was a girl, and a young one at that. She didn't blame him for feeling that way, and she didn't want to tell him why she had to be the one to get away from his family.

"Don't worry about that. Look, I'm sure what just happened weakened it, but that will only last so long. We have to move, now," she said.

Greg pulled at his hair. "Jesus fucking Christ. I feel like I'm losing my mind."

"Then lose it later. Right now, your daughter needs you."

Her sharp words stunned him, and he fixed her with a dubious stare before grunting and heading back into the house.

"Harsh," Eddie said.

"We don't have time to be nice. You said you know where he is. Tell me. I'll find him."

As they walked to the front yard and her Jeep, Eddie described the house.

"It's a split level house with dark blue shingles. There's a red brick chimney on the right side and an attached garage with a solid white door on the left. The Thunderbird's in the garage, if you want to check that first to make sure you have the right house. I've seen a lot of split level houses in this neighborhood, and in the dark, it's going to make it even harder to discern one from the other."

She opened her door and climbed in. "Then give me something else to go by. Is there a lawn gnome in the front or some other odd feature that'll make it easier for me to spot?"

Eddie closed his eyes and thought, then snapped his fingers. "Yes! The top five or more shingles on the upper right hand side of the house are partially torn away. Must have been from a storm or something. The house is close, I'd say within ten blocks. The EB got toasted by Selena's doppelganger, so it's gone back to lick its wounds. That's not to say you have all night, but if it does make another attempt before you find it, I think it's weak enough for me to hold it back."

"Have you ever stopped a spirit from attacking someone?"

He shook his head. "Can't say that I have, but I can always try. I'm learning more about myself in just a few days with you than I ever did at The Rhine. We go together like gunpowder and matches.

"Are you okay with this?" he asked. "I mean, knowing that if all goes well, you're going to find yourself in a house with a dead body and his very pissed off spirit? He died in the throes of his twisted fantasy about Selena. It's not going to be pretty."

He looked sick with worry. She needed him to be able to concentrate all his efforts on Selena and her safety, and not waste a single iota of energy on concern about her wellbeing. It was time to tell him about her father and Alaska, at least the abridged version. It took her a moment to collect her thoughts, because this was a story that was shared with no one, aside from Angela, so she'd had no practice in its telling.

She said, "As bad as this has been, Eddie, I've seen worse. Much worse. If you really want to know who I am as a person and why I do what I do, then you have to know about Alaska."

He held up a hand, assuring her that she didn't have to tell him anything she didn't want to. She continued anyway.

"My mom died in her sleep when I was just a baby. Her death broke my father. Even though they had just won the lottery, nothing could change the fact that he had lost the one woman he ever loved, and was now a single father to a baby. He felt if anything ever happened to him, I would be left an orphan, and was in fear of dying just like my mother. Her death showed him that it could come at any time. I think that's part of the reason why he stepped into studying the paranormal. By surrounding himself with stories of death and what lay beyond, he was searching for proof that my mom was still somewhere, waiting for him, and he was also hoping to face his fears enough to make them go away.

"When I was six, he took me, my aunt Eve and my cousin Liam to live in a huge mansion of a cabin in this town called Shida, Alaska. It was part of his therapy, leaving the house where my mom had died and taking on a sort of adventure. The house was said to be haunted, so he thought it would be great to live in it and study it for a couple of months. It was a vacation for me, as much as it was work for him. Things didn't take long to fall apart. I remember seeing weird lights in the hallway at night and talking to a man in the yard who just up and disappeared. My aunt says a lot of other things were happening, but when you're six, you only notice the things that directly affect you. The town itself didn't want us there. It was exclusively Native American, with the exception of this guy, Judas, who was the one who had asked my father to come in the first place."

"So you lived in a haunted cabin, surrounded by living people that didn't want you there?" Eddie said. "How come your father didn't take you all right back to New York?"

There was a split second where she was going to ask him how he didn't know all of this when he had made contact with her father, a contact stronger and more intimate than she had been able to make over the years, including her annual pilgrimages to Alaska. Then she realized that her father had been a man who played his cards close to his vest, showing them only to those he loved. He had found Eddie so he could guide him to her. Maybe he saw tonight coming, and knew she would need Eddie to get them all through to the dawn.

She shook her head slowly, her eyes looking past the Leigh house in front of her, back to the cabin nestled amidst the forest in Shida, reliving the last night she had seen her father alive. "Eve said that when things went bad, they went bad fast. My dad realized that there were different forces at odds in the cabin, and that some of them were attracted to the townspeople. So, he planned a final night where he invited a bunch of guys and girls, like our age, who were some sort of gang or something, but on the outer fringes of the town itself. No one else would talk to us, much less come to the house."

"They were bait," Eddie said.

"Yes. But there was no way my father could know what they would attract. He was hoping to get voices on EVP, maybe even record a shadow or something, but nothing like what happened."

Jessica's stomach cramped and she had to swallow to hold back a rising tide of acid in her throat.

"None of us realized that there were bodies, dozens of them, buried right outside the house. All of them had been murdered over the years when Shida was a growing town. You see, Shida was a kind of hideaway for criminals of all tribes, a place to disappear and get a fresh start. But many of them were tracked, and when they were found, the town took care of them. Their spirits were angry, and having the residents of the town in the house fed their hate. There were shadows, anthropomorphic, but four times larger than any man. They assaulted the cabin, trying to break through like a shark struggling to get at a diver in a submerged cage."

The caterwaul of two fighting cats broke her concentration. They hissed and wailed at one another, and for several seconds sounded as if they were in a fight to the death. When silence returned to the dark streets, she continued.

"Some of the spirits managed to possess the town's sheriff, and while the shadows tried to get at us, they had him murder all of the founding members of the town, house to house, one by one. And when he was done, they brought him to our house to finish the job. I was upstairs with my aunt when the worst happened, while the shadow people downstairs started to tear people apart. And that's when the spirits of another family that had been killed in the cabin before us came to my father, and told him what he needed to do. He knew then, when death was all around us, that he couldn't get the genie back in the bottle, and there was nothing he could do from this side to stop them. So he asked one of the gang to kill him. I...I'll never know why he did it, but when he died, my God, the light was blinding, but it drove all of the shadows back to their graves. Everything stopped."

Jessica wiped a lone tear from her eye and turned the key in the ignition.

"I came back to New York with my aunt, who had been given full custody in my father's will. She had the Alaska house razed, and the rest of the town collapsed after seeing a good percentage of its population murdered. It's a true ghost town now, in every sense of the word. I go there every year and when I'm lucky, I can capture my father's voice as an EVP. If I'm lucky."

Eddie leaned into her window, unsure what to do or say. She had broken down her wall as far as she ever had for him, and she felt raw and sore in the places where she housed the darkness.

"You see, I'm not afraid of dying," she said. "Because I know there's more to come. I know my father and my mother are waiting for me. That's why EBs don't scare me. Most of them are just lost and scared themselves. And ones like this? I'm angry, just like I would be if it was alive and preying on young kids. Do whatever you have to and keep Selena safe. It's time I took care of things."

She sped out of the driveway, stopping just short of plowing into a car across the street. She saw Eddie in the rearview mirror, still standing there, watching her leave, processing everything she had confessed.

He looked up when the streetlight outside the house suddenly blinked off.

"Oh no you don't," she said with a slight growl, punching the accelerator and turning down the first street to begin her search.

Chapter Fifty

When the streetlight died, Eddie felt a breaker of venomous intent overtake him. It was a weak salvo, meant to let him know that it hadn't gone for good. It would be back, and soon. He ran into the house.

"I need everyone to sit on the floor in a circle, holding hands," he said.

Several candles had been lit and were spaced throughout the room, creating undulating shadows that danced along the walls. It made him think of Jessica and her family in a cabin in the middle of nowhere, struggling to keep the shadows at bay. He shook the images away. This was *not Alaska*, and he would damn well make sure nothing else would happen to this family.

Selena had stopped crying and Rita had a hard look about her, as if she was willing to take on the devil himself to protect her daughter. She hauled the coffee table away and brought Selena and Ricky onto the floor with her. Greg, who had been standing by the front window, joined them.

"We're going to have to form a ring of protection," Eddie said. He'd heard about his great-grandfather doing something similar for a woman who was being accosted nightly by the angry spirit of her abusive, deceased father. D.D. Home had been a voracious diarist and the majority of his notes had been kept within the family, handed down to each successive male Home that had shown signs of possessing *the gift*. Eddie wished he'd been less preoccupied with pretty girls in school and had devoted more time to studying those notes. At the time, they just seemed cool and creepy, like reading Poe or Lovecraft. He didn't realize then the real life applications D.D. Home's accounts could have.

"Okay, join hands."

He sat between Selena and Ricky, the ones most vulnerable to the EB. He hoped that their closer proximity would give him a better chance at fending off any attacks. Selena's hand was cold and clammy, while Ricky's was firm, resolute. Brave kid. He gave him a quick smile and Ricky lowered his eyes and nodded, like he would do to his baseball coach when the game was on the line and it was his turn at bat.

"Do we have to close our eyes or something?" Rita asked.

"No. As a matter of fact, it's best you keep them open, so you can notice if anything happens around us. I'm going to have to close *my* eyes, but that's only so I can concentrate."

There was tension in the room, but it was emanating from the living like summer heat off metal siding. He couldn't do anything about that. What he had to do was conjure an image of white light around their circle. This wasn't the searing bright light at the end of the tunnel of death with angels singing, like so many people with near-death experiences reported to have seen.

This light had to have substance, an impenetrable barrier that was as hard to behold as it was to break. He looked at their faces, studying the way they were sitting, holding one another's hands. Closing his eyes, he recreated the image in his mind, while another part of him was back in his childhood bedroom, reading the old book his father had lent him as part of his fledgling psi education.

The woman's name had been Dorothea, and his great-grandfather had managed to both protect her and dispel her father's angry spirit all on his own over the course of a weekend in some small hamlet in England. All Eddie had to do was protect Selena while Jessica did the heavy lifting. Of course, D.D. Home at the time was a man in his psychic prime who had devoted his life to honing his abilities. Eddie's thin resume as a guinea pig and a young man struggling to understand what he could do and what his limits were left a lot to be desired, but it would have to be enough tonight.

He started with a small pinprick of light that began to circle them like a toy car on a plastic track, going faster and faster, leaving a white contrail in its wake, the contrail itself growing in thickness as it went round and round.

Yes, it was working!

Young Eddie read on to him, guiding him, while he pushed the light in an ever-intensifying spiral. The light rose up the contours of their backs to the tops of their heads, until they were ensconced in a glowing, pulsating cocoon.

When he felt the cone of light was complete, he sought out Jessica, offering her what little strength he had left to give.

Keep going, Jessica. Find him. We're safe. You want to kick some EB ass? Now's your time to do it.

Jessica had just turned down Scott Street, a dead end that was six blocks away from Greg and Rita's, when she heard a whisper behind her ear.

"We're safe."

She jammed on the brakes, put the Jeep in park and whipped around to look at the back seat, expecting to find a passenger that had stowed away unseen, until now.

There was nothing there.

"You want to kick some EB ass? Now's your time to do it."

The voice startled her. She was about to step out of the car until she realized it was familiar.

Eddie.

"How the hell are you doing this?" she said aloud, not sure if he could hear her or read her mind.

There would be time to ask him later. Right now, the message had been received. She resumed her recon of Scott Street, searching for a split level house with blue shingles, some of them hanging off. The neighborhood was filled with split level homes of varying colors. She had spotted a couple of blue ones, but in each case, the shingles were in place.

She turned around at the cul-de-sac and sped down the street, confident that the road would be clear of pedestrians in the dead of night. At the corner, she made a hard right onto Hall Place and slowed down, swiveling from left to right, searching.

Jessica felt time slipping away as easily as a silk blanket between her fingers. Selena was under Eddie's protection, but even he admitted he had no real experience doing anything like this. And he looked physically exhausted. How much more could he take?

"Where are you, you sick bastard?" she muttered, leaning close to the steering wheel and peering at the darkened houses.

The farther she got from the Leighs' block, the smaller and more run down the houses became. It wasn't exactly poor, but definitely on the lower middle-class end. Most of the front lawns were well-tended, but a few looked as if they could use an industrial weed whacker.

At the end of Hall, she could only make a left and found herself on a very small street that ended at another cul-de-sac. There were seven houses in total—three on each side and one at the very end. Two were small Capes, one a ranch in need of a paint job.

Her heart stammered for a beat and her mouth went dry when she first heard, then saw a pair of dark blue shingles on the last house on the right slap against the upper corner of the house as a salty gust of wind swept through the street.

It was also the lone house with an attached garage.

She pulled the Jeep right up to the garage door. It was cracked and flecked with peeling bits of paint. The passing wind left utter silence in its wake. The house looked cold and empty, as did most houses in the night, but this one even *felt* abandoned.

So as not to make any noise, she left her door ajar and pressed her face against one of the square windows in the garage door. The glass was too filthy to see through. She pulled out a penlight and shined it inside. Its light was just strong enough for her to make out the shape of a car, and a large one at that, but she couldn't tell the make or color.

She moved to the next window, which was grimier than the first, then the next, skipping past the two that had been filled with plywood.

"Dammit."

Even though the house looked exactly as Eddie had described it, a part of her needed the additional proof of the car before crossing the line into criminal breaking and entering. Eddie had proved to be the real deal, but no one was infallible.

She went back to the car and opened the hatch, finding a screwdriver in the toolkit she kept in the spare tire wheel well. Looking around to make sure no lights had snapped on in the nearby houses, she went to work, digging the flat end of the screwdriver into a corner where the plywood met the window frame. Softly grunting, she wiggled it back and forth, trying to loosen the wood. There was a crack, then a fibrous tearing as the plywood began to give way.

It popped out and landed inside the garage. Jessica froze, sure that the muffled noise could be heard for miles. After waiting for a ten count and seeing that no one had come to find the source of the sudden noise, she clicked on the penlight and poked her head inside.

The red Thunderbird filled most of the cramped garage. The windows were heavily tinted and she could see through the clear windshield that the leather interior was jet black. A perfect stalker car.

"Got you, asshole."

A battered metal door, partway open, led to the interior of the house.

She pocketed her penlight and screwdriver. Reaching her arm through the window, she searched for the door lock, holding the end outside with her other hand. When she found the latch and turned, she eased it open so it didn't make a sound. Lifting the door, inch by agonizing inch, seemed to take forever. Someone must have been watching over her, because despite most of the house appearing to be in need of repair, the springs on the door were well oiled and silent.

The garage smelled like old motor oil and grease. All of the tools, and there were tons of them, were carefully hung on pegs or put in marked storage bins. The man who had lived here had made his car his priority.

The metal door opened up into the kitchen, and another smell overwhelmed her like a punch to the nose. Images of rotted road kill on the side of the highway flooded her brain, only this was worse as it was mingled with the scent of shit and the putrescence of festering garbage.

Something had died in there. Or better yet, some*one*.

Jessica pulled her shirt up over her nose.

"Dad, I know you've been with me the whole time here. Your squeakpip could use a little extra courage right about now. I'm used to seeing things after they've left a body, not the body itself."

Stepping into the kitchen was like entering a walk-in freezer. The temperature outside was in the upper seventies, but none of the warmth of the day had permeated this house for a long time. She winced in disgust as a pair of cockroaches skittered past her foot, in hasty retreat from the full garbage pail.

The floor above her creaked as if someone was unsuccessfully trying to sneak about. Cautiously, she left the kitchen and walked into the living room. It was bare, with just a reclining easy chair, tube TV on a press-wood stand and small tables on each side of the chair. A pair of binoculars rested atop one table while the other held a stack of newspapers and the remote for the TV.

A deep, masculine groan, dripping with reproach, a warning to her that contained a promise of dire intentions, echoed down the nearby stairs.

She looked up the dark staircase, unable to see anything above, though the smell was even more pungent, a breadcrumb on the trail for her to follow if she dared. A near painful tingling started at the nape of her neck and she had to rub it to make it subside while still holding her shirt up to her nose. She hated when her body's natural reactions tried to hijack will.

"I know you don't want me here," she called up the stairs. "But we both know it's too late for that. Time to find out who you really are."

She was alone, in a strange home that housed an evil EB and a dead body. There was finally a direction to take. She knew what she was up against. For the first time since she'd come to New Hampshire, she felt she was in her element.

With the tiny beam from her penlight leading the way, Jessica ascended the stairs.

Eddie rocked back when he felt the EB slam into the protective cocoon of light he had constructed around them. Selena and Ricky tugged on his hands to keep him from rolling out of their circle.

"Is something wrong?" Rita asked. He could see her squeeze her daughter's hand a little bit harder, as if to let her know that she would not let any harm come to her.

"Just our friend trying to get in. It didn't work," Eddie said. He closed his eyes again and concentrated on keeping the EB out. He laughed to himself when a thought floated past for just an instant. *I feel like a spam blocker.*

Since he'd never done this before, he wasn't sure how long he could maintain it or how much he could withstand. It was his hope that when Jessica found the body, the EB would have to divide its energy, leaving it too weak to get past his novice psychic wall.

Hope was all he and Jessica were going on now.

He could hear Greg and Rita talking to the kids, though it was as if they were several rooms away, behind closed doors.

Greg shouted, "Kids, I need you to stay calm!"

Eddie opened his eyes and saw that all of the candles had been snuffed out. The rising panic in the room was almost tactile.

He said, "Your father's right. It can't get at you, so it's directing itself at little things it can control. It wants you to be scared, to break the circle, to be vulnerable. Don't let it inside your head. It's going to try to get your attention in other ways. Just ignore it. If you want, close your eyes and think of your favorite place to be. If you're not paying attention, then nothing it does can affect you."

It was easier said than done, but he needed to reassure them all that the EB was impotent, for now.

A lamp scraped across an end table, tottered and crashed to the floor. Everyone but Eddie jumped. "See, candles and lamps," he said. "That's all it can do now."

"Mom, I want to get out of here," Selena said.

"I know, honey, I know. Don't let go of my hand. I'm here."

There was a rattling of glasses in the kitchen cabinets, followed by another futile attempt at getting through to Selena. Her fear was riling the EB up, but there was nothing Eddie could do about it. He just had to hold steady.

And hope that Jessica had found the house.

Chapter Fifty-One

The old stairs creaked like an ocean-battered pirate ship. The smell of decay was so strong it pierced the cloth of her shirt that was pulled over the lower half of her face, clogging her nose until it felt as if it were fouling her brain, settling in so it could blossom into a dark, malignant tumor.

Jessica had to fight back the urge to puke. She gagged twice, but managed to keep everything down. The second floor was small, with only two rooms and a bathroom. As much as the thought repulsed her, she had to follow her nose to the source.

The first bedroom was an obvious junk room, filled from floor to ceiling with boxes, card tables, discarded chairs and mounds of magazines and other junk.

A hoarder's paradise.

It was an odd sight, considering the neat garage and Spartan living room. She got the feeling that the man who had lived here wasn't even sure *what* he was—an obsessive neat freak or a cluttered pack rat?

As an EB, he was focused and repugnant. It was as if death had granted him clarity of his tortured, confused soul. She had to remind herself that not everyone wanted to go to the light. Bad people made for bad EBs.

Up next was the bathroom. She pictured a tub full of blood and water, a bloated body within the vile soup, one arm dangling over the side, a straight razor still in its grasp.

She exhaled when she saw it was empty.

There was one room left, and the stench was definitely strongest at the threshold.

She paused before stepping into the room. A high-pitched humming noise came from deep inside. The shades had been pulled down, so no light permeated the darkness. Her hand flew to her covered mouth when her penlight settled on the dark shape sitting with its back to her on a plush chair by the closed window.

The humming was the buzzing of thousands of flies. They swarmed over the body, making it look as if its flesh were alive and crawling off its bones. She couldn't see anything beyond the writhing black bodies of the flies.

She dry heaved, dropping her penlight. Her shirt pulled away from her face. When she sucked in a great lungful of air, several flies darted down her throat. Coughing to spit them out, she reeled into the wall. She knew it was just her mind playing tricks on her, but she swore she could feel them wriggling around in her lungs, their tiny wings scraping against the soft tissue.

The flies streamed from the dead man in a dark mass, covering her in mere seconds from head to foot. Jessica swatted at her arms, her hair and face, used her fingers to scoop them out of her mouth. The thought of being enshrouded by flies that had, only seconds ago, been feasting on the rotted flesh of a corpse broke her will, and she screamed as she stumbled out of the room, tripping on the pulled-up edge of an area rug and landing on her stomach. She heard the crunch of a hundred fly bodies, felt their pulp and blood splash against her skin.

Laughter exuded from the room as wave upon wave of flies descended on her, seeking her blood, driving her to madness.

"Shit," Eddie muttered.

He'd felt the EB leave the house, which could only mean Jessica had found the body and it was not falling for his divide-and-conquer plan. His sole consolation was that she had done this before, was, in fact, much more experienced than him. And if she was at the source, she would find what she needed to end the nightmare.

"It's gone," Selena said. She had become so familiar now with the EB that she could sense its coming and going as easily as watching a living person walk in and out of a room.

Eddie wanted to connect with Jessica, but it was impossible to do so without breaking down the cocoon. Fatigue, the kind that would take him a week in a warm bed to recover from, had settled in.

He heard Greg say, "Just stay put, honey. Eddie will tell us when it's clear."

I hope your confidence is justified, he thought.

His shoulders sagged and his stomach roiled when he saw that the light had dulled. There was no telling how much longer he could keep it up. Seconds? Minutes? Not much longer than that.

It's all you, Jess. It's all you.

The laughter built and built until it became a steady cackle that would have raised the hairs on Jessica's head if she hadn't been wrapped in a buzzing, undulating cloak of flies. No matter what she did, no matter how many she killed, there seemed to be an endless supply of others to take their place.

Knowing that just seconds earlier they had been resting on the flesh of the decayed corpse worked her mind into a furious panic.

She managed to get to the bathroom and turned on a faucet with a shaky, desperate hand. Splashing cold water on her face drove away some of them, but they reclaimed their purchase once the water sluiced off.

They were biting her, digging into every crevice they could find, feasting on her like a thousand vampires. Her skin felt as if it were on fire and she was so dizzy, it was hard to stand, much less think straight.

Her only thought was to get away from the flies. There were so many crawling over her eyes that she couldn't see and was afraid of breaking her neck falling down the stairs.

Splashing more water on her face so she could at least find the stairs, she recoiled when the bathroom door slammed shut.

Oh God, no!

The bathroom was pitch-black. She fumbled in her pants pockets for the lighter she kept as a backup in case her penlight batteries went out.

When her fingers found the smooth, plastic lighter, the answer to her dilemma came to her fully formed, as if it had been secretly stored in the lighter, waiting like a genie in a bottle for someone to rub it and release their reward.

Smoke.

Flies, like bees, hated smoke.

She fumbled forward and grabbed a dry, matted towel off the wall rack. The flies were back on her face, but she didn't need to see to push the small metal wheel on the lighter. She heard it *whoosh* to life and moved the towel close to where she imagined the flame to be.

When she smelled the sharp tang of burning cloth, she had to keep from screaming for joy and letting more flies into her mouth.

The towel went up fast, and the smoke built up even faster in the enclosed room. She could see again, and grabbed another towel to add to the fire. She swatted the flies in the air with the flaming towels, lighting their little bodies as they sought to escape. As the smoke and flames intensified, she dropped the towels, coughing hard, and had enough presence of mind to bend low and reach for the door handle.

At first, it wouldn't budge.

"Not again, mother fucker!" she shouted, tugging on the door with all of her strength.

The door wouldn't budge. She could hear the continuous laughter outside.

Fool me once, she thought with a sneer.

After pulling the bath mat from the floor, she threw it in the tub and ran cold water over it. While it was soaking, she kicked one of the burning towels near the bottom of the door. It took seconds for the dry tinder of the door to ignite.

As the fire grew, she dropped the soaked bath mat over her head and waited, her lungs spasming from both the smoke and the flies that had descended within her and died.

She cloaked herself in the soaked bath mat. Once the door was engulfed in flames, the stench of burning paint and varnish riding hard, she grabbed the metal waste pail by the sink, held it in front of her and charged at the door. The fire-stressed wood gave way and she crashed through it and into the opposite wall in the hallway.

This made the laughter stop. Smoke poured out of the bathroom and into the room with the corpse. The flies feared the smoke more than the commands of the EB and fled to other parts of the house. Jessica dropped the wet bath mat onto the floor.

"Nice try," she said. Every inch of her skin itched and the room began to spin. She shook her head and retrieved her penlight.

"Time to find out who you are and send you to the hell I know will be happy to have you."

The dresser was bare. A single folded piece of paper rested on it. She opened it, scanned the first few sentences, then stuffed it in her back pocket.

She needed his wallet. If it wasn't on the dresser, it was most likely in one other place.

His back pocket.

Her revulsion pushed away for the moment, she stood before the corpse. He had used a handgun to end his life, placing it in his mouth and blowing a small hole into the top of his head, shattering his left eye in the process. Part of his skull and brain matter was encrusted on the wall behind him. The gun lay on the floor. What was left of his skin was nothing more than a gelatinous ruin. Maggots squirmed in the cavities of his mouth, nose and eyes, spilled out of his ears.

Not allowing herself time to consider what she had to do, she grabbed the corpse by the collar and threw it off the chair, onto the floor. It hit with a dull, wet smack.

A small framed picture flew from the wall, just missing her head. It was a feeble attempt at best, and only gave her strength.

She reached into his back pocket, felt the flesh beneath the fabric burst, and wrapped her fingers around his wallet.

"You're toast."

Loose change, a tie tack, pencils and random papers flew through the air, converging on her.

Jessica flipped the wallet open, ignoring the objects that pelted her like rice on a wedding day. She lifted her light and found his license.

After taking a glance at the fire that had now crept into the hallway, she read his name to herself at first, then smiled.

"Guess what, *Christopher P. Harlan*? It's time for you to go! Do you hear me, *Christopher Harlan*? Leave this house, leave this world and never return!"

The EB howled with rage. Jessica could feel it within her bones as much as she could hear it punishing her eardrums.

"You're no longer wanted here, Christopher Harlan. The world is a better place without you. I hope you have to face the souls of all those you tortured, and I hope they have no mercy!"

The EB's wailing began to diminish, like turning the volume knob down on a stereo. It grew fainter and fainter, until it dissipated into silence.

And that was it. The cold in the room was replaced by the heat from the fire. Things stopped flying around the room.

Most of all, she sensed the emptiness that told her he was no more. A part of her wished for more dramatic exits, possibly even a glimpse of their world to come, but did it really matter?

He was gone. Selena was safe.

Eddie felt a battering ram of rage pummel the circle. His stomach tightened and the bones in his spine cracked from the sudden rush of energy.

It had fled from Jessica. *She must have its name,* he thought. The wretched coward took off before she could work her hoodoo and send it to whatever waited for it on the other side.

Rita screamed as the back of her shirt was pulled from her neck. As she raised her hands to pull the collar away from her throat, her body was snatched backward and she tumbled out of the protective ring.

"Rita!" Greg shouted.

He scrabbled to her side and was lifted a foot into the air, as if he'd been kicked in the midsection. His body tipped the coffee table over.

"Mom! Dad!" Selena screamed.

Eddie was quick to secure hers and Ricky's hands.

"You can't let go," he said.

The EB was playing to her weakness. It wanted her out of the safe zone he'd created.

Rita scooted across the carpet, brushing something from her pants. Eddie saw phantom finger depressions move up her thigh.

I have to help her.

No! Concentrate. It wants Selena. Protect the kids.

It felt as if every cell in his body was going into shutdown mode. His heart danced an unsteady beat. He was pretty sure his bladder had just let itself go. The muscles in his legs and arms tightened into a painful cramp, then loosened, too weak to hold on. Worse was the pain in his head. It was as if little bombs had been placed throughout his brain and were being detonated one after the other.

He had to get the EB out of here, back to Jessica. He could feel that she was still alive, still strong, or at least stronger than he was at the moment.

There was only one way to expel it.

He had to let it all the way in again.

Focusing the light around the kids, he conjured his barn totem. The doors were wide open, inviting. As much as it sickened him, he filled the barn walls with the images of Selena that the EB had forced upon him earlier. Her nude, helpless, broken body was everywhere.

It was too much for the EB to resist.

Eddie watched the dark mass slink into the barn, huffing like an incensed bull.

The light around Selena and Ricky dissipated as he brought all of his power to the center of his mind.

The last moments of the EB's life pulsed within the barn walls. Eddie knew its impotence, its rage against God and the devil and anything else that had a hand in its creation.

Eddie felt no pity.

"You like what you see?" he said to the shapeless form.

It chortled. *"I knew once you experienced my lust, you wouldn't be able to resist."*

"Yes, she is one sweet piece of meat." It pained Eddie to even think it. *"Come over here. I've improved upon your fantasy. I think you'll like it."*

He motioned for the EB to join him in the center of the barn.

It crept forward, too riled up by the vivid display of its hunger to resist.

That's a good pedophile, Eddie thought.

The moment it stopped, Eddie threw open the barn's roof with a wood-rending eruption.

A cyclone of white energy whirled beneath the EB's pulsating form.

"What is this?" it roared.

"Your ride home."

"Noooooooo!"

With an ear-shattering *whoosh*, the light exploded, sending the EB through the open roof and into the darkness. Eddie felt Jessica's energy, and with everything he had left, pushed the EB straight to her.

When the EB broke away, everything went black. He felt his stomach heave, and thought he heard frantic voices around him.

He opened his eyes and saw Selena leaning over him. Her arms shook and tears streamed down her cheeks.

He wanted to tell her it would be all right. The bad EB was about to have its ass handed to it by the brave, self-destructive girl.

Speech was beyond his abilities.

The lancing pain in his skull made him wish he were dead.

He wouldn't be so lucky.

The adrenaline drained from Selena's body as quickly as it came, and her legs threatened to give way. She compelled them to run through the fire, feeling its hot tendrils lick her bitten, defiled flesh. The floor and walls crackled as the flames ate away. Her insides were singed when she breathed, and black spots formed at the corners of her eyes.

A section of the floor gave way, and her leg fell through up to her ankle. She pitched forward, held by the sharp, smoking planks like a bear trap.

She glanced up to see the fire dance across the ceiling. It looked and sounded as if the entire hallway was about to collapse.

Jessica tugged at her leg to free her foot.

"No, no, no, not like this!"

A heavy, flaming two-by-four came crashing down, landing inches from her face. She smelled the sharp tang of burning hair and swatted the blue flame from her head.

The heat was overwhelming. Sweat stung her eyes. The more she moved her leg, the more the wood pinched shut on her ankle. It was like quicksand.

A tingling sensation prickled along her lower back.

Her stomach clenched and her body froze.

She wasn't alone.

Harlan's EB was still here. She felt it watching her, waiting for the flames to engulf her.

Crying out with exertion, she grabbed her leg and pulled, but it accomplished nothing. The fire roared throughout the hallway. It was as if it, too, was alive.

Looking up, she saw what was left of the ceiling was close to total collapse. When it did, it would crush as well as set fire to her.

Her strength sapped, she lay flat on the hot floor. The hair on the back of her neck vibrated as the EB came closer, savoring its victory.

I'm sorry, Selena, she thought. She shut her eyes against the roiling smoke. Then, *I love you, Daddy. I'll be with you, finally, soon.*

Jessica's exposed skin started to blister. It didn't matter. She knew this wasn't the end. There was so much more to see.

"Squeakpip! Get up!"

The sound of her father's voice startled her. Her eyes flew open and she looked around for the source.

Turning around, hoping to see her father, she instead came face to face with Christopher Harlan, deceased and stronger than ever.

The EB was a solid black mass, with a vague hint of shoulder and a head. A pair of violet eyes glared at her from within its stygian depths.

A smoky appendage stretched toward her. It touched her forehead and pushed down, trying to pin her to the floor. Its touch was colder than the depths of the ocean.

Sinister laughter seeped into her skull.

"So pretty. I could have fucked you, too," it hissed.

No.

She was strangely okay with burning to death.

But not in the company of Harlan's EB.

Not knowing it would remain free to torture poor Selena and her family.

Screw this!

She wasn't going to let Harlan win. Her father told her to get up, and that's what she would do.

But first, she needed to be a little more forward with this EB from hell.

Staring into its hateful eyes, she shouted, "I thought I told you to go away. Christopher Harlan, your evil soul isn't welcome here anymore!"

It shrieked at her while its edges grew soft, more translucent.

"Nice try, asshole," she spat. "I'll say it one more time. Christopher Harlan, go...to...hell!"

The black shape shattered into thousands of fragments, the force fanning the flames.

The pair of violet eyes hovered in the air for a moment, then faded to pink, then white, and closed in on themselves.

Now he was gone.

She pushed her leg forward, hoping to change the position of her foot, and felt the wood crack as she yanked her foot free. With the EB gone, the dying house hadn't the strength to hold her. After scrambling to her feet, she ran down the stairs, feeling the fire rage at her back. Her shoulder slammed into the kitchen doorway but she barely registered the pain.

Yanking the garage door open, she sucked in a huge lungful of clear, night air. The pain and pleasure almost made her pass out.

A few lights had come on in the surrounding houses.

She stumbled to her Jeep. Her fingers trembled as she fumbled to get the key in the ignition. She looked out the window to see that most of the smoke had remained contained, thanks to Christopher Harlan's shutting every window tight before he offed himself. If she was lucky, the neighbors wouldn't have time to register the fire or the strange Jeep with the frantic girl inside before she sped off.

She started the Jeep and backed out of the driveway. Her skin felt as if it were electrified and pulsing, thanks to the innumerable fly bites. On the way back to the Leighs' house, she tried to call 911 and report the fire, but dropped the phone onto the floor.

Everything after that was black.

Chapter Fifty-Two

"Knock, knock."

Jessica had been dozing, the television turned down low so it was just background noise. She turned to face the door.

Eddie walked in holding a bouquet of flowers and a full plastic bag.

"How you feeling?" he asked as he grabbed the chair near her bed.

"Like shit, but it's an improvement from total shit."

Eddie looked at her standard issue hospital gown and chuckled.

"What?" she said.

"They couldn't find a Metallica gown for you?"

"Don't make me laugh. It hurts, too much."

"Okay, how about this? You hungry?"

"Starving."

He pulled her tray over and took out two Styrofoam boxes. One had Chinese food, the other a cheeseburger and fries.

"I wasn't sure which you'd be in the mood for," he said, putting the flowers on the windowsill.

"I think both," she said.

She had collapsed when she walked into Rita and Greg's house, part of an adverse reaction to what the doctor said was the most insect bites he had ever seen. She was also dehydrated and exhausted, with what looked like a bad sunburn on her arms, so she was given a two-night stay at Seabrook General. Her memory after leaving Christopher Harlan's house was sketchy at best. Eddie had promised to fill her in on all the details when she was up to it. All that mattered was that Selena and her family were safe and would never again be harassed by Harlan's EB.

Her face and arms looked as if she had a bad case of the chicken pox, with red, raised bumps everywhere. The doctor said they would go away after a few days, though some would leave small, lasting scars.

Jessica piled pork fried rice onto her burger. Eddie looked on with mild revulsion.

"Really?" he said.

"Really," she answered, and took a huge bite.

"Greg, Rita, Selena and Ricky came by earlier but they said you were out cold. They left this for you." He pulled a three-foot-tall teddy bear from the side of her table. It held a heart to its chest.

"That was real sweet of them."

"Yeah, well, they're real sweet on you. I think Greg might petition the Pope to make you a saint."

She ate a handful of fries. "It's funny how things change, isn't it? Greg hated me when we got here."

Eddie nodded. "He had every right to be skeptical. That is, until it was impossible to deny the truth."

"Has the doppel...double walker come back? Is Selena sleeping okay?"

"I think her double walker accomplished what it came for. As for her sleeping, that'll take some time before she feels comfortable again. Can't say that I blame her."

When she had eaten every morsel of food, she lay heavily against her pillows. "Did you find out any more about Christopher Harlan?"

"The news reported a little about him when they covered the fire. By the way, they have no leads on who or what started the fire. One neighbor thought they saw a car drive down the street around the time it started, but didn't get the make or model. I think you're in the clear."

"Was anyone hurt? I don't think I could live with myself if that happened. I had to do something and at the time, I didn't think of consequences."

Eddie touched her hand reassuringly. "They put the fire out pretty quickly. No one, other than you, was hurt."

Jessica sighed. "Thank God. So, tell me about Harlan."

"He was bad, Jess, as bad as we thought. The entire neighborhood is shocked that he lived in their midst for so long without so much as an inkling of the monster that he was. He was a pedophile, through and through. The rescue team found boxes of child porn, spy cam pictures, you name it. He had a room full of the stuff. Harlan was an uber-predator who escaped the system. But in the end, he tried to make things right, though it didn't work out that way."

"You mean by killing himself?"

"Yep. I read the note that you had in your pocket. It fell out when I went to hang up your jeans. Did you know it was his suicide note?"

"To tell you the truth, I barely remember taking it. I was busy looking for something with his name on it. I must have known at the time. Why else would I have saved it?"

"Sometimes, our actions aren't necessarily our own."

"You get that from a fortune cookie when you bought me lunch?"

"Ha-ha. Anyway, Harlan's obsession with Selena went on for a year. He followed her from school, took pictures of her when she was in stores or the park with her friends. It got so bad that he began to impersonate her, to dress like her, to walk like her, to try to *be* her. As sick as it sounds, he liked to masturbate *as* her. And when that wasn't enough, he knew that he had to take her.

"Now, here's where it gets even stranger. About two months ago, in the middle of his planning to abduct Selena, he goes to his doctor because he feels a pain in his..."

Eddie paused, uncertain.

"A pain in his what?" Jessica prodded. "I'm a big girl, I can take it."

He exhaled. "Okay, well, something was wrong with his dick."

He flushed red, but Jessica needed to know the rest. "Can't say that I feel sorry for him," she said.

"It turns out, he had cancer. Within a week, that whole area would have been as useful as a ball of silly putty. So now his plan to kidnap and rape Selena is ruined. He can't have her the way he craves. His own body rebelled against him, and it throws him into a rage. The last thing he did before putting the gun in his mouth was watch Selena walking home from school one last time. Feeling like the impotent bastard he'd become, he scribbled a quick suicide note and pulled the trigger."

"You got all that from the note?" Jessica asked.

"Some of it. The rest I got from his spirit as you started to use his name against him. I had been trying to connect with him, and made solid contact just as you found his driver's license." His shoulders shook. "Worst contact I've ever made. I may need therapy."

Deep down, he knew that wasn't far from the truth. He still couldn't get over the way his physical body reacted when he was tethered to Harlan's energy. The carnal fantasies about Selena should have turned his stomach, which they did. But there was that part of him that responded all too eagerly to the images. He knew it was all Harlan, but the violation to his own body was a tough one to handle.

They sat in silence, overcome by the enormity of events that had led to this.

Jessica finally said, "Holy crap."

"Yeah, holy crap is right. Christopher Harlan couldn't have Selena in life, but he was damn sure he was going to make good on his desire in death."

Jessica watched the IV drip, felt the weight of his words add to the contemplation of her future, something she had been doing a lot now that she had time to think in the hospital.

She found his hand and said, "I can't thank you enough. I couldn't have done this without you."

"We were a pretty good team. Maybe one day I can help you with your own abilities, especially if you plan to do more of this. I don't think you need to create hurricanes wherever you go. You are truly your own worst enemy. But on the flip side, you have a pretty remarkable gift. I'd like to try to figure out what makes you tick, help make your life a little easier."

Jessica smiled. "I'd like that, too."

She squeezed his arm and exclaimed, "Oh my God, I hope you still have a job. I'd hate to see you lose it over coming here with me to get our asses kicked for a week."

He laughed. "Surprisingly, my boss is letting me come back. I think he likes the way I arrange the B vitamin shelf. Skill like that is hard to find. I told him I'd be back tomorrow. I'm going to take the Amtrak to the city."

"At least let me pay for the train ticket."

He waved her off. "Don't worry, it cost less than the gas to drive home anyway."

Eddie kissed the back of her bruised, swollen hand and walked to the door.

"Call me when you get back. Remember, I've been inside your head now. I'll know if you try to give me the brush off."

She laughed, rolling her eyes.

"And I do believe you have some more visitors. Take care of yourself, Jessica. You know, despite everything, I'm really glad I found you."

"I'm glad you did, too. Thank my father for me next time you talk to him, okay?"

And maybe you could connect him to me like you did with Christopher Harlan's EB, she wanted to add. It physically hurt to hope there was a chance she could talk to her father again. There would be time.

Eddie nodded, and was gone.

To her surprise, she was sad to see him go. *Maybe this one-girl show needs a partner,* she thought. *That is, if the show goes on at all.*

She yelped with surprise when Aunt Eve and Liam swooped into the room, toting balloons, flowers and a host of other gifts. Eve put her arms around her and pulled her tightly to her chest. Even Liam managed to hold her hand and give her a kiss on the cheek.

"I swear, you're trying to put me in an early grave," Eve said, kissing her forehead and nose.

"It's not intentional, I swear," she said.

"Hey, you look like a before picture for Proactiv," Liam joked. It felt good to laugh and she didn't threaten to beat him for making fun of her.

"I should have never let you come here," Eve said, smoothing out Jessica's blanket.

"I'm a grown woman, and I would have come anyway," Jessica said. "There was no way of knowing it would get like this."

Eve gave her a look that said, *you of all people know how bad it can get.*

Jessica changed the subject. "Now that you're here, did you pack your bags so we can go on that trip to Maine?"

"Not a chance. You're coming home the second they discharge you. And your ghost hunting is suspended until further notice, you hear?"

She knew Eve was expecting resistance. Hell, it was what Jessica did best, but she only nodded and said, "I could use the rest. I have some required reading I have to do for the next semester. It'll be good to get caught up."

Later that night, Eve sent Liam to the hospital café to get some coffee. She had informed the hospital staff that they were not leaving after visiting hours and a nurse had brought a pillow and blanket for her and her son. As she tried to make the plush vinyl chairs a little more comfortable, she said, "I met Eddie this morning. I figured I'd let him say his goodbye first. You didn't tell me he was so handsome."

"Oh boy," Jessica said with a sigh.

"Seriously, that boy seems to care for you. I don't pretend to know what the two of you got mixed up in, but I have a strong feeling that you needed each other to get through it. You'd be doing yourself a favor by keeping him around, that is, if I can talk some sense into you both to behave like normal people your age and leave the ghosts to the movies."

Jessica pulled her blanket up to her chest and settled onto her side.

"You never know," she said. "Stranger things have happened."

She closed her eyes, and slept.

About the Author

Hunter Shea is the author of the novels *Forest of Shadows, Evil Eternal, Swamp Monster Massacre* and *Sinister Entity*. His stories have appeared in numerous magazines, including *Dark Moon Digest, Morpheus Tales* and the *Cemetery Dance* anthology, *Shocklines: Fresh Voices in Terror*. His obsession with all things horrific has led him to real life exploration of the paranormal, interviews with exorcists and other things that would keep most people awake with the lights on. He is also half of the Monster Men video podcast, a fun look at the world of horror. You can read about his latest travails and communicate with him at www.huntershea.com, on Twitter @HunterShea1, Facebook fan page at Hunter Shea or the Monster Men 13 channel on YouTube.

The dead still hate!

Forest of Shadows
© 2011 Hunter Shea

John Backman specializes in inexplicable phenomena. The weirder the better. So when he gets a letter from a terrified man describing an old log home with odd whisperings, shadows that come alive, and rooms that disappear, he can't resist the call. But the violence only escalates as soon as John arrives in the remote Alaskan village of Shida. Something dreadful happened there. Something monstrous. The shadows are closing in…and they're out for blood.

Enjoy the following excerpt from Forest of Shadows…

They screamed.

And impossible as it seemed, George Bolster was grateful for his family's unbridled cries of terror as they masked the other unearthly sounds that ghosted their every move.

Whump. Whump. Whump.

The steady beat of an unseen giant's footsteps up the stairs.

"Into the bedroom, now!" George shouted at his panicked wife and sons. They scrabbled into the room at the end of the hall while the floor quaked beneath their feet. Once inside, George slammed the door shut and braced his back against its oak frame. His sons, Cory and Matt, clung to Sharon's sides, their eyes wide and terrified, darting around the room, looking for death in benign shadows.

"Sharon, push the dresser over."

Stifling a sob that made her entire body shudder, she reluctantly pulled away from the boys and ran over to the large dresser. George grunted as the unseen force in the hallway pounded against the door.

"Hurry!"

Matt leapt to his mother's side to help push the heavy piece of furniture across the floor and against the bedroom door. Cory, who was only six and barely forty pounds, could only curl up into a corner and whimper. A clap of thunder made the entire house quake and they all shrieked in unison. George still pressed his weight against the door while Sharon and Matt gathered as much bulk as they could find and piled it as high and as fast as they could on top of the dresser.

The door shook as it was rammed again and again, so hard that the arch above the doorway began to crack. It wouldn't be long before the entire wall would collapse and then where could they go?

A deep thrumming emanated from beyond the door, a sonorous hum that was not so much heard as it was felt. It hurt like hell. They felt it vibrate their chest walls, disrupt the hammering rhythm of their hearts. It crept up their spines and exploded in their skulls, threatening to liquefy their brains.

So they screamed. Fighting fire with fire. The pile of debris stashed against the door shook as the pounding on the door continued. Staggering on jellied knees, George peered out the sole window into the moon-bathed woods outside. It was only a drop of twenty feet or so. Maybe, if he jumped first, he could catch them one at a time and they could run into the woods. But it was so damn cold, well below zero, and they didn't have a coat between them. Could they possibly navigate their way through the snow-steeped forest to their nearest neighbor a mile away?

Suddenly, everything stopped. The pain ceased and they all dropped to their knees. What sounded like a thousand tiny claws ticked across the hardwood floor of the hallway, retreating to the other end and descending the staircase that lead to the living room below.

George shook his head and went back to the window.

"Is it gone, Daddy?" Cory whispered.

"I don't know. Everyone stay quiet."

He kept his eyes on the faintly illuminated yard and his ears tuned for any sounds within the house. Matt and Cory muffled their cries into their mother's breast.

"What are you thinking?" Sharon mouthed.

George pointed out the window and used two fingers to simulate running. It was their only chance.

"George, we'll freeze to death."

One look from her husband ended any protest. Gently pulling the boys from her sides, she went over to the dresser and found two blankets, several pairs of sport socks and one wool hat. She worked in silence, wrapping the boys in the blankets and putting an extra pair of socks on their shoeless feet. Cory, being the youngest and frailest, got the hat.

George gathered his family by the window.

"I'm going to jump into the snow out there. Matt, I want you to go next, then Cory, then Mom. Once we're all out, I want you to stick close and run as fast as you can. We're going to try to make it to Glenn's house."

"But that's really far and it's so dark out," Matt protested.

George hugged him and felt close to tears. "I know, little man, I know. But we have to get out of here, and Glenn's house is the closest to us."

"Maybe it's gone away," Cory said. They all looked towards the door. The entire house had been silent for almost five minutes now.

Sharon placed a hand on her husband's shoulder. "It might not be a bad idea to wait a while and see."

George wanted nothing more than to run like hell from his house. Freezing to death was a welcome option to the thing downstairs.

"I'm not sure—"

The floor exploded just five feet from where they sat as the assault recommenced, this time from below. A fist-sized hole opened up between the splintered wood. A maniacal rush of thrashing and clawing blasted from the fresh portal as the floor shook from repeated efforts to widen the gap.

"Everyone up!"

George threw the window up hard, shattering the glass. Without a moment's hesitation, he jumped out into the cold night. He landed in a three-foot pile of snow that cushioned his fall. His right leg throbbed a little and his lungs hurt as he sucked in his first draft of frigid air.

"Okay, Matt, jump!" he shouted.

Sharon plucked her youngest son and aimed him into his father's waiting arms. George caught him and they both fell back into the snow. He was back on his feet by the time Cory had himself perched on the windowsill. Cory looked back at his mother, afraid to leave her alone, even if it was only for a moment.

"Go, Cory. I'll be right behind you."

The opening in the floor grew wider as more shards of wood shot out of the hole like lava from a volcano. Cory sprang into the air and almost sailed past his father. After a quick tumble in the freezing snow, George was back up and waiting for Sharon.

Heavy moaning filled the room. Sharon lost control of her bladder. Something was trying to find purchase on the jagged edges of the hole. Something huge, black and evil.

"Sharon! Come on!" George and the boys were shouting to her from the yard. Momentarily mesmerized by creeping fear, she turned back to the window and placed a foot on the sill.

As she prepared to jump, a trio of shadows stretched from the trees like a sentient ink spill and engulfed her family. One second they were there, calling for her to jump, and the next instant they were gone as the shadows retreated back into the forest.

"Nooooooo!"

She never noticed the presence behind her.

Available now in ebook and print from Samhain Publishing.

SAMHAIN
PUBLISHING

It's all about the story...

Romance

HORROR

Retro ROMANCE

www.samhainpublishing.com